HEADLESS

TAYLOR FENNER

ALSO BY TAYLOR FENNER

The Haunting Love

———

Finding Elizabeth

———

The Eternals Trilogy:

Out of Darkness

Into the Light

Through the Fog

Eternal Fire (Eternals Trilogy Novelette)

———

Night of Terror & Other Assorted Stories

———

CurseBreaker: An East O' The Sun and West O' The Moon Retelling

———

Monsters & Mist

———

No Check Out

It Rose From the Ashes (Coming 9.13.2024)

Headless

Print Edition

Copyright © 2018 by Taylor Fenner

This is a work of fiction. Names, characters, businesses, places, events, and incidents are either the products of the author's imagination or used in a fictitious manner. Any resemblance to actual persons, living or dead, or actual events is purely coincidental.

Print ISBN: 979-8-8693-4813-5

Second Edition Published 2024

❀ Created with Vellum

To my cousin Billy, thank you for your generosity and support.

HEAD LESS

TAYLOR FENNER

Forget everything you know about the Legend of Sleepy Hollow…

NENFABRIK
CHEMNITZ

CATALYST

<u>CHANCE</u>

Son,

You'll soon learn that nothing in this town is as it seems. Men have been dying in this town under mysterious circumstances since I was a boy. And I saw "her" again - Cora Whitt, the girl that got away. She looked the same as I last saw her: young, vibrant, and beautiful. Chance, I don't know what she is, but it isn't possible to look twenty years old when I haven't seen her in nearly thirty years. She may be dangerous. She may be the one behind these killings - I don't know. But I doubt I'll live to see the truth. Come home, Chance, and find out the truth. Stop the killings. You are the only one who can.

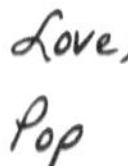

———

Chance folded the letter, worn from a hundred readings, and tucked it back into the map on the passenger seat. Beside it lay a half-eaten, half-discarded tuna sandwich he'd picked up at a gas station where he'd stopped to fill his tank. The bread was stale, and all signs pointed to his vintage Mustang needing an oil change. He didn't drive much. Living in New York City meant he didn't need to. Most people took the train or the bus from the city into Tarrytown and Sleepy Hollow, but something made Chance think this wouldn't be a quick weekend visit to check on his pop. No, this stay would be infinitely longer.

CHAPTER ONE

CORA

My story started with a blade, and someday, it will end with a blade. It was the sharp blade of a scythe, wielded by someone other than the Grim Reaper, and not a pumpkin carried by a headless horseman that truly scared poor Ichabod Crane enough to drive him from our sleepy village. But nobody tells that story.

Contrary to what you might think, Ichabod was far from the scrawny, bookish type you might think him to be. He could best Brom Bones any day in the looks department. But let's face it, nobody in the eighteenth century looked like what Hollywood depicts. People weren't that sexy then. Men didn't have steroid-filled sculpted muscles or have perfect tans from working the fields, and you'd rarely see a woman of any virtue wearing the cleavage-enhancing bodices you see in movies. This was New York State in the pre-nineteenth century; people were plain, modest, and, for the most part, boring.

I'll be the first to admit that immortality made me beautiful. But even so, Ichabod and Brom were both fairly attractive for their time. In any case, Ichabod was shy—not in the peculiar

Johnny Depp kind of way—but in the modest never-knows-when-to-make-a-move way, and Brom was the type that always got what he wanted. *Always.* From women to lie with to positions in the community, I'm not sure Brom ever heard the word no.

I've spent the last two hundred years trying to eradicate all traces of Brom from my memory and my life, starting with his descendants. After managing to wipe him and his male heirs from the world, I was less than satisfied, and as time wore on, I used my gift on others.

If my dearest friend, Irvie were still alive, he'd find my drive for revenge almost amusing; just like he would find Tim Burton's interpretation of his most beloved story amusing. He was always calm and always able to find the joke in things. That's why I loved him as fiercely as if he were my brother. I've missed him and felt his loss like one would feel a phantom limb every day since they laid him in the ground. And I've not let another soul get that close to me in all the years since.

———

As dawn approaches, I sit astride my faithful buckskin horse, Blood, and watch my latest victim trip and stumble his way home after a long night of partying.

A low, disgusted growl escapes my lips as his pitiful wife or girlfriend races out to help him inside, peppering him with questions about where he's been all night as she leads him indoors. This wasn't the first time he came home late, definitely not the first time she stayed up all night waiting and checking the time on her phone every other minute. Nor would it be the last, I'm sure. She knows it, too; she just won't admit it.

The first pale rays of sunlight appear over the horizon, and I realize I'm out of time. My task will have to wait another night. I sigh and pat Blood's silky black mane as we turn back toward

Sleepy Hollow Cemetery. I know we won't get there in time, not before the sun turns me back to dust, returning me momentarily to the darkness I hate.

———

A few minutes later, I wake up inside the dark, dank crypt of my dearly departed best friend, Irvie. To the rest of the world, he's the famous author Washington Irving, best known for writing *The Legend of Sleepy Hollow*, but to me, he will always be plain old Irvie, the first, and for a time, the only person who knew the truth about me and loved me anyway.

I know what you're thinking; you think I'm the Headless Horseman. Ha! What if I was to tell you there was no headless horseman? No, there is no headless Hessian out for revenge on his fellow man, just me, the headless horse*woman* with a completely different reason to want revenge. Oh, the legend is real, alright, but I'm no Katrina Van Tassel. Let's just say I had a vested interest in the man she chose, the man that spurned me – the man that ended me.

I stand up, shaking away the past like the cobwebs covering my mortal body. I have just enough time to shed last night's skimpy clothing and slip into a floral skirt and a loose-fitting magenta blouse. Since I have to get to my photography studio to meet with an enthusiastic bride who wants me to photograph her wedding, I don't have enough time to run up to my apartment above the studio and scavenge up something more professional.

I hate weddings. Then again, maybe that's because of my past.

———

CHANCE

An ominous chill crawls over me like invisible spiders even before I turn onto Pop's tree-lined street. Pop's neighborhood sits on the edge of town, with enough distance between homes to give privacy without being completely desolate, but today, the area gives off an eerie vibe. Even in broad daylight, my mind conjures visions of the famed headless horseman lurking in the shadows, waiting for an unsuspecting victim.

When I pull in, Pop's car is missing from the driveway, but that doesn't strike me as odd. When I was a child, he often hid the car in the garage to fool potential visitors into thinking we were away. I doubt that's changed in the ten years since I've been gone.

I lay my head against the cracked headrest as I survey the house. Pop still hasn't finished the screened-in porch he started building when I was ten. He used to say he was waiting for summer to come and then a sunny day project, and then it became his retirement project as if he'd ever close up the shop. The pathway to the house, gravel wore down into a haphazard walk from dozens of repetitive tracks to and from the house, has begun to sprout calf-high weeds, and I wonder why Pop hasn't yanked them out.

Finally, I bite the bullet and shove the car door open. I swing my duffel bag over my shoulder and force myself to put one foot in front of the other until I'm standing in front of the crooked screen door that I knocked off the hinge in my hurry to escape this house, my Pop, and this town years earlier. Pop never fixed it.

I tug the screen door open and twist the storm door's door-knob. For a brief second, I'm met with resistance, and then the door pops open with a creak. Air rushes out like an exhale after a long period of holding one's breath. I push the door open further and am met with a temperature frigid enough to fog up my breath.

"Pop, I think the heater's busted," I call out as I breathe into my cupped hands and rub my palms together. Even with a busted heater, the house shouldn't be this cold yet. It's only October.

My comment is met with strangled silence.

"Pop?" I call again, straining to hear signs of him puttering around inside the tiny house. "The door was open. Are you alright?"

I didn't think anything of the unlocked door. After all, this is Sleepy Hollow, New York. Nobody locks their doors because nothing ever happens here. I move down the hallway, and the sound of my stomping feet echoes in the small space as I pass boxes upon boxes of books for Pop's shop and old photos hanging crookedly on the wall. Next to the doorway to the kitchen, Pop's fishing rod lies forgotten and collecting dust.

I push forward, passing the kitchen and heading for the living room. Pop may have nodded off in his old recliner, or perhaps he didn't hear me.

As I step onto the threshold of the living room, I'm once again met with a rush of cold air, and the air around me drops ten degrees. My eyes dart around the darkened room, the trees outside the picture window blocking out the sunlight from the east. That's when I spot Pop lying face down on the living room floor.

"Shit," I exclaim as I drop to my knees at Pop's side, "Pop, wake up! Come on, don't do this to me. I'm here, Pop, I'm here."

I fumbled around, trying to find his pulse as all recall of the training I had to do for the lifeguard job at the local pool I took the summer I was sixteen flees my mind. I'd only half paid attention in the first place because I only took the job because Stacey Jensen, the hottest girl in my grade, said she liked to hang out there and maybe she'd see me there. Now, I wish I had paid attention instead of fantasizing about a girl who had never shown up at that stupid pool.

When I find his pulse point and don't feel a pulse, I curse

under my breath and yank my phone from my pocket. My hands shake as I dial 911.

"911, please state your emergency," the aging dispatcher's voice crackles as the call is picked up.

"I need an ambulance. My father isn't breathing. I came in from out of town and found him face down on the living room floor." The fingers of my left hand tap out a frantic rhythm against my thigh as I speak to the dispatcher.

"Calm down; I'm tracking your call and sending help your way," the dispatcher's voice is soothing like a comforting grandmother's voice might be. I hear her typing information into the system as she asks, "What is your name?"

"Chance Jordan," I answer quickly. "My father is Chancellor Jordan Junior."

"Alright, Chance, hang on," the dispatcher murmurs, and she types something else into the system. "Can you check to see if your father's pulse is strong or weak, honey?"

"I checked, but I couldn't find a pulse," I explain as worry colors my tone.

"Alright," the dispatcher types something more. The sound of her fingers on the keys makes my stomach churn. "I have EMS and police on the way. The ETA is two minutes out. Stay on the line until they get there."

"Thank you," I whisper, even though I can tell from the change in the dispatcher's tone that things don't look good. I've seen enough medical dramas on television to know that if there's no pulse, you're most likely dead or soon to be dead.

"They're coming, Pop, just hang on," I plead as my voice breaks.

I hear the shrill sound of sirens filling the air in the distance, growing closer. "They're coming," I tell the dispatcher.

"That's good, honey," the dispatcher sounds sympathetic. "I'll let you go let them in."

"Thank you," I say, though I'm not sure what I'm thanking her for. Maybe it's just for listening.

On autopilot, I get to the front door as the police chief and the paramedics trudge up the front steps.

He's in here," I motion for them to follow me as I quickly weave between boxes to get to the living room.

"The EMTs will take it from here, son. I need you to step out of the room." Chief Devries places his hand on my shoulder to get my attention as EMTs hurry to get to work. He's been the police chief since I was fifteen, but it sounds like he still hasn't lost the thick accent acquired somewhere far in the south where afternoon garden parties are held beneath fragrant magnolia trees and dripping Spanish Moss and Weeping Willows blow gently in the breeze.

I begin backing away to follow his directions when a young female EMT who'd been beginning to check Pop's vitals raises her head, making eye contact with Chief Devries, and shakes her head gently.

I don't need to be a genius to figure that gesture out. "No," I exclaim as I try to push past Devries to return to Pop's side. Devries's hands shoot out, gripping my shoulders and holding me in place as I shake my head angrily. "No, that's not right. He can't be dead."

"I'm sorry, son." Devries's mouth hardens into a grim line as I watch the paramedics move Pop to a stretcher and begin placing a white sheet that's materialized from out of nowhere over Pop's face and body. Devries rubs the back of his neck nervously. "It's been a long time since you left town, Junior. Was your old man expecting you?"

The only thing I hate more than someone addressing me as Junior is the look of suspicion in the portly sheriff's eyes as they dart between Pop's covered body and me, still in his clutches.

"I got a letter from him asking me to come home," I answer around the lump forming in my throat as my eyes drift back to the cloth. My stomach lurches, and I regret my earlier tuna sandwich. "He can't be dead, he just can't be. You have to do something for him," I urge.

"He's gone, boy. We won't want to make any assumptions until the coroner can examine the body," Devries exhales loudly through his nostrils, "but it was likely a natural death. Unnatural deaths don't happen around these parts. That's more likely in that big ole' city you're living in. Your father hasn't been well for some time, but even so, it *is* the department's procedure to eliminate any other possible cause. Starting with how long you've been in town and why you've returned."

"I told you, I got a letter from Pop asking me to come home," I reply shortly as the hair on the back of my neck raises. Something isn't right here.

"Do you still have the letter?" Sheriff Devries asks, his tone sharpening.

Something about the way Devries asks makes me feel the need to be defensive. Without understanding why, I find myself saying, "No, I left it back at my apartment in the city; why?"

Devries shakes his head dismissively, "Might have given us an insight into his frame of mind, that's all, son."

My skin crawls, "but you said you thought it was a natural death. You're acting like it was a suicide or murder or something."

"Now, why would you say murder, Chance?" Devries tries to loom over me intimidatingly even though there's not even a hair's width difference in our heights.

"I didn't say it was murder," I say, frustrated by his tone. "I said that's what you're acting like it is."

Devries's face shutters into an unreadable mask. "I think it would be best if you came down to the station and answered a few questions."

"What? You've gotta be fucking kidding me," I exclaim. "You actually think I did something to my Pop?"

"I know you and your father have been estranged for some time," Devries replies smugly, "and I find it a little unusual that you blow back into town on the same day your father is found dead."

"But I found him," I remind him. "I'm the one that called 911."

"A likely story," Devries muses. "Now, we can do this the easy way or the hard way."

"No way," I exhale hard. "I didn't do anything wrong, and you're treating me like a suspect in a crime."

I try to back away, but the police chief grabs my wrist and twists it and me around before I can react.

"I didn't want to do this," Devries murmurs as he produces a set of handcuffs from his belt. "Chancellor Jordan the third, you are under arrest for the suspected murder of your father. You have the right to remain silent. Anything you say can and will be used against you in a court of law. You have the right to an attorney; if you cannot afford an attorney, one will be provided to you. Do you understand these rights as I've read them?"

"This is insane," I mutter as Chief Devries hauls me out of the house I grew up in and shoves me into the back seat of his cruiser.

Back in my Mustang, Pop's letter lies hidden out of sight, tucked away in the map.

CHAPTER TWO

My phone starts ringing the moment I step out of Dark Brews, the coffee shop down the street from my apartment and studio. I stack and balance the cups I'm bringing back to the studio between my chin and the book I'm carrying as I fumble around the pocket of my faux leather moto jacket, trying to wrap my fingers around my slippery smartphone.

By the time I pulled it loose, the caller – an unknown number – had hung up, leaving no message. I blow a loose strand of my wavy strawberry-blonde hair out of my eyes and look up, scanning the quiet streets. For mid-afternoon, on an October Saturday, the streets are shockingly sparse. During the autumn season, it's common to see tourists flooding the town and surrounding area to take walking ghost tours and visit other locations geared up for Halloween.

It's funny how, all because of a story, an area can transform from a small farming area to a tourist destination. It's also amusing that I've been here to see it all.

A car alarm down the block interrupts my musings. I stuff my phone back into my pocket and walk past the seasonally decorated storefronts until my small studio, Sleepless in Love Photography, comes into view. I step out of the cold and into the cozy warmth of the studio as my eyes adjust to the dim lighting inside.

Just twenty minutes earlier, I had to mediate an argument between a bride and her mother over pre-ceremony photographs with her groom. The superstitious mother of the bride tried to warn her daughter that the groom seeing her before the wedding was bad luck, but the bride wasn't hearing any of it. The mother might have worn the girl down until she also reminded her it was tacky, and she shouldn't want to be a tacky bride like her matron of honor. Then the gloves came off. I was lucky to slip out with the excuse of needing to meet with the editor of the Sleepy Hollow Gazette at Dark Brews to go over some proof photos for the weekend edition. I freelance with the newspaper when their usual photographer has other engagements. Those other engagements, more often than not, involved a large bottle of scotch.

"Andi, I'm back," I call out to the back of the studio space, "And I brought you a caramel macchiato."

"Mmm-mmm, come to Mama," my assistant, Andi, looks up from the computer on his desk and coos as he looks past me to the steaming sugary drink clutched in my right hand. Andi, born Andreas, then changed to the non-gender specific Andi, who has the type of androgynous good looks that should have him staring up at me from the pages of Vogue if only he had the ambition. He begged me to hire him after he graduated high school last fall and, so far, was proving better in front of the camera instead of behind it. I've caught him admiring himself in the oval mirror that hangs on the back wall of the studio more times than I can count, and he's constantly taking selfies on his phone.

"Here you go," I murmur, handing him his drink as I pass him to reach my desk. "Have there been any calls or drop-ins?"

"Not a peep the entire time you were gone. Hey, did you hear the old man that runs Hollow Books died?" Andi asks as he inhales the inviting steam rising from his to-go cup.

"Chance?" I ask as a lightning strike of pain breaks through to my stone heart. Chancellor Jordan is my one regret of the past two centuries. Unlike the male company I usually keep, he wasn't a cheater, just a man who fell in love with a girl who could never be tamed.

"I don't know his name," Andi shrugs nonchalantly. "He was old, though, and really weird. It must be all the books he was surrounded by all the time. Do people actually read anymore? For fun, I mean?"

"I believe they do. And Chance – I mean Mr. Jordan – is only in his early fifties," I correct as I roll my eyes.

"Fine," Andi amends as he juts out his bottom lip, "he wasn't old old, just parent old."

I shake my head and pull up the files from the wedding we photographed last weekend as Andi continues, "Now his son, though, he is one fine piece of ass. What I wouldn't give to get me a piece of that."

I look up from the thumbnails on my screen as Andi waves the morning paper in my face. "I can't believe the police actually thought he had killed his old man. Good-looking people just aren't capable of murder."

I snort but choose to remain quiet. I love Andi like family, but sometimes, his comments make me wonder about him. I squint to look at the grainy black-and-white photograph situated above the fold of the Gazette. The man whose photo stares back from the front page of the newspaper is a striking copy of his father, far from the boy he'd been the last time I saw him.

Chance Jordan, called "junior" by no sane person ever, had snuck into Beau's Bar one Friday night hoping to score a beer or two. I had taken pity on the young-looking sixteen-year-old with skinny arms and long, wavy hair. He'd tipped his head back and laughed when I brought him a bottle of Budweiser and told him he should have been the one buying me a drink. I'd smiled and disappeared into the night, and that was the end of that.

The man in the paper's hair is short on the sides yet long on the top, styled into a messy pompadour. His hooded eyes tell the story of secrets he keeps closely guarded, and the chiseled line of his jaw suggests he doesn't smile as often as he should.

Andi chuckles knowingly, and I look up from the paper and see him staring at me mischievously. "Come on, boss lady; don't even try to tell me you don't think he is yum-my."

"He's attractive," I admit reluctantly as I tuck a strand of hair behind my ear nervously.

"He's more than attractive," Andi clucks his tongue. "How long has it been since you had a date? Six months? A year?"

"My dating life is not a subject open for conversation," I look down and shuffle some papers on my desk.

"Honey, this is for your own good," Andi raises his voice into a high falsetto. "You need to get out more and have some fun."

If only Andi knew how often I did go out at night or the things I did without a care.

———

By ten at night, I'm putting the finishing touches on my outfit and getting ready to go out for the night. A sheer red lace dress hugs my body with only artfully placed panels concealing my bra and panties from view. In the city, this dress wouldn't be anything to stare at, but here in the Hollow, it may cause a heart attack. I tousle my hair so that it looks like I've just crawled out of bed and add a swipe of pale red lip gloss to my lips, the type that looks as if I've just wet my lips.

As a creature of comfort over fashion, this outfit is a million light years from my everyday style, but for what I'm about to do, it is necessary.

Red 'fuck me' pumps slip onto my feet, and I wobble for a minute at the height they give my five-foot-four-inch frame before tucking the matching clutch I bought with the rest of the outfit from an online retailer under my arm. One last glance at my reflection in the mirror, and I twist the apartment doorknob three times and step into the hallway.

Across the street from my studio and apartment, in a historically preserved building, sits Beau's Bar. Patrons steadily pour in and out of the front door, spilling fragments of the twenty-year-old rock music blaring inside out into the night.

The air seems to shift as I enter my usual hunting grounds. Suddenly, I feel pressure on my shoulders, as if someone or something is waiting to see what I'll do next. Running my left hand through my hair and ruining my careful styling, I lock my emotions away in the metaphorical box I shove everything personal into and scan the bustling bar. My eyes lock on the muscular back of the one person I'm looking for, and a predatory smile slips into place on my face.

"Do you know where a girl might get some refreshments around here?" I tease as I lean against the bar, tilting away from the overworked bartender and focusing on the man I came here for.

"Hey," an attractive man with short blonde hair and cerulean blue eyes turns his attention to me. "I was hoping I'd see you here tonight."

"And here I am, so what are your other two wishes?" I watch his eyes dilate in thought as I rest my elbows on the bar and clutch the underside of the thick, shiny wood. I met him here last night, and he called himself Wild, but I had five dollars wagering that that was just a nickname. His clothing, fake tan, and demeanor screamed player, and I nearly had him under my spell by the time the bartender called last call last night.

"I'm not sure you could handle my wishes, baby girl," Wild flashes me a toothy grin.

"You'd be surprised," I lean in closer to whisper, playing along.

"Barkeep, give this beauty a lemon drop," Wild calls as he waves the bartender over.

I swivel around, make eye contact with the weary bartender, a balding man in his mid-forties, and say, "Actually, I think I'll take a whiskey, neat."

"Comin' right up," the bartender slings a wet bar rag over his shoulder and reaches under the bar for a rocks glass before pouring me two fingers of the amber liquid I prefer.

"Now you are my type of woman," Wild salutes me with his shot of tequila before tipping it back.

After the bartender places my drink on the bar beside me, I wrap my fingers around the glass, inhaling briefly without breaking my eye contact with Wild. Without taking a sip of my drink, I lay my hand on Wild's muscular thigh and squeezed gently, "I can't believe a stud like you doesn't have a girlfriend."

Wild leans in closer and winks, "Just haven't met the right girl, I guess."

———

Two shots of tequila later, Wild is stumbling across the street to my apartment. His hands are in my hair and running along my curves as his lips and tongue blaze a trail down the side of my neck to where the sleeve of my dress has slipped off my shoulder.

"Easy there, big guy," I laugh as he leans a little too heavily on my side.

"I can't wait to get inside," Wild murmurs, "you're absolutely intoxicating."

As I deftly unlock the door to my apartment, I briefly wonder if he's ever told the woman he lives with that. We spill inside, with only the dim light of a lamp I left on before I left to illuminate us. I guide him toward my bedroom, walking backward as our lips and tongues tangle. I shrug his jacket and shirt off his shoulders hurriedly as his impatient hands struggle with the zipper on the back of my dress.

"Mmm, patience, babe," the meaningless endearment slips off my tongue easily as Wild groans against my ear.

"Can't, need you now," his words slur together as I shove him onto my bed and straddle his hips.

I leave a trail of kisses on his chest as I reach between us and free him from the confines of his tight jeans. He hisses in pleasure as I guide his hard length into my core and sheath him in my wetness.

"Oh fuck, baby girl, you feel so good," Wild groans as his hips buck up to meet mine.

As he loses himself in the movement and the moment he doesn't notice me bring my fisted hands up on either side of his neck. They never notice, nor do they see the invisible blade I place upon their throats and wait for the right moment. Should they notice, it would only look like I was gripping the sheets on either side of their head, overcome with my own enjoyment of our shared pleasure.

The moment Wild becomes lost and untethered in his climax, I bring the blade down hard against his throat. His groans of pleasure turn to panicked gasps as his windpipe is severed beneath my weapon. I lean back as his eyes bulge in terror seconds before the light drains from their cerulean depths. I feel his soul filter into my pores and shutter in my own sadistic pleasure as his body disintegrates into dust before my eyes.

I roll over and catch my breath, saved for the night from waking up in the darkness of Irvie's crypt, knowing that tomorrow morning Wild's girlfriend will find his body, mysteriously whole and lifeless, in their bed; another victim of the strange deaths that have plagued our little village for several centuries without any explanation or sign of foul play.

***

CHANCE

It took me twenty-six hours, a call to a friend of mine who is a criminal defense attorney back in the city, and four snarky remarks to attempt to convince Chief Devries that I did not murder my father. And even then, he didn't believe me. Not until the preliminary coroner's report came back this morning indicating Pop most likely died of a massive heart attack, which he did have a history of heart trouble to back up.

"You're free to go," Devries mutters gruffly as he returns my wallet and wristwatch to me in a Ziploc bag, "but don't leave town just yet. We might have a few more questions for you."

"Aye, aye, Captain," I mock salute him as my attorney friend Neil corrals me toward the police station's front door.

"He was trying to bait you," Neil rubs his hands over his face tiredly. I can see his exasperation with me written all over his face. I'm the one he usually calls to complain about one of his reckless clients, and now I'm just as bad as they are.

"I know," I hang my head as Neil adjusts the silver cuff links his father bought him the year he made partner in the family law firm.

Just as Neil moves to exit the station, an excited voice crackles across the police scanner, "Chief? Chief Devries, you're not going to believe this. There's another one."

"Another what, Deputy?" Chief Devries growls impatiently.

"Another dead man found in his house," the deputy relays eagerly. "Two deaths in two days, ain't that something?"

"Did you remember to call in the coroner and the forensic team this time?" Devries pinches the bridge of his nose.

"Oh, that sounds like a really good idea," the deputy's voice breaks a little over the connection. Neil has to elbow me to stop me from snorting, but I can tell he's holding back laughter, too.

"Just give me the address, and don't touch anything," Devries commands. The deputy reads off an address on the other side of town, and Devries scribbles it down onto a pad of paper. When he looks up again, his eyes narrow as they land on me.

I hold my hands up in mock surrender. " It wasn't me. You've had me here all night, remember?"

Chief Devries shoots me a sour look before pushing past me through the station door and climbing into his cruiser. He is in such a hurry that he doesn't notice that he's about to drive over the curb, and the car drops down onto the street with a soundless thud before disappearing down the street.

"This is some town," Neil remarks as he walks me out of the station. Parked crookedly across three parking spots is his sleek black sports car, and I wonder how Chief Devries missed that. He takes proper parking procedures very seriously, if I remember correctly. I wait for Neil to click open the doors as he frowns regretfully, "In case I forgot to mention it, I really am sorry for your loss. I know things between you and your father were strained; it's just unfortunate you didn't get the chance to patch things up."

"Thanks, man," I rub my chin uncomfortably. The stubble that grew up over my jaw overnight itches like crazy, but I shove my hands into my pockets to stop myself from scratching away.

Inside the car, Neil fiddles with something on the dashboard touchscreen that controls everything from the seat temperature controls to the radio and clock. Without looking at me, he says,

"You know I want to stay and be there for you at the funeral, but I have a major case going on back at the office. I have to be in court on Monday morning."

"Who are you defending this time?" I ask.

"Do you remember that rash of murders in Washington Square Park about six months ago? The ones that imitated Jack the Ripper?" Neil asks as he pulls onto the road.

"Yeah, wasn't that some weirdo middle school English teacher or something?" I strain to remember the details of the case. "Dude, you're not defending him, are you?"

"Someone has to defend him properly," Neil says defensively, "otherwise he'll just get out on appeal."

"Whatever you say," I grin. "So, did he do it? Or is this one of those things where he's going to claim temporary insanity?"

"Chance, you know I can't discuss anything with you about the case on or off the record. Attorney, client privilege and all that," Neil replies automatically, but the corner of his right eye twitches, telling me that his client did, in fact, do what the papers said he did, and he's worried about the case.

"I'm only ribbing you, Neil. Chill," I smirk as we pull up to the curb in front of Pop's house.

"I know," Neil murmurs as he looks past me to the house. "Be serious for a minute, Chance. Are you going to be okay in there all by yourself?"

"I'll be fine," I nod, even though I'm not so sure.

"Call me if you need anything," Neil makes me promise as I move to get out of the car.

"I will," I promise as I tap the side of the car with my open palm. And damn if Neil doesn't look relieved to be driving away a few seconds later.

I sigh and rip down the crime scene tape covering Pop's front door, taking a deep breath before stepping inside.

Two hours later, I'm sitting in Pop's home office with stacks of papers spread out on the desk in front of me. The coroner's office called to inform me Pop's body would be moved to the local funeral home, and I made tentative arrangements to meet with the funeral director tomorrow to finalize Pop's funeral plans. Plans he'd had in place for some time, apparently. Now, I just needed to find the paperwork the funeral home needed about the burial trust Pop had set up.

In my search, I found stacks of past-due notices on medical and household bills and Pop's random scribblings about current and previous inventory for the bookshop he owns downtown, but not the papers I was looking for.

How had things changed so much since I'd left? Pop's shop has always been a place where collectors travel far and wide to search for rare and unusual books, which gave us a comfortable enough lifestyle, but the bills for expensive medical testing stopped my heart as they climbed into the mid-six-figures. What am I going to do? Am I responsible for the bills now that Pop is gone? Will I have to sell the shop and the house? Why did my old man have to be so damn secretive about everything?

CHAPTER THREE

I caught sight of the sickle a little too late. One minute, I had been begging Brom not to do this to me and not to leave me for her. Sure, perfect, beautiful Katrina Van Tassel had money and status, but she really wanted Ichabod. Couldn't Brom see that she was only choosing him because her father wouldn't permit Ichabod to marry his only daughter?

I was arguing that point when Katrina urged Brom to "do it."

We'd been in the burned-out barn where Brom and I often met for stolen moments, and some of the displaced farming tools were still on hand.

I saw Brom raise his arm, and in my confusion, I initially had no idea what he was holding in his hand. At the last possible second, I saw the blade of the sickle. I didn't have time to duck, any time to react at all, before I felt a sharpness choking me. That's all I remember before everything became dark and silent.

I felt like I was floating, and I couldn't see anything but darkness. For the first time in my life, I was genuinely terrified.

"That's because you're dead, girl," a raspy female voice reached out to me in the darkness.

"Is this the... afterlife?" I remember asking hesitantly.

The raspy voice laughed coarsely and humorlessly, immediately putting what was left of me on edge. "No, girl, this isn't the afterlife. Think of it as a suspended plane of existence."

"Brom did this to me," I murmur, my voice coming from everywhere and nowhere at once.

"Aye, that he did," the voice concedes. "Took yer head clean off. T'was a gruesome sight to behold."

"How could he do this to me?" I ask, rage coloring my tone. "I loved him. What's going to happen to me now?"

"Tell me, girl, what do you want to happen to you? What do you want the most right now?" The raspy voice asks sharply, waiting expectantly for my answer.

"Revenge," I hiss, the first thing that comes to mind. The word sounds drawn out when spoken through my suddenly parched lips.

"Then revenge you shall get," the raspy voice replies, sounding pleased with my answer.

I wake up in my bed in my studio apartment for once. I grasp my throat and gasp for air, much like I did the first time I came back to life.

I told you before that there is no headless horseman. However, there is a headless horsewoman, and I'm it. Like it or not, forevermore—my immortality is my curse.

Thoroughly sick of my melodramatics, I shove those unpleasant memories into the tiny mental box they belong in and stumble around to get ready for the day.

So often, I wake up in Irvie's crypt after an unsuccessful night of hunting, and it feels strange to start my day as if I were any other ordinary person.

After a quick shower and half a pot of coffee, I throw myself into some clothes and make it down to the studio just as Andi is letting himself in. Technically, the studio is closed on Sundays, but I always end up doing one thing or another to keep on track. Andi's gotten in the habit of coming in and hanging out until he can convince me to come out for brunch with him.

"Morning, boss," Andi says without really looking at me.

"Morning," I reply groggily as I shade my eyes against the morning sun that slants through the front windows invitingly.

Finally looking up and noticing me, Andi lets out a low whistle, "damn, girl, you look like shit. Did you finally take my advice and go out last night?"

"Something like that," I grumble as I pull a pair of sunglasses from my desk drawer and slip them over my eyes.

"Why didn't you call me?" Andi clasps his chest, pretending to look hurt. "We could have gone to the city and gone dancing!"

"I'm sorry, Andi." I smile ruefully. It was a last-minute decision, and I just went across the street to Beau's."

"Oh, a local bar," Andi's face turns sour. "I guess I didn't miss anything."

"Probably not," I laugh tiredly as I boot up my laptop to check for business emails. I usually don't handle a soul reaping this badly, but this morning I feel and certainly must look like I'm in the middle of a killer hangover. Hmm, killer hangover, I snort at my joke.

"You okay over there?" Andi asks as he looks me over curiously.

"Absolutely," I lie as I busy myself with work.

———

Within a day, word spreads about the two mysterious deaths in town, although in my defense, I can only take credit for one.

And people easily dismiss Chance Jordan Sr.'s death as natural. Older people with heart conditions die all the time, apparently, even though Chance was only in his early fifties. Wild's death is considered much stranger in the eyes of the town. Young men in excellent health don't go to sleep and not wake up the next morning.

As per my routine, I lie low and don't go out hunting. Not that anyone could tie Wild's death to me, but on the off chance that the police department actually realizes any of my victims were the target of foul play, I usually wait between six months and a year between killings.

Usually, I can make the souls I've absorbed last without any adverse effects, but I'd pushed myself a little too far this time, waiting fifteen months between kills. Now, fresh off a kill, I can tell the toll it had taken on my mortal body. The dark circles I'd covered with makeup have faded, and I look healthy and whole again. I can't make myself wait that long again.

The Gazette's website informs me that Chance Sr.'s funeral is scheduled for Wednesday afternoon.

It's a strange day for a funeral, I decide, as I give Andi the rest of the afternoon off so I can go upstairs and change before heading to the cemetery. I pull on a black vintage wrap dress and secure it tightly at my waist. My reflection in the mirror stares back at me uncertainly, telling me perhaps this isn't a good idea. And still, I keep getting dressed.

While it wouldn't make sense for me to really attend the funeral, who says I can't say a final goodbye to someone I once cared about from a safe distance?

I rethink my decision for the tenth time and fear that I've made a foolish mistake the minute I step out of the covered bridge and past the Old Dutch Church into Sleepy Hollow Cemetery. What was I thinking? I can't do this.

I'm about to turn and leave before anyone catches sight of me when my eyes hone in on a man with broad shoulders and short espresso-brown hair standing over an open grave, and my heart falters ever so slightly. My mind plays tricks on me, taking me back to a day just like this, twenty-five years ago, as my Chance stood over his young wife's grave with his three-year-old son at his side. My heart broke for him that day. And for some reason, I'm seeing it all over again.

This cannot be happening. A ghost, which I genuinely believe myself to be at times, cannot be haunted by another ghost.

I edge around the cemetery under the cover of tall oaks and brightly tinted maple trees, trying to get a better look at the man's face. I clutch the trunk of a thick, red-leafed maple tree and hazard a peek, holding on so tight that the bark bites and scratches at my palm, reminding me that I am entirely corporeal.

For a moment, all I see is the Chance I knew thirty years ago —the man I let my guard slip for before I realized how foolish I was being. Then, in the span of a blink, the man changes slightly. The strong Roman nose, full lips, and hooded eyes are the same, but there is something haunted in those eyes, something completely distrustful of the world around him.

I can see him speaking to the open grave, but I'm too far away to make out his words. As he speaks, he waves his hands around animatedly, and I get a glimpse of elegant black tattoos running up his long fingers and blending into another design at his wrists. My eyes rove up over his suit jacket, the color so dark the naked eye might mistake it for black before realizing it for the dark blue it truly is until it ends at his neck, revealing the hint of more colorful ink. Half-inch thick stubble, the same color as the hair on his head, covers his chiseled jaw, and he pauses to scratch it, almost as if he can sense my eyes lingering on him. Finally, I noticed the inch-and-a-half wide gauges in his earlobes, and my hunch was confirmed.

The man standing over the grave is the new Chance, the

young Chance, my Chance's son. My hunch is further confirmed when Gil Lindstrom walks through into the cemetery and joins the man at the gravesite.

Gil Lindstrom was Chance Jr.'s partner in crime when they were teenagers. He was there in the bar the night I bought Chance that drink, ready to create any mischief he thought would catch the eye of the older girls home from college for the summer.

Like Chance Jr., Gil, now sporting a thick black mustache and beard, has changed so much since he was a teenager. From a reed-thin boy, he worked out until he transformed himself into the ripped and toned man women drool over. Luckily for everyone, Gil also learned manners and became responsible enough to get a seasonal job on one of those crabbing boats that they feature on *Deadliest Catch*. I've seen Gil in Beau's plenty of times since he turned twenty-one and quickly learned that he likes to use the show to pick up women. But since he's single, he's safe from me and the revenge I take. And I believe once he finds a woman who can tolerate him long-term, he will remain faithful to her. I have an eye for those sorts of things; I have to after all this time; otherwise, my world would be chaos.

At the grave, I watch as Gil supportively pats Chance on the back. A few minutes later, the minister arrives and begins to speak. Since no pallbearers show up to bring in a casket, I can only assume the casket has already been lowered into the grave, though I have no idea why.

I listen in on the small, personal funeral service, feeling slightly voyeuristic, but make sure to take my leave before Chance, Gil, or the minister has the opportunity to spot me in the trees.

CHANCE

"Thanks for coming," I mumble as the gravedigger begins to fill Pop's grave with dirt. Other than Father Zeal, Gil was the only other person to show up for his funeral. When did Pop become such a loner? I wonder briefly as Gil and I turn back toward the parking lot by the church.

"I'm here for you, buddy," Gil replies firmly, his tone devoid of the happy-go-lucky charm he's known for. After a long pause, he asks, "Do you want to grab a beer at Beau's?"

"Shit, yeah," I exhale hard. "I think I need one. Or two."

"That's the Chance I know," Gil's grin is barely visible behind the bushy black mustache and beard growing out of control on the lower part of his face. "We'll have a drink for Pop."

That was the thing about my father. All of my friends were so comfortable around him that they called him Pop or sometimes Papa Jordan. Not that Pop minded. No, he usually found it amusing.

"Meet you at the bar in ten?" I ask when I reach my car.

"Are you slowing down with old age, Chance?" Mischief glitters in Gil's eyes. "I think I can make it to Beau's in five and piss old Devries off in the process."

"That might be," I nod in agreement, "but I don't need him crawling up my ass again. I know he still thinks I'm guilty of something."

"Devries is an idiot," Gil snorts. "He's been trying to pin something on one of us since we were freshmen in high school. Suspicious redneck."

I smirk at Gil's description and realize it's true. There wasn't a moment since Devries blew into town that Gil and I or any of our other friends didn't have to be looking over our shoulder, waiting for the red and blue lights to flick on in our wake.

"I bet I can get there in three minutes." I counter Gil's earlier challenge. Some might say our behavior is inappropriate so soon after Pop's funeral, but this is Gil's way of making me feel better. Neither of us has been particularly good at expressing ourselves – except in the angsty way we did as teenagers.

"Is that so?" Gil cocks his eyebrow.

"Yep," I reply, but by that time, we're both leaping into our cars like we're fifteen years old again, about to drag race with only our learner's permits.

———

I beat Gil to Beau's by a few seconds. I got out and leaned against the hood of my car. "So, the loser buys the winner's first round, right?"

Gil laughs, "Tonight, I think that can be arranged. But only if I can choose what you're drinking."

"Should I be afraid?" I ask dubiously as I follow him into the dimly lit bar. It's been years since I've seen Gil. He was the troublemaker when we were kids, and I can only imagine what he's like now that we're actually old enough to be served at Beau's.

"Oh yes, be afraid. Be very, very afraid," Gil guffaws as he parks himself on one of the cracked barstools at the bar. He motions to Beau, the bartender and bar's third-or-fourth-generation namesake, with a two-fingered salute, and he gets to work making whatever Gil's gesture treats us to. It's early and the middle of the week, so other than a few regulars, we have the bar to ourselves.

"I wasn't sure you would still be in town," I comment as Beau begins pouring a flaming blue liquid from one metal tankard to another. My eyes widen as I hold my breath, anticipating the moment that Beau will miss and set the bar ablaze.

"I'm just back for a few days," Gil shrugs, his back turned to the fire show going on over his right shoulder. "I gotta be back in Anchorage by the weekend."

"What is he making?" I interrupt. My index finger shakes as I point at Beau's careful pouring.

"A blue blazer," Gil says as if I should know what that is. "It is scotch and a few other things."

"Drink up, boys," Beau grins as he slams two identical tankards down in front of us. Seeing my apprehension, he adds, "Don't worry, it won't kill you. Don't they make exotic drinks down in the city?"

"Not in the dive bars I usually frequent," I reply as I raise the tankard in appreciation.

"How are things back in the city?" Gil asks as he sips his drink, "seeing anyone worth mentioning?"

"Nope, nobody special," I frown into my tankard. There was someone, but the whole thing is too screwed up to tell Gil about. "How about you? Still scaring the women off?"

Gil laughs, "I don't know what you're talking about. Women line up to spend the night with me. I have the sweetest personality and roguish good looks, can't you tell?"

I choked on my drink and let it drip back into the tankard. " Who told you that?"

"I believe her name was Sarah Jean," Gil thinks back, "she had some pretty fine assets if you catch my drift."

"She must have been blind," I pause, "and potentially crazy."

"Oh shut up," Gil grins, "you're just jealous."

I tip back the rest of my drink and slam the tankard down on the bar. The drink felt like fire all the way down, and my senses already felt duller. "So tell me," I start, feeling bolder with the alcohol in my system. "Has there been anything weird going on around here since I left?"

"What do you mean?" Gil asks, confused by my change in conversation.

"I don't know," I feign innocence. "There have been two deaths, including Pop's, in less than a week. Have there been a lot of suspicious deaths in the past ten years?"

"I thought you said Pop died of a heart attack," Gil looks at me questioningly.

"He did," I nod. "But what about the other guy? He was young and in good health. It is weird that he just dropped dead of natural causes."

"Maybe he was a drug addict," Gil counters, "or maybe he had some undiagnosed health problem the coroner hasn't discovered yet. Shit happens. Why do you ask?"

I shrug nonchalantly, "No reason, just curious."

Gil sets his tankard down slowly, "are you working on a story or something? Is something going on that I don't know about?"

I shake my head noncommittally, "I'm not sure yet."

"Well, be careful," Gil cautions. "Sometimes what sounds like innocent fun can uncover something dark and unnatural, or don't you remember?"

Do I ever. I've been running for ten years trying to forget.

CHAPTER FOUR

CORA

I wait until dark, sitting in my window seat and watching people come and go from the bar across the street. I see Chance and Gil enter the bar early; then Chance leaves alone a couple of hours later. On a Wednesday night, the bar will most likely be half-full of men looking for a drink after a long work day. It's not exactly the young crowd Beau sees on the weekend, but it is good enough for my purpose.

I threw on a pair of curve-hugging bell bottoms I pulled out of a bin at the Salvation Army and a floral tunic before heading for the bar. Out front, Beau has stacked up three bales of hay and topped them with gruesomely carved jack-o-lanterns. Beneath them, on a chalkboard sign written in glow-in-the-dark chalk, Beau's sister has scrawled, "Don't lose your head. Take a safe ride, or we'll send the horseman after you!"

I smile at the joke before yanking open the heavy bar door. I've been haunting Beau's Bar since the current Beau's grandfather, Beaufort, opened it in the mid-fifties. Maybe it's because they feel like family to me in a way. Somewhere down a twisted family tree, Beau and his family are distant relatives of Irvie.

Beau even looks like Irvie with his boyish face, long, brittle hair, and thin form. You know, if Irvie had worn Rolling Stones t-shirts and pierced his eyebrow.

"Hey there, pretty girl," Beau grins at me as he dries out a beer mug behind the bar.

"How is my favorite bartender tonight?" I lean forward and peck his cheeks briefly before settling onto a barstool. He wasn't working over the weekend, so it's unlikely that he saw me with Wild, but that doesn't matter. The true story about the inspiration for The Legend of Sleepy Hollow has been passed down from one generation of Irvie's family to the next. Beau knows precisely what I am and what I've done.

"You might not want to say that too loud," Beau leans forward, and I catch a whiff of his pine-scented aftershave. "It makes it sound like you're an alcoholic."

"Don't all cheaters look for a ditsy blonde who has had too much to drink?" I wink.

"Fair enough," Beau chuckles as he pours me a shot of whiskey.

Down the bar, in a dark corner, Gil sits surrounded by women vying for his attention.

"You look so good in a suit, Gil." A brunette wearing Daisy Duke shorts over black fishnet stockings rubs Gil's arm appreciatively.

"This?" Gil gestures to the suit. "This is just a little something I pulled out of the back of my closet. You should see me when I'm really trying."

He winks, and his adoring fans swoon. I'm serious. One even becomes a little unsteady on her feet, although whether that is from the Gil effect or the alcohol is anyone's guess.

I shake my head in amusement and glance around the rest of the bar as I sip my whiskey. A few old war veterans sit at a table next to the ancient jukebox, reminiscing about one war or another. By the door, a woman waits for a blind date; if the fact that she keeps pulling up a dating app on her photo to glance at a picture is any indication, and around the pool table in the back, a group of guys stand gossiping like old women.

Then I spot him. A young guy, maybe twenty-five or twenty-six, with tawny hair and broad shoulders, slumps in his chair. In his hand, he twirls a glass of clear liquid over and over while staring down at the table intensely.

I motion to Beau, "I'll be over there if you need me."

Beau smirks and shakes his head, "whatever you want, Cora."

I lip my lips teasingly before walking over to the table. The soul I've absorbed thrums within me, keeping me strong, but who's to stop me from having a little bonus fun?

"You're going to burn a hole in this table if you don't stop staring at it," I murmur by way of greeting as I slide into the seat across from the guy.

"Good," the guy answers darkly.

"Something bothering you, honey?" I ask as I try to get him to look up at me.

"Do you ever wish you could just disappear?" The guy scratches at the scarred table top with his middle finger.

"Perhaps," I pause, "but why would you want to do that when I'm here?"

By now, I'm sure some of you might be tempted to ask why I only go after young men who cheat or look likely to cheat. My answer? I don't. Remember that middle-aged businessman they found at that inn in Piermont a couple of years ago? That was totally me.

"I didn't ask you to sit down," the guy mutters dismissively.

I roll my eyes at Beau's album covers glued to the ceiling, find Nirvana's Nevermind album filling the tile right above my head, and contemplate giving up.

"Now that's no way to treat a lady," I try again.

"I don't think you're much of a lady," the guy replies as he finally slowly, painstakingly looks up at me.

I gasp and lurch back from the table as I come face-to-face with Brom's dead eyes, set into a slightly different-looking face. The very eyes I plucked from his skull the night I exacted my revenge. I petrified one and put it into an Ouija planchette that I now wear around my neck as a trophy from my first kill.

My stomach lurches, and I feel nauseous as the man who cannot possibly be sitting in front of me keeps eye contact, not so much as blinking. I try to swallow, but I feel my heart pounding in my throat, choking me. Little beads of sweat break out on my hairline as I struggle to breathe. I'm on the verge of hyperventilating as the spell freezing me in place bursts, and I leap from my seat, knocking the wobbly three-legged chair backward in the process.

Whoever this man is, he keeps staring at me smugly as I back away and stumble out of the bar, bumping into a couple of tables in my path. I hear Beau calling my name, but all rational thought has deserted me, and my mind is screaming to get as far away from the guy at the table as possible. For the first time in over two hundred years, I'm terrified.

CHANCE

I wake up the morning after Pop's funeral with a marching band of elves playing in my skull. Forcing open my eyes, I realize the music is coming from the obnoxious ringer on my phone and swipe at it to stop. In my hungover state, all the swiping accomplishes is to knock the phone onto the hardwood floor with a thud.

I groan and reach onto the floor to retrieve the offensive object while brushing hair out of my eyes with the back of my arm.

I tap the screen a few times to light it up and read: new missed call; Carlotta. Ah, just as well. Carlotta is the last person

I need or want to talk to. All she'll do is try to convince me we haven't been doing anything wrong and that we belong together. I'm not sure her husband—my former boss—would agree with that.

That's why I thought Pop's letter's timing was perfect. I could get out of the city, clear my head, and get to know my father again. So, I sublet my apartment, put my stuff into storage, and quit my job. But then I got here and walked into this mess.

I've searched the house from top to bottom, but I haven't found any trace of what Pop might have meant by the suspicious deaths occurring in town nor any sign of the woman he mentioned in his letter.

Maybe Pop confused the girl he saw for someone who just looked like someone he had known thirty years ago. Perhaps she was a relative – a daughter, a niece, a cousin – of the woman he had once known. Pop has always been a little eccentric, and he had a wild imagination. Maybe, in his last illness, he just thought he had seen her.

When I was a kid, I used to hang on Pop's every word as he told me grand stories about being a descendent of Ichabod Crane and how, as if by magic, he'd been drawn back to Sleepy Hollow, a place he'd spent summers in as a child, a year or two before he met and married my mother. As I grew older, I realized magic wasn't real and that Sleepy Hollow was a small, ordinary town like any other. The grand stories faded into fables, just another bedtime story a single father told his son, like Peter Pan or the one about the little toy soldier.

I dissect Pop's letter for the millionth time and run possible scenarios through my head again as I take a shower and get dressed. I realize too late that Pop is out of coffee, and I groan before grabbing my car keys off the hook next to the door.

I'll have to give in and buy a cup of overpriced coffee from the coffeehouse down the street from Pop's bookstore. The cool air penetrates the thin cotton of my thermal, looking for warmth as I stroll down the sidewalk from Pop's shop to the coffeehouse. Brightly colored leaves fall from the trees artfully planted in front of storefronts for atmosphere faster than the shopkeepers can sweep them away. A bright orange one lands on my shoulder, but I quickly flick it away.

Ten minutes later, made whole by a to-go cup full of strong coffee, I fumble with the lock keeping me out of Pop's shop. Hollow Books resides in one of the preserved early nineteenth-century buildings on Main Street and comes complete with an old-fashioned wooden door that only opens with a skeleton key. I've been after Pop for years to replace the door. It isn't safe not being able to see who's coming into the store. But Pop always shrugged off my concerns, citing historical landmark guidelines as the reason the door couldn't be changed.

The key finally clicks into place and releases the lock so I can open the door. Turning the brass knob in my hand, I let myself inside and wonder when the last time Pop came into work was. Did he open on the day that he died? Did he lock up the night before, fully intending to come in early the next morning to shelve new inventory, not knowing that his heart would give out before he was able to return to his beloved bookstore?

I inhale deeply, the scent of paper, old books, and candles filling my nose; the smell of the familiar, the scent of my childhood.

Just like the house, Hollow Books is organized chaos. Everywhere I look, I see books—books shoved messily into over-stuffed bookshelves, books stacked up precariously on the floor, books stacked and open on the front counter—books as far as the eye can see.

"Shit." I groan and shake my head as I weave down the narrow aisles to Pop's office in the back of the store.

If possible, Pop's office is an even more horrifying sight.

Loose papers cover every surface, including random sheaves of paper tacked up onto the walls. I think I've finally found what I'm looking for.

———

Two hours later, I collected a box full of Pop's notes on what he considered 'strange goings on in the Hollow' and restored the office to a semblance of order.

I'm just about to leave when a file under a stack of books on the desk catches my eye. I slide it out and try to decipher the hurried scribbles written on the cover. A piece of paper flutters out of the file to the ground, and I bend down to pick it up.

Turning it over, I find a picture of a young woman. She's very young, in fact, probably not more than in her late teens to early twenties. My heart begins to pump a little faster as I study the girl's pretty face. From the angle the photo was taken, she was looking toward the camera, but not quite. Her full, pouty lips are twisted down into a frown, and her almond-shaped eyes are narrowed – from emotion or the sun, I'm not sure. She's frozen in time, shoving a hunk of strawberry blonde hair away from her face.

Though the photo is slightly out of focus and cuts off at her collarbone, I can honestly say that the girl in the picture is stunning. Something tugs within me, and I suddenly need to know who the girl is.

Is this Cora Whitt, the girl from Pop's letter? Could someone who looks like a goddess like she does really be dangerous? In my experience, it's not only possible, it's probable, but this girl could be anyone. The time stamp on the back of the photo says the photo was processed the day before Pop sent his letter. She has to be the one. But who is she?

There's only one person I can think of who could tell me where I can find her.

———

"Beau," I call out as I enter the bar. The lights are dim as usual. Beau must save a bundle on his electricity bill, keeping the lights this way.

Standing at the bar, Beau is flipping through the channels of the small television hanging in the corner. At the sound of my voice, he looks over and tips his chin in greeting, "Hey, Chance. What can I get you?"

"I was actually hoping you could help me with something," I tell him as I pull the photo of the girl out of my pocket. "I found this photo in a file in Pop's office. He took it right before he died, and I was hoping you could tell me who she is."

Beau was two years ahead of me in high school, and his family owned this bar for a few generations, which means Beau knows almost everyone in town.

"I can try," Beau replies as I slide the photo across the bar. He glances at it as he pours me a beer I didn't ask for and freezes mid-pour.

"Beau?" I prompt when he doesn't immediately respond. He hasn't exhaled in precisely one minute and forty-five seconds. Please don't ask me how I know that. Sighing and trying again, I ask, "Well, do you know her?"

Beau snaps out of his daze and clears his throat a couple of times before finally saying, "Uh, yeah, I've seen her around a few times."

"Do you know her name? Or where I can find her?" I ask eagerly.

Beau scratches his head nervously, "Um, I think her name is Cara or Cora or something. I don't know much about her—I've just seen her, you know, around, here and there. Here's your drink; you don't want it to get warm. I should get back to work; it will be getting busy soon."

Beau hurries away to get a drink order from a weathered old

man sitting at the other end of the bar before I ask him anything else. The way he evades my questions and can't even make eye contact tells me he knows more than he's saying.

I shove the photo back in my pocket and drain my glass so quickly that I feel the rush of a buzz hit me immediately. I throw some money down on the bar, and as I'm turning to leave, I hear a voice say, "That girl may be pretty, but she's a beautiful danger."

"What was that?" I whirl around and find a middle-aged man hiding in the shadows. He raises his beer to me in salute, his face coming into the light enough for me to see the black eye patch covering his right eye. It's Fall-Down Dan, the local loon —other than Pop, of course. "Do you know this girl?" I ask as I pull the photo out of my pocket once more.

"I don't need to see it again," Dan says, shoving the photo away. She's pretty unforgettable."

"Do you know where I can find her?" I ask, hoping to get a lead. "I just want to ask her a few questions."

Dan shakes his head. " The girl is as easy to capture as the wind. She appears when she wants to, goes home with who she chooses—but never lets anyone close enough to know a thing about her. I tell you, there's something wrong with a girl like that—something wild and untamed."

"You're drunk, Dan," Beau announces as he comes up behind me. He shakes his head at the old drunk and crosses his arms over his chest to look menacing.

"I am not," Dan protests. "I've only had this one beer."

He holds the half-empty drink up as evidence, and Beau groans and shoves his hand out, palm side up. "Just hand over your keys, and don't think about sneaking behind the bar to get them when I'm not looking."

"You youngins take the fun out of everything," Dan grumbles as he reluctantly hands over a set of keys.

"That's what I'm here for," Beau smirks at me before bustling back behind the bar. It's weird like the strangeness of our earlier encounter never transpired.

"Well, thanks for your help, Dan," I wave goodbye and head for the door.

Dan's next words leave me frozen in the doorway, "Don't forget what I said, Chance. Your father didn't listen, and look what happened to him."

When I turn back to ask what Dan means by that, I find him slumped in his seat, snoring softly.

It's time to see what else is in the box of files I collected from Pop's office.

CHAPTER FIVE

CORA

There's only been one murder in the past fifty years that I'm not responsible for. About eleven or twelve years ago, a sixteen-year-old girl was strangled and thrown from a girder of the covered bridge, made famous by Irvie's story and most commonly referred to as Headless Horseman Bridge, to the rushing waters of the Pocantico River below. It's common knowledge that teens sneak out there, trying to be brave and daring, and make out there while the water rushes by just a few inches under their dangling feet.

Eventually, the girl's boyfriend, a guy with an extensive juvenile record from over in Tarrytown, was charged and convicted of her murder. To this day, he maintains that he was nowhere near the bridge or his girlfriend that night. I've always wondered if there was a possibility he could be telling the truth, but what kind of judge of character am I? I thought Brom actually loved me. Look at how that turned out.

If I had been lurking around that night, maybe I could have saved her, but I was throwing back shots of whiskey and flirting with tourists at Beau's until I was so drunk Beau had to carry me across the street to my apartment.

That night and that murder are often on my mind as I ride Blood through town. My favorite time of day is the stretch just before dawn, when the sky is lightening but not quite dawning into a new day, and the world around me is quiet and still.

There's never anyone around to see me, though I cling to my ghostly invisibility like a safety blanket. If there were anyone able to see through the cloak of my invisibility protection, nobody would believe them if they told what they'd seen. A headless woman riding a horse through town; I don't even carry a pumpkin, flaming or otherwise.

I haven't been able to sleep since my encounter with the Brom lookalike in the bar. So I've been wandering restlessly.

This morning, my subconscious led me to Sleepy Hollow Cemetery. I stopped for a minute and brushed a layer of fallen leaves from the top of Irvie's grave. The crypt I wake up in sometimes only holds a plaque with his name on it; his actual remains lie among the other residents of the cemetery grounds.

"Hello, my old friend," I kneel and pat his headstone lovingly. "I miss you. I think you'd get a kick out of this unbelievable world. I wish you were here experiencing it with me, but I guess immortality is only granted to the bitter and vengeful."

Blood steps closer to the grave, and I feel his hoove brush against my lower back as he nuzzles Irvie's grave.

"You miss him too, don't you, boy?" I ask as I stroke the side of Blood's head. He snorts into my hand, his breath coming out in curling tendrils as he looks for a treat.

I still remember the day I returned in my ghostly form to peek in on Irvie and how surprised I was that he could see me in return.

"Cora?" Irvie asks excitedly as he runs to his open window and grips the window sill.

"You can see me?" I ask in astonishment.

"Of course!" Irvie exclaims, "You're still you – just a ghost! Well, except for not having a head."

"Unfortunately, I seem to be missing that," I feel the grin in my voice.

"And who is this fine fellow?" Irvie motions to Blood.

"This is my new mount," I explain. "His name is Blood."

"A fitting name for an unusual circumstance," Irvie chuckles and rubs Blood's massive nose. Blood's ears perk forward, and he snorts in pleasure.

Along with everything else Irvie had going on in his life, he spent the rest of his life keeping me company. He was the one who convinced me to try out being corporeal again. After a bit of experimenting, I was able to appear lifelike again. At first, it only lasted for a few minutes, then a few hours, but we learned over time as I took my revenge that my killings granted me a sort of half-life. After these killings, I could remain whole for months on end.

Irvie was my best friend and my strongest supporter. I might have loved him a little, although mostly, he was like the brother I never had. When he told me he wanted to write my story, with a few changes to protect me, I laughed it off. I didn't realize it would become what it did. I still have a first edition of the Legend of Sleepy Hollow hidden in one of my cedar chests in my apartment, and I like to think it's like having a piece of Irvie with me always.

———

I spend some time with Irvie before brushing the dirt off my transparent knees and remounting Blood.

Back at my apartment, I coax my body to become a physical thing again and cringe as my head seals back into place. After a shower and a change of clothing, I see that I have just enough time to hit up Dark Brews for my daily caffeine rush.

"Good morning. What can I get started on for you?" The barista asks as her brunette ponytail swings back and forth behind her head. The motion reminds me of Blood's tail swishing when he's waiting for a sugar cube.

"Can I get a large mocha to go?" I place my order as I search for the appropriate change in my purse.

"Coming right up," the girl smiles. Ugh, morning people. Something should be done about them.

I go to the other end of the counter to wait for my drink as my eyes wander around the spacious coffeehouse. A businessman sits by the door, sipping from a coffee mug as he reads the New York Times. Two teenage girls hurry in and place an order before spreading out on the couch by the front window for some last-minute studying.

In the cozy corner in the back, a young couple sits with their heads bent together as they enjoy a romantic breakfast. The guy hand-feeds his girlfriend one of Dark Brew's famous pumpkin spice scones before sipping from his mug. A drop misses his mouth and drips down his chin, and his girlfriend grabs a napkin and wipes it away. Then they kiss – one of those sappy romantic movie-type kisses. It makes me want to gag. It's too early to be forced to witness something that sweet, especially when it's all an act. Nobody is that in love with their significant other. Or maybe I'm just so cynical I can't appreciate romance anymore.

"Large mocha to go," the barista calls out my order, sparing me from one more second of witnessing the manifestation of my worst nightmare. I thank her and throw a dollar in the tip jar before grabbing my drink and stepping back into the early morning sunshine.

I take a long sip as I begin walking back to my studio when I hear someone call out to me in a thick New York accent, "You! Wait up; I've been looking for you."

I spin on my heel, my eyes automatically narrowing in suspicion as I come face to face with Chance, the second generation. So, this is why Beau left me a message in the middle of the night to tell me that someone was asking questions about me. I keep quiet as he approaches, wondering what he wants from me and how I should play this off. Does he know who I am? Of course not; I mentally shake myself. That's not possible.

"Can I help you?" I ask, deciding to play it cool.

"I've been looking all over for you," Chance pants after sprinting up to me to close the rest of the distance between us.

"Um, do I know you?" I ask, playing dumb.

"No, but I think you might have known my dad," Chance explains as he falls into step beside me. I keep walking toward the studio, and he continues, "You see, my father moved here when he was twenty, and he just recently passed away."

"I'm sorry for your loss," I murmur sincerely. Lies take shape in my head as I continue, "But I don't know how I can help you."

"I thought perhaps you might have known him. He ran Hollow Books." Chance gestures in the general direction of the bookstore. His tone turns coaxing, "Please, what's your name? I promise I'm not crazy."

"Cordelia," I reluctantly tell him. Squinting up at him, I add, "I go by Cora, though." A smirk sliding into place on my lips, I decided to play with him, "What is your name? Or should I just call you 'crazy guy from the street?'"

A dark, unreadable look travels across his face as he follows me into the studio and trails me to my desk. The look passes quickly before transforming into a blank, expressionless mask. "I'm Chance, Chance Jordan. I'm named after my dad. Are you sure that name doesn't ring a bell?"

"I can't say that it does. I'm sorry. Besides, I'm not much of a reader." The lie slips easily off my tongue.

He walks over to the decorative bookcase behind my desk and runs a finger over the spines of the top shelf of books on the overstuffed bookcase. "I can see that."

I shrug, unfazed by being caught in the lie, "I mostly buy books online."

"What happened to the 'Shop Local' initiative?" Chance's lips turn up in a teasing smile.

"I thought Hollow Books only sold old and rare books. I doubt your father kept much in stock in the way of Stephen King." I smile sardonically into my drink.

"He might have been stocking him if it was a first editi–," Chance pauses when he sees the cover. " Oh, this is the television adaptation cover, so no. Ugh, Under the Dome. I hate that one."

"What's wrong with Under the Dome?" I demand.

Chance shrugs, "The tv show sucked."

"First of all, never judge a book by its television show," I intone. "And secondly, the first season wasn't bad. It got weird after that. I can relate to feeling trapped in one place with no escape."

Ignoring my comments, he keeps reading off my titles, "Carrie, The Dark Tower, It - they made a remake of that movie, you know."

"I know," I murmur, but he's not listening.

"What? Not a single romance novel in this entire bookcase?" Chance looks up at me, his eyes brightening mischievously. "What kind of woman are you?"

"Romance is for idiots," I mutter darkly into my drink. "It gives women the false sense that men aren't all a bunch of one-track-minded pigs that don't have any feelings or emotions above the belt."

"Whoa," Chance holds up his hands defensively. "Not all men are quite that bad. And what about women? Women can be so fickle sometimes."

No, not all men are bad, I think, sadly. Not that I could tell Chance that.

Oblivious to my thoughts, Chance continues, "Although I'm

right there with you with romance novels. They're just commercialized fluff. Give me a heart-pounding thriller or a bone-chilling horror novel over romance any day."

I grin at his description, "So, did you attack me on the street to ask me about my taste in books?"

"Oh," Chance shakes his head as if trying to remind himself of the reason he's standing in my studio. "No, I found a photo of you in one of my father's files. It was taken just before he died, and I wanted to know if you knew him."

"No," I answer quickly. "Like I said, I haven't shopped at Hollow Books. I'm kind of a homebody. I don't go out much."

"Do you know why he might have had a photograph of you?" Chance asks.

I shake my head, "I have no idea. Maybe he was taking photos of people out and about. Or maybe he took the photo by accident."

"If that were the case, why would he have processed the photo?" Chance crosses his thick, muscular arms over his chest, trying to look intimidating. I don't know what he thinks he knows, but it likely isn't much. I'm not lying. I haven't seen his father in years, and I don't understand why he'd have a current photo of me in a file in his office. My studio has been across the street and down the block from Hollow Books since I started my business about five years ago, but I've always been careful to make sure he never saw me. It would be too confusing for him. For example, when Harrison Ford sees Blake Lively again in The Age of Adaline, she tries to pretend that the girl he knew is her mother. That lie didn't turn out so well for them.

"Your guess is as good as mine," I mirror his stance, crossing my arms over my chest as I lean back in my desk chair.

I fight the urge to flinch under Chance's scrutiny. His copper-colored eyes are intense and unrelenting. Finally, he breaks the connection and strides over to my open equipment cabinet.

"You're into photography, right?" Chance asks as he picks up my most prized possession, my H6D-50c camera. He turns it over in his hands, examining it like it's a disposable camera and not the most expensive thing I own. "Maybe he hired you to take some photos for him. Or maybe you gave him some lessons."

"Do not touch that camera," I snarl through gritted teeth. I have a thing about people touching my stuff, especially my cameras. Andi isn't even allowed to handle them, and he works for me.

"This thing?" Chance holds it up for emphasis. "Why shouldn't I touch it?"

"Because it costs almost as much as a midsize sedan," I explain as I dig my fingernails into my palm in an effort to calm myself down. "If you drop it, I'll be forced to kill you."

"Oh," Chance turns slightly green as he sets the camera back down on its shelf. "Sorry."

"I've already told you that I don't know your father, and I have no idea why he was photographing me. Is there something else you need, or are you just here to drive me crazy?" I glare at him.

Chance matches my glare, "You don't have to be so uptight. I was just curious."

I growl and throw my hands up in the air in exasperation. Finally, Chance gets the hint and heads for the door. "I guess I'll see you around."

"Not likely," I mutter as the door clatters shut behind him.

A heartbeat passes before Andi comes charging into the studio wearing dark, oversized sunglasses and a designer T-shirt tucked into a pair of jeans. "Ohmigod, what was that smoldering creature doing in here, and why didn't you text me? He is so hot! I'm dying to meet him in person."

"Chance?" I groan as I shuffle some papers around on my desk. "You weren't missing much. He was driving me insane."

"You kicked him out?" Andi looks outraged.

"This is a photography studio, not a coffeehouse. He wasn't a prospective or current client, so he didn't need to be here," I rationalize.

"Are you crazy?" Andi asks. "What did he want? What did he say? Was he asking you out? Please tell me you didn't give him the cold shoulder you give every other guy in the world."

"He was not asking me out," I assure him. "He was just asking me a few questions about his dad, that's all. I'm not interested, but I'm sure you can still catch him if you hurry."

"How can you not be interested in him, Cora?" Andi puts his hands flat on my desk, interrupting my restless shuffling. "He is so perfect."

I shrug, and Andi sighs in disappointment as he flops dramatically down at his desk. "I don't know what I'm going to do with you, girl."

I try unsuccessfully to hide my smirk. Driving Andi crazy with my apparent lack of interest in relationships has become a sort of pastime for me since he started working in the studio.

In true Andi fashion, his attention drifts to something else as he wakes up his computer. "Ooh, I almost forgot. You have to check out this guy I met online."

I look up from my screen, where I'm checking my e-mail, to see that Andi has pulled up a headshot photo of an attractive guy with curly blonde hair, full, almost feminine lips, and rectangular gray eyes. "He's cute," I concede. "Just be careful, not that he's one of those Tunafish people."

"They're called *Catfish*." Andi shakes his head, "and he's not. We had a Skype date last night."

I scrunch my nose, "why are they called Catfish, exactly?"

"I don't know. I think it has something to do with fishing," Andi waves his hand dismissively.

"Awesome," I deadpan. "Can we get to work now, please? I need you to get those proofs ready for the Downing wedding.

The clients are coming in at three to pick through which ones they want us to make prints of."

"Sure thing, boss lady," Andi salutes me saucily.

———

CHANCE

She lied to me. That beautiful, frustrating, insane girl lied to me with nearly every word she spoke in that strange, musical, almost foreign accent. I twist the gauge in my ear angrily as I stand on the sidewalk next to my car, trying to process what just happened. Around the girl in Pop's photo – the one and only Cora – I felt slightly drunk, intoxicated. Like I was floating on a cloud, and I didn't care where I was or what I was doing as long as I was in her company. Fuck.

I could kick myself for rushing her without a solid plan, but when I saw a girl step out of Dark Brews, resembling the girl in Pop's photo, I found myself darting across the street before I could stop myself. I'd gotten a slight look at her in the image, but the girl striding down the street with an air of confidence about her was on the short side, maybe five-foot-three or four. One could even describe her as mostly leg except for the generous curve of her hips and her ample chest. Her long, wavy strawberry blonde hair had kept blowing into her hazel eyes as she looked at me like I was a deranged mental patient. But I could see through her; her ignorance was all a beautifully constructed lie, and damn if my body didn't respond to her, begging me to lay her down on the nearest flat surface and take her despite it all.

Cora is feisty. When I picked up her camera, I really thought she was going to clobber me with a blunt object. I've worked with plenty of photographers on assignments, so I know how uptight they can get about their equipment, yet for some reason, I just wanted to mess with her.

Somehow, some way, I know she knew Pop. That much was evident from her avoidance and body language. I'm still trying to puzzle out how she can look so young when Pop claims to have known her thirty years ago.

Getting an idea, I hop in the car and head back to Pop's. This is the digital age. I should be able to find out anything I want to know about this girl online.

Ten minutes later, I sit down in front of Pop's computer with a pen wedged between my clenched teeth and an unlit cigarette tucked behind my ear, habits I picked up while working for various publications. I don't smoke anymore, but something about the unlit cigarette being within reach calms me down. And I keep the pen handy in case I need to scribble something down in a hurry. I don't need paper when I can take notes all the way up the inside of my arm. Most of my coworkers thought my scribbles were just part of one of my tattoos.

I tap out a melody with my fingertips on the dusty wooden desk Pop used at home. Pop was a bit of a Luddite, and sitting at his desk, it conjures images of him swearing at the computer because it didn't do what he thought it should do. I can't count the number of times he ranted that computers would be the demise of our modern society and how, if he had his way, we'd all go back to doing everything by hand.

When the computer finally flickers on, I pull up a search engine and type in the name Cordelia "Cora" Whitt plus Sleepy Hollow, New York, hoping that Pop was right about her last name.

The search returned nearly five thousand results, but only one of them actually connected with the girl I met earlier today, a website for her photography studio, Sleepless in Love Photography.

I click on the link, and a dark-themed website fills the

screen. In the top left-hand corner is an animated headless horseman, the logo of nearly every shop or business in town, and the studio's name. I sift through the various pages and find useless information on the location of her studio, a portfolio of her work, and the type of photo sessions she hires out to do, but nowhere do I find anything personal about her – except for her name on the contact page.

Next, I pulled up Facebook and Instagram, but they came up empty except for a business account on Instagram. What twenty-something-year-old doesn't use social media? Even as anti-social as he was, Pop used Facebook to keep track of family and old friends.

I lean back, biting my lower lip in frustration, and then decide to take a different approach. I pull up the family history website I've used in the past to track down people for stories and type in Cora's name. I came back with one result and excitedly clicked on the link to see what the website had uncovered.

My excitement quickly deflates when I realize the result is for a twenty-one-year-old woman who lived and died in Sleepy Hollow in seventeen-ninety. A public records search yields the same result, and a search on a background check website with the slogan "We can dig up dirt on anyone for one low price of fourteen-ninety-nine!" comes back with no results at all.

Who is this girl? It's like she's a ghost or something, like she doesn't exist. Maybe her name is an alias, but if so, what is she hiding?

I decided to pull up the contact information of a friend of mine at the New York Times. Just because I have never managed to land a job there—yet—doesn't mean that I don't have some contacts in their superior ranks.

"Hello?" my friend Eli sounds harried when he picks up after five rings.

"Hey man," I greet him as I visualize him sitting in his cubicle buried under a pile of work, "busy day?"

"Somebody's got to write all of these damned obituaries," Eli grumbles, and the sound of shuffling papers filters through the receiver. "What's up with you? You've been like a ghost since you quit the Post."

"My dad died, and I'm trying to figure some stuff out back home," I explain.

"Shit, I'm sorry to hear that, Chance," Eli clears his throat uncomfortably.

"Thanks," I cough awkwardly. Say, I'm calling to find some information on this girl—her name is Cordelia Whitt, but she might go by Cora. Can you do a little digging and help me out?"

Eli's startled laughter breaks in and out across the line. I've always gotten spotty reception at Pop's house. "You want me to use the Times's resources to look up information on a girl you want to nail?" Eli sounds incredulous.

"Actually, it might be for a story," I correct. "Nothing definite, just something I'm thinking of freelancing. I'm trying to piece out a few things, but I can't find anything about this girl. It's like she's a fucking ghost or something."

"Hmm," Eli sounds thoughtful as I hear the clinking of the ceramic mug on his desk. He usually keeps no fewer than fifty pens in that mug because every writer knows not to be without writing material when an idea or a lead pops up. "Cordelia – or possibly Cora – Whitt, you say?"

"That's right," I confirm. She'd be from Sleepy Hollow or somewhere in the surrounding area. She's probably in her early twenties right now."

"Got it," Eli murmurs as he takes notes. I'll see what I can dig up. So, what kind of story is this? Is it anything I might find interesting?"

"I'm honestly not sure yet," I shake my head even though Eli can't see me. "It's just something strange that my pop wanted me to follow up on."

"How are you handling things up in the boondocks?" Eli asks

cautiously. To him, even Brooklyn is considered lower class. He's strictly Manhattan with its' upscale bars and restaurants where he can lounge around in his overpriced clothes and pretend like he's not drowning in student loan debts.

"It's different than I left it," I pause, "and yet it's the same at the same time."

"I hear Grankowski has been having a mental breakdown since you quit," Eli gossips.

"Really?" I ask as a twinge of guilt hits me. I loved my job at the Post, and my boss was good to me, but outside forces forced my hand. I had to quit. There was no other way. All because I made one stupid, selfish decision when I was drunk and thinking with my dick, a decision that became leverage to an evil bitch that wanted to keep me under her thumb – or just under her in general.

"Yeah, man," Eli's voice pulls me out of my dark memories. "He's completely lost it. He's a total mess without you. Why the hell did you walk out anyway? You never told me."

"It's kind of a long story," I mutter.

"I have time," Eli's tone perks up eagerly.

I snort, "Maybe when I get back to the city, you can take me for that beer you owe me, and I'll tell you all about it."

"I'm going to hold you to that, Chance," Eli sounds amused yet intrigued.

"Call me when you find something, okay?" I corral him back to the point of my call.

"Will do," Eli promises before clicking off.

I set the phone down next to Pop's desk lamp and flipped through the photos Pop took of Cora right before he died. I don't know why I find her so fascinating. About all I know is that I need to talk to her again. At the thought, my heart begins to beat faster, and all the blood in my body rushes to my cock. I can't get too attached to this girl, no matter what my body wants. I ruin things, ruin lives. I always have and always will.

CHAPTER SIX

CORA

At five after five, Andi yawns loudly and stretches his long arms over his head, "Whew, that was one long-ass day of making ugly people pretty."

"Andi," I chastise as I try to stifle a grin, "You shouldn't make fun of the clients."

"There's only so much that Photoshop can do," Andi argues as he points at his screen. "Sometimes people just gotta admit that they're unattractive."

"You're incorrigible," I cover my mouth as a giggle escapes my lips.

"I'm adorable, and you know it," Andi retorts as he slides his oversized sunglasses over his eyes. It's not worth mentioning to him that the sun set a half hour ago. He comes over and sits on the edge of my desk. " So you know that guy I was telling you about? The one I met online?"

"Yes?" I reply cautiously.

"Well, he invited us to a party at a friend of his over in Tarrytown." Andi's eyes are filled with hope and excitement as he looks at me over the top of his sunglasses, and he bites his lip.

"Us?" I echo, sounding like a broken record.

Andi sighed, "Well, technically, he invited me, but this is the first time we're meeting in person, and I'm nervous, so I thought maybe you wanted to come with me. Give him the 'Cora Whitt' seal of approval."

"You want me to crash your first date with your dream dude?" I ask incredulously.

"I don't know," Andi says, adjusting his slouchy knit hat. What if he doesn't like me in person? What if we're only good in cyberspace?"

I put my hand on his knee reassuringly, "Come on now, where's the confident Andi that I know and love? Of course, he'll like you in person! What's not to like?"

"I am pretty amazing," Andi concedes as he looks down at his gold designer sneakers.

"See? That's better," I smile. "You know you don't need me."

"I guess," Andi mumbles. "Are you sure you don't want to come, though? All you ever do is work. You never allow yourself to have any fun."

"Don't worry about me," I shrug off Andi's invitation. "I have a hot date with Stephen King waiting for me upstairs."

"You have a guy upstairs, and you didn't tell me?" Andi shrieks, looking momentarily wounded before that flirty glimmer is back in his eyes. What are you doing sitting around here with me? Go get him, girl!"

Andi practically shoves me through the back door of the studio into the corridor that leads both to the back exit and the stairwell to my apartment. He blows me a kiss and says, "Go on, I'll lock up on my way out."

He's so excited that I don't have the heart to tell him that Stephen King is the author of the book I'm planning to stay in and read tonight.

———

Despite a full day's work and Andi's invitation to go to the house party in Tarrytown after work, I'm still so keyed up from my earlier encounter with Chance that I can't focus on the words on the page I'm trying to read. I try to concentrate harder on Bag of Bones, but my thoughts keep wandering back to Chance running his strong hands over my bookshelf downstairs and critiquing my taste in books, and without my permission, my thoughts drift off to where I'd rather have his hands. Curse it. Why does he have to look so much like his father? A half-hour passes fruitlessly before I sigh and shove my well-worn bookmark into the page I've been staring at and slide the book onto my overflowing coffee table.

Realizing how much clutter I've allowed to pile up on its surface, I grab a garbage bag and start tossing in old magazines and catalogs I kept for no reason at all other than maybe at some point I'd order something from one. I blush with embarrassment as I realize one of the catalogs dates back to three Christmases ago. Once the garbage is off the surface, I straighten the books left behind into two stacks: books I'm reading and books I want to show off. In the center of the coffee table, I set a bowl of dried rose petals and hollow, dried-out pumpkins. It's a strange combination, but it fits my personality.

I stand back and admire my handiwork, but I still can't escape my feeling of restlessness, so I head downstairs, careful to make sure Andi really has left for the night and isn't lurking around waiting for details on my imaginary date. Then, I disappear into the dark room I converted from a small windowless office space. Professionally, I work mainly in digital, but I still enjoy using my film-only Nikon and capturing life through my lens in the old-fashioned way.

I've been fascinated with cameras and photography since they were introduced to the general public. I scoured the area looking for a shop owner who could order me one, but it took some time. Many thought I was crazy, a woman with such an odd passion. Still, I've been carefully capturing the world around me, first on daguerreotypes, then tintypes, and finally on paper, for nearly one hundred and eighty years.

I still have all of my original cameras on display in the studio, though most assume I picked them up at garage sales or antique shops.

In the dark room, I process and manipulate a strip of negatives, first developing one layer, then cutting it out and laying it over another negative to create an entirely new photograph. A few years ago, I read an article about an exhibit at the Met dedicated to the history of manipulated photography before the digital age. They posted some of the photos on their website, and the work was amazing. It inspired me to try something new. I've been hooked on the idea and experimenting with different methods ever since.

I work silently until my vision begins to blur, and my head starts to swim from chemical-induced dizziness. Being what I am, I can withstand being locked in an enclosed space with the chemicals used to develop film photographs for long intervals, but I'm not immune. It was part of the reason I didn't make much of a fuss when digital became the new big thing in photography.

I run up to my apartment and grab a bottle of water, then decide to take Blood for a ride so I can get my fill of fresh air.

Soon, Blood and I are flying down the street toward Sleepy Hollow Cemetery. I swear Blood is one morbid horse. This is always his favorite place to visit on our nighttime rides. He speeds up into a canter as the gates come into view, and in one majestic leap, we cross the barrier between the sleeping village on one side of the gates and the silent cemetery on the other.

Something weird happens every time I cross the cemetery boundary. My vision switches from normal seeing-in-the-dark vision to a luminous green night vision that allows me to see my surroundings. It makes me feel like a cat or maybe a bat.

When I was first resurrected, I was able to find Bathsheba, the *volva* that brought me back to the world of the living, wandering the depths of the cemetery. She is an immortal being like I am, though much, much older. She mentioned once that she was born during the rise of the Vikings back in Scandinavia. Her kind was highly respected before Christianity drove Paganism from the cold lands. She'd fled her home and lived a nomadic existence ever since, eventually settling in our village of Dutch settlers because it reminded her of her homeland.

Over time, my meetings with Bathsheba became farther and fewer between. She insisted that I was capable of caring for myself and that I didn't need her anymore, but now it seems as if so many strange things are happening at once, and I need her more than ever.

A horse on a mission, Blood trots toward the back of the cemetery to the old, forgotten graves, stopping dead in his tracks in front of two weathered graves covered in thick, soft moss. Though the names have nearly faded completely, as if time wishes to erase their existence altogether, I can still see the names as if they were freshly carved onto the stone. Bromforth Bones and Katrina Van Tassel Bones died in 1790 and 1791, respectively.

Though it seemed like only minutes spent in the dark with the raspy voice I learned belonged to the village witch, in truth, my soul lingered in the dark in between for several months before I was resurrected into the monster I'd become.

My headless body wasn't even cold in the grave a fortnight before Brom made Trina his wife. Apparently, Brom had framed Ichabod for my murder, telling the village that Ichabod was my lover and he had killed me in a rage when he learned I had ruined his chances with Trina. The rumors of my impurity and dirty bloodlines were the only things that saved Ichabod from being hunted down and facing the gallows' noose. You know, because a whore's life wasn't worth anything.

Ichabod was abandoning town the night I rose from the dead, a headless horsewoman on a menacing steed waving about a scythe as if I might tear the world apart if I could. I wasn't after him, but he didn't take it that way. I scared him so severely that he rode as fast and as hard as he could from town, never to return. Not that he had anything to return to. His love had married another and was already showing signs of carrying his baby, and Ichabod's true love had always been knowledge anyway.

On the night I rose, I headed straight for the home that Brom had been near finished building when I died. On hot nights lost in breathless whispers and naked flesh moving as one in the hay loft, Brom promised me he'd make me his wife as soon as the last floorboard was in place and he'd finally be able to lay me down in a bed made of feathers like an honest woman. It was those stolen promises that had once kept me going. The light at the end of the tunnel for my miserable life, but on that night under the full moon, I approached his house with a more bloodthirsty purpose.

I'd stood at his window and lured him from her bed. Trina never even stirred, nor had she on any of the nights he'd snuck out to bed any of his other mistresses. If she hadn't been such a heartless witch, I might have pitied her.

Instead, he'd followed my headless form to the barn, disbelieving the eyes that told him I was still walking among the living. When he reached out to grab me to cure him of the silly delusion that I was really there and found solid flesh, I drew him under my spell.

I gave him one last long, hard ride before I gouged out his eyes, keeping one as a souvenir, and stole his soul, and afterward, when he had turned to dust beneath me, I basked in my first kill. I'd gotten revenge on my murderer, but I wasn't nearly done yet. Brom had two sons on the way, one with Trina and one with her poor cousin, and since my power only works on adult males, I had to wait.

I'd only returned to that house once, on the night that Trina gave birth to Brom's son. As soon as the midwife took the baby away to clean him, I snuck into her dark bedchamber. In her exhausted post-delivery state, Trina mistook me for the midwife and didn't have time to react or utter a cry before I raised my scythe and opened her throat, spilling her traitorous blood all over her bedsheets.

I always wonder if, in those months after Brom's death, Trina knew that Brom had had other lovers and if she knew that he had fathered her cousin's child. She must have. She couldn't have been that obtuse. If Trina honestly thought I was the only other one, she was sorely mistaken.

"Revisiting your past?" Bathsheba's raspy voice pulls me from my memories.

"Trying to figure out a puzzle," I murmur, my words nearly getting lost in the wind. I don't bother looking over into the face of the crone standing at Blood's flank. I knew I would find her here just like she knew I would come seeking her out.

"Aye, what might that be, girl?" Bathsheba sounds disinterested as she seats herself upon Brom's headstone. Sometimes, I wonder why she resurrected me and what she gained from bringing me back. Bathsheba can be nurturing like a mother and, at other times, unfeeling and ruthless.

"I killed them," I mutter. "I killed them all. One generation after another, until there were no descendants of Brom left alive. Or at least I thought I did."

"And what is making you question that, Cora?" Bathsheba asks gently, honing in on the bewilderment in my voice.

"I ran into a man with Brom's eyes and his face," I furrow my brow. He not only resembled him, but he bore such a strong resemblance that if I did not know it to be untrue, I would think Brom was still alive. Then there was the chilly, calculated look of a predator that he stared me down with—as if he knew me, knew exactly who I am and what I've done."

A shiver of unease slides down my back as I recall the memory.

"And you are sure you did not imagine such an encounter?" Bathsheba inquires.

"I am certain," I nod. "He was made of flesh and bone."

Bathsheba hisses in resignation, "It could well be that you encountered your *Crooked One.*"

"My what?" I ask as I turn to face the old crone fully. I blink uncomfortably as I take in the sight of her. Bathsheba once explained to me that if an immortal does not restore some of the energy needed to keep them going at least once a decade, then the immortal may become withered and wraithlike. The very picture of nightmares – and before me, my savior appears as frail and horrifying as the malicious spirits the village children, and I would tell stories of on harvest nights many moons ago. "Bathsheba," I whisper, "what has happened to you?"

"Nothing for you to worry about, girl," the cranky old crone waves off my concern. "What you should be worried about is the Crooked One."

"What is a Crooked One?" I ask, unsure if I really want to know.

Bathsheba sighs, "'tis the entire reason you were able to be resurrected; a dark spirit, a restless spirit whose rage has drawn the attention of the dark gods. In turn, they've been blessed by their gods, allowed a mortal life to bring death and destruction on anyone they choose."

"Like me," I ask carefully.

"No, dearie," Bathsheba shakes her head furiously. "I resurrected you, and though you have a thirst for revenge, you were born with a pure heart. You're a Gatekeeper. Keeping the living world protected from the Crooked Ones is the entire purpose of a Gatekeeper. Crooked Ones were born with dark souls, and when they met their end, their souls drew the attention of demons who breathed new life into them, turning them into mindless, soulless horrors. A plague upon the earth. Each Crooked One has a Gatekeeper counterpoint, usually a victim of their cruelty."

"What does this Crooked One want?" I ask, not wanting to understand what she's telling me as I angle my body closer to Bathsheba. I feel an uncontrollable hunger for information stirring within me. "And why did it wear Brom's face?"

"Your murder was just the accelerant that illuminated Brom's existence to the underworld. And when you were resurrected and exacted your revenge on Brom, you initiated the demon's ability to breathe new life into him." Bathsheba explains. "He has probably been waiting centuries for the right time to show himself to you, to seek revenge against you. Be careful, girl. This won't be the last you will see of him. You'll have to kill him before he has the chance to kill your spirit forever."

"You're telling me that my revenge is what caused this rotting of his soul? Yet you were the one who resurrected me and told me to get my revenge," I huffed angrily. "How can you say this is my fault?"

"I'm saying no such thing, dearie." Bathsheba's lips are set in a grim line. "I'm saying it was inevitable. Brom was off from the moment he took his first breath. If he hadn't murdered you, it would have been someone else, and that person would have set things in motion. Your death was merely the catalyst. It's your entire purpose in this half-life of yours to end Brom and drive him back to the underworld."

"How? How can I kill something that is not alive?" I demand.

My vision swims, turning foggy, and as I blink to clear my eyes, I realize Bathsheba is becoming faint and unfocused.

"Your heart will know how. It's what you were resurrected

to do," Bathsheba says simply before she fades from sight completely.

———

<u>CHANCE</u>

I'm standing in front of the fogged-up bathroom mirror, mindlessly shaving the stubble from my jaw, when I hear my phone ring in the other room.

Gripping the soft, butter-colored towel around my waist tighter, I quickly slide into my old bedroom and grab hold of my phone. An unfamiliar New York City number flashes across the screen, and I hurriedly answer, hoping Eli has tracked some information down on Cora.

"Hello?" I answer eagerly.

A rich laugh that used to immediately have my cock stiffening answers my greeting. "I knew you would be happy to hear from me, honey."

"Fuck," I groan as I slap a hand over my eyes. Carlotta Grankowski. Some women can't take a hint.

"Hello, Chance," Carlotta purrs.

"What do you want?" I ask through clenched teeth. I should have hung up, but I know she'll call back.

"I had a dream this morning that you were buried inside me," Carlotta begins, and I feel my body tightening and responding to her words against my will, "and then I realized it's been too long since you made that a reality."

I can hear her clicking her fake fingernails against her phone case. I still have scars on my back from those fingernails. Continuing, she added, "I want you over here in ten minutes."

I sigh, "I told you, Carlotta, we're over."

"Is that so?" I can hear the wheels turning in Carlotta's head as she tries to think of a way to manipulate me into coming back to her. "Come on now, baby, you know that you still want me. I can tell from the sound of your voice. And if you don't do what I want, I'll have to tell my husband that you took advantage of me. He loves you, but he won't hesitate to blackball you all over the city, Chance."

"Tell whoever the hell you want, Carlotta. I don't care," I snap before hanging up on her and blocking her number. I learned a long time ago just how empty her threats were. Unfortunately, it wasn't until recently that I got tired of her moods and her games.

I met Carlotta at her and her husband's Fourth of July cookout at their house on Long Island. I'd been back in the city for a month, and her husband had hired me at the Post only two weeks earlier, but I loved my job and the freedom I was given to write whatever I wanted.

At thirty-nine, Carlotta was eleven years my senior, though not old enough to be considered a true cougar. It had been a while since I'd gotten laid, and when she stepped out onto the patio with those long legs and surgically enhanced tits, all I could think about was those legs wrapped around my waist and her long black hair caressing my shoulder as I fucked her against the wall. I realized too late that she was a manipulative viper who was never going to let me go willingly. I figured if I quit my job and stayed away from the city long enough, she'd get bored of waiting around and find a new victim. I guess I haven't been away long enough.

I toss my phone and the damp towel onto the bed and yank on a pair of jeans, feeling frustrated that I allowed Carlotta to get me all worked up again.

Barefoot and shirtless, I pour myself a mug of coffee and steel myself to deal with the task I've set out for myself today: going into Pop's room.

Pop was notoriously private. After my mom died, I can't remember the door to their bedroom ever being open. He never locked it, exactly, but I knew enough not to try to step foot inside. Even when I was a teenager, Pop's room was always off-limits, though I don't exactly know why. That hasn't changed since he died. I've left the door shut like he liked it.

Today is the day that changes, and I'm afraid of what I'll find.

I pace in front of the door, sipping my coffee and trying to work up the courage to wrap my hand around the doorknob and open Pandora's box. I feel paranoid like Pop's ghost is watching me over my shoulder, silently waiting to see whether I'll break his unspoken rule or not. I can almost feel his warm breath against my neck.

Man up, idiot, I scold myself. *He's gone. He can't yell at you now.*

Sighing heavily, I set my mug down on the floor and opened the door before I could talk myself out of it. As I pushed the door open, a burst of cold air rushed out of the room as if the room was exhaling after holding a long breath.

I nudge the door open further with my foot and step inside. Blackout curtains cloak the room in total darkness as I run my hand along the wall, searching for the light switch. Finally, finding it, I blink as my eyes adjust to the change in lighting.

Pop's room is pretty sparse. A king-size bed monopolizes much of the small master bedroom, flanked on one side by a Tiffany lamp atop an antique cherry wood nightstand. The only other furniture taking up space in the room is a glass-fronted barrister bookcase stuffed with classic novels and a beat-up dresser whose drawers don't quite close.

I run my hand over the top of the dresser and it comes away grimy with dust. Wiping my hand against my jeans, I sit down on Pop's lumpy mattress and stroke the quilted comforter lovingly. My grandmother sent us both one when I was seven years old. Dad's was more practical, but I remember mine being covered in squares of train and spaceship fabric. It hits me suddenly that I'm alone now. I don't have any family left on either side, and the thought drowns me in a sea of sadness.

Swallowing hard, I rub my eyes with the back of my arm. I

must have dust from the top of the dresser in them because my eyes are watering. I blink a few times, and my eye catches the corner of something white sticking out of Pop's nightstand drawer—a piece of paper.

I try to pull the paper free, but it's thoroughly stuck, so I grab the paper in one hand, the drawer pull in the other, and pull. When it doesn't immediately release, I place the lamp on the floor and tip the nightstand forward while pulling on the drawer pull, figuring that something is stuck in the drawer.

After a few tries, which made me rethink canceling my gym membership, the drawer finally fell open and clattered to the floor, narrowly missing my feet.

Sighing, I reach down to retrieve the drawer and its contents and spot the reason the drawer refused to open. A small, thick leather book is taped to the underside of the drawer. Peering into the base of the nightstand, I realize there is a three-inch well under the drawer where the book must have fit.

Curiosity tugs at me as I remove the tape from the book and run my fingers over the cover. A leather cord and a gold button keep the book securely closed, and my big fingers fumble to unwind the cord.

Inside the book, I find pages upon pages of Pop's hand-written notes. At first, I assume it's another one from Pop's inventory books or maybe a customer order ledger until I take a closer look.

The little book contains names, ages, and a single date. The dates go in order, popping up from the year my father was born up until six months ago, about two listings a year. In the corner of the pages are three coded identifiers circled in red pen. Some pages have an "S" in the corner, others an "H.A.," and more marked with a "U."

I flip to the end, looking for some legend or key, and come upon a few entries written in a shaky hand. Pop's writing has always been beautiful. He always grumbled that it wasn't right that letter writing has become obsolete in a world obsessed with emails and text messaging. This looks nothing like his writing, yet I can still tell that it was written by him by the way that he forms certain letters in his cursive script.

The top of the first entry explains the codes: S for stroke, H.A. for heart attack, and U for undetermined. The twice-yearly dates now stand out to me as dates of death. Finally, I'm getting somewhere. This has to be what Pop wanted me to look into.

The following entry is addressed explicitly to me.

Chance,

If you're reading this, then you arrived too late. This damn ticker of mine finally gave out, and I'm sorry that we never got the chance to mend things up before the angel of death came to deliver me to the other side. There's so much I never told you, so much that I should have told you but never thought it was the right time.

The fact that you're here reading this means that my letter found its' way to you, so you know some of what I meant to tell you, though I'm sure you have more questions than answers at this point.

Perhaps it is best if I start at the beginning. Though I moved to Sleepy Hollow when I was twenty, I first came to the village as a boy. Like any adventurous eight-year-old, I became intrigued by the ghostly story about a headless horseman, so as a young man, I decided to move from the city and make this my home. What I didn't realize at the time was a pattern of death in this village. Young, healthy men die of seemingly natural but unexplainable circumstances every six months, but I'll get into that later.

When I first arrived in town, I went to have a beer at the bar owned by the grandfather of your school friend, Beau. That night, I met a girl, a mysterious, beautiful, seductive girl who didn't give me the time of day. Being young and relatively confident in my looks and my charisma, I didn't let the girl's rejection dissuade me. For a whole month, I pursued that girl, and yet each time I asked her out, she'd tell me that she had been hurt before and wasn't the type of girl a guy like me should get involved with.

I should have listened to her, but I was already half in love with her. I told her I'd prove to her that not all guys were like the one who had hurt her. After another month, I finally wore her down.

For four months, that girl was my entire world. I shared every part of myself with her: my hopes, dreams, and plans for the future. I'd discuss those grand plans of marrying her and opening my bookstore before having a few children with her at length, too wrapped up in my ideas to realize that while I'd been opening up to her, she hadn't been sharing herself with me.

One night, I finally worked up the courage to present her with the simple ring I'd bought with half of my savings. I thought she was happy with me, but when I woke up the following day I found the ring on my dresser and a letter telling me she was sorry, but she couldn't be with me. I didn't see her again, not for a long, long time. I was all twisted up inside, but eventually, I met your mother and put my memories of that girl in my rearview mirror, though I've never forgotten her.

That brings me to recent events, part of which I mentioned in my letter. Yesterday, I was coming out of the store when I spotted a glimmer of strawberry-blonde hair. Over the years, every time I'd see a girl with fair hair, my heart would seize up, and my memory would be flooded with images of my time with that girl.

I waited, hoping for the young girl I saw to turn around and remind me that I was just an old fool pining over what could have been. To my shock, when the girl turned around, it was her; not a fantasy or an illusion but the very girl I met and fell in love with thirty years ago. Instead of looking like a fifty-year-old woman, though, she appeared to be still as young and vibrant as the last time I saw her.

I know what you're thinking; you're thinking I've lost my damned mind – that in my recent sickness, I've begun having delusions – but that's not the case. If you don't believe me, there's a flap on the back of this book that contains pictures of me with her. I'm printing off a photo I took yesterday with that i-telephone thing you bought me last

Christmas, and I'm placing it in a file in my office at Hollow Books. Hold the photos side by side and see for yourself. It is the same girl.

Her name is Cordelia Whitt, but she answers to Cora. You're a journalist, son; you need to find out what's going on in this town. How can a girl I knew thirty years ago still look the same as the last time I set eyes on her?

Why are these seemingly natural and unconnected deaths occurring? There's something not right about them. One hundred men in the past fifty years between the ages of twenty and thirty-five dying of heart attacks, strokes, and other undetectable means is not natural, no matter what the police or the coroner claim. There are more, Chance, I know there are. Who knows how far this dates back? I have a bad feeling about this, son. There may not be a headless horseman striking people down in this village, but something sure is.

I don't know how Cora fits into this if she does. That's what I need you to figure out. Find out what's going on and put a stop to it if you can. Keep your eyes open and your ears peeled, and above all, be careful who you trust.

I'm passing my legacy on to you. This book or the files in my office contain everything you need to know about my research. Godspeed, my son, and good luck.

Love,

Pop

———

The book falls from my hands onto the dusty hardwood floor. Whether from his obsession with the Legend of Sleepy Hollow or something else, Pop really believed that something was going on around here. It sounds unbelievable, but this book lists dozens of names with corresponding dates.

If what Pop says is true, why hasn't anyone looked into this before? So many deaths by those circumstances are unusual. Even if there isn't anything hinky going on, shouldn't someone have done some investigating into this? There could be a massive drug operation causing natural-looking deaths for decades, and nobody has done a thing about it.

If this story pans out, I could be looking at a story that will turn my career around. New York Times, here I come. The thought raises my spirits, making me feel slightly twisted, as I retrieve the book from the floor, look up the obituary for the young guy who died right after Pop, and add another name to Pop's death scrolls.

CHAPTER SEVEN

"I can't believe this," Andi complains as he stomps ahead of me into Beau's, "I finally get you to come out for the night, and we end up going to a local bar." He says *local bar* like they're dirty words.

I shrug, unconcerned, "It's close to home."

Andi looks at me like I've lost my mind, "Um, yeah, right across the street from your apartment."

"Don't you want to go where everyone knows your name?" I tease as I spot two barstools open up at the bar and drag Andi along behind me. I realize belatedly that he does look a little out of place at our local dive bar, wearing his silver sequined tank top and tight white jeans. I opted for a more casual approach when I threw on a denim skirt and a silky black V-neck sweater before we left the studio.

"I wanted to go somewhere that I can dance," Andi replies.

"Well, maybe Beau will turn some music on, and you'll have your chance," I mumble as I hoist myself onto the barstool. I felt so bad for all the times I turned Andi down for after-work drinks that I finally said yes as long as I could pick the place. If I had known this was how he was going to act, I would have just hung out in my dark room, experimenting with new exposures.

Andi snorts, "Not likely."

I spot Beau at the end of the bar and wave my finger in the air to let him know to come over when he gets a chance. He nods and tips his head toward one of his patrons, silently telling me he'll be over when he's done.

"Are we going to get service anytime soon?" Andi whines as he drums his long, manicured nails against the bar's surface.

Beau swoops in before I can respond, "Hey, Cora, you want your usual?"

"Yes, and he'll have a–" I pause as I gesture to Andi, waiting for him to tell Beau what he wants.

"I'll have a cosmopolitan," Andi fills in the gap smoothly.

Beau snorts, "Nice try, kid. You want a soda?"

"No, I want a Cosmo," Andi argues. I roll my eyes at Beau, who is trying to hide his amusement.

"You can want it until your face turns blue, but I know you're not twenty-one," Beau lets him down lightly as he pours my whiskey on the rocks and fills a tall glass to the brim with Coke for Andi.

"This blows," Andi mutters as Beau slides the glass over to him and goes to wait on other customers.

"Hey, how did your date go last night?" I ask as I sip my whiskey.

Andi shrugs, "It wasn't bad. I wish we could have had some downtime to hang out and really connect, you know? I asked him if he wanted to go somewhere quieter, but he thought I wanted to hook up and got kind of upset about it. He said he didn't want to move too fast."

"Maybe that means he thinks you guys have the potential to be something serious," I suggest, but Andi's raised brows tell me he's not impressed.

"Hey, Cora," A familiar yet unwelcome voice calls out to me

over the noise of the bar as a large, long-fingered hand lands on my shoulder. "How is business?"

I turn around slowly, even though I know who I'll find. Behind me, Andi perks up and says, "This night just got a whole lot better."

"Hello, Chance," I look up at him unhappily through my eyelashes. He towers over me with his height even as he wraps one jean-clad leg around the barstool behind him and sinks onto the seat.

"You look nice," Chance murmurs as his eyes rove over my body. He tries to appear lecherous and unaffected, like a player, but I can see the honest interest in his eyes.

"Thanks," I mumble awkwardly.

"You know," Chance continues, "I was just thinking that you're awfully young to own your own studio. That's a big accomplishment; what are you – eighteen or nineteen?"

"I'm twenty-one," I correct through clenched teeth. I know he's baiting me, but I can't stop the snarl that comes through in my tone. I say, "The same age Annie Leibovitz was when she landed a job at Rolling Stone."

"I'm not knocking you," Chance snipes back defensively as he pushes up the arm of the left sleeve of the heather gray thermal he's wearing, "You just look so young."

"And you look like you've been run over by a freight train," I lie, which causes Andi to gasp behind me. Chance doesn't look bad at all. He just looks too much like his father as he looms over me with his chiseled jawline and sexy hooded eyes, partially obscured by a stubborn strand of hair that has fallen over his eyes. Unamused by my comment, a muscle in his jaw ticks as he stares down at me.

He pushes the strand of hair out of his eyes as he growls, "Do we really have to bring out the worst in each other all the time?"

"I don't know," I smirk, "this is only the second time we've met."

"And yet each time we've seen each other, one of us ends up angry," Chance reminds me.

"Maybe we're just two chemicals that shouldn't be mixed," I raise my eyebrow at him in a challenge.

He leans forward and places one of those strong hands on my hip. I tense up as he whisper-yells into my ear, "Then why do I have to fight the urge every time I see you not to take you into a back room and see if I can make you scream my name while I'm thrusting deep inside you?"

I gulp hard as his dirty words cause a tingling between my legs. "Must be part of my charm," I rasp through suddenly dry lips.

CHANCE

I watch the thunderclouds storming in her irises clear up as her pupils' dilate and drown out her irises completely at my words. She's trying to act unaffected by my touch and my presence, but her body tells another story.

I don't know what made me say those words. They were out of my mouth before the thought had even fully formed in my brain, but I have been thinking about all the things I want to do to her ever since I first walked into the bar and saw her seated next to the young guy who works at her studio. Cora seemed utterly oblivious to the eyes of every man in here watching her every move as she sat on her bar stool in that damned short skirt that shows off more of her long, lean legs than should be legal. A glance down at her now also causes my insides to tighten as I get a better look at the low-cut sweater she's wearing that pushes her impressive rack up and out for anyone in this bar to admire. I swallow hard as I try to tamp down my attraction to her.

Instead of allowing myself to savor her, I decided to mess

with her, get her hackles up, and see how she reacted. What I didn't expect was the scorching heat I felt when I grabbed her hip and pulled her against my body. I need a cold beer to cool me down, or I'm in danger of walking into another potentially messed up relationship when I know damned well that's not what my interest in Cora really is. I need answers more than I need to lose myself in her.

"Is everything alright here, Cora?" Beau asks as he saunters up to where we stand at the bar.

"Everything is fine, Beau," Cora assures him without tearing her eyes from mine.

"If you say so," Beau doesn't sound convinced. He shoots me a dark look as he rests his hands palm side down on his side of the bar.

I raise my eyebrows at him in a silent challenge, "I didn't know you two were such good friends, Beau."

Beau grunts, looking smug.

"Alright, I've had enough excitement for one night," Cora announces as she drains the rest of her drink, grabs a small purse off the bar, throws some cash down to cover her drink, and says, "I'm out of here."

"I think we should go on a date," I announce as I follow her out of the bar and into the street.

My proposition stops her dead in her tracks. A car speeding through town swerves to avoid hitting her, and I pull her back toward me as the driver honks the horn and yells a few obscenities through the closed window. Cora recovers quickly, shoving my hand away and saying, "I'm not the type of girl a guy like you should get involved with."

I bristle, remembering the exact words were spoken to my father thirty years ago. "And what kind of girl are you?" I venture.

"I'm the kind of small-town girl who has no plans to leave

the area. I don't fit anywhere into your city lifestyle or your aspirations for the future." Cora retorts.

"You have no idea what my aspirations are," I challenge.

"Oh, really?" Cora smirks before crossing the street to her studio. "Let me guess, you have some hot shot job, but it's not enough, and you have your eye on a corner office by the time you're thirty, and a trophy wife would make that all come a little easier."

"Actually, I'm more at a crossroads career-wise, and I've had enough bimbos on my arm to know that isn't what I want long-term." I correct her. I watch as she lets herself into the studio before asking, "Isn't it a bit late to be working?"

"I live in the apartment upstairs above the studio and the candy store next door," Cora explains as she jerks her head to the darkened windows on the second floor, sounding bored with our entire conversation.

"That's convenient," I murmur as I shadow her into the dark studio space and through another door into a dimly lit hallway in the back.

She looks over her shoulder at me and arches one fair eyebrow. "I don't remember asking you to come up."

"I invited myself," I shove my hands into my pockets and follow her up a steep, winding stairwell that is so hazardous it must violate at least a dozen health codes.

Cora sighs as we reach the top of the stairs, stopping in front of her apartment door. No number adorns the door, identifying it as an apartment unit, but at some point, someone painted the door black because, underneath the chips in the paint, the door is light wood. I wonder how long she's lived here and if she lives alone.

Turning my attention back to her, Cora says, "Look, Chance, I'm exhausted, and I'm not in the mood to keep arguing."

"Do you ever relax and let someone in?" I blurt.

"Let someone in? To my apartment?" Cora purposefully misinterprets my meaning.

"Into your life," I amend, "You're so closed off. I mean, it's mysterious and sexy, and it definitely makes a guy want to work harder, but you're too young to be so closed off."

Cora shrugs, "I don't trust men."

"Ah," I hum as I look her up and down, "so you're a lesbian?"

Cora snorts, "Definitely not."

"See," I grin, "so you do let some people into your life, sometimes."

"Sleeping with someone and having a relationship with someone are two completely different concepts," Cora points out.

"I know," I nod thoughtfully as I take another step closer to her. She licks her lips and narrows her eyes as I groan, grabbing her chin in one hand and the back of her head with the other, pulling her toward me so I can capture her lips. I feel her body squirm as I kiss her roughly, claiming her without words.

Her kiss burns, sending heat through me from my head to the soles of my feet as our bodies align. I push her against her door, deepening the kiss as my hands move to capture hers as I lace my fingers through hers to hold her in place. Her kiss is the kind that makes men do stupid things, even when her heart isn't invested in the act.

She lets me kiss her at first before coming to her senses and shoving me back and glowering at me as I grin unashamedly.

Without missing a beat, I add, "Which is why I think we should go on a date before we hit the sheets. You know, see if we have chemistry outside the bedroom first."

"We don't have chemistry anywhere," She protests through lips swollen from our kiss.

"We'll see," I comment as I run the pad of my thumb over those red, kiss-swollen lips and wink, "I'll pick you up tomorrow night at eight."

"No, you won't," Cora yells after my back when I make it halfway down the stairwell.

Laughter is my only response, and without turning around, I can tell she's still standing there at the top of the steps, fuming.

CHAPTER EIGHT

<u>CORA</u>

He kissed me. The jerk had the nerve to kiss me even though my body language was screaming that I wasn't interested. And yet I let him, like some weak, lust-driven girl, I let him kiss me.

What's worse is that it was possibly the hottest kiss I've ever had. Unlike his father, Chance is the type of guy who is confident in his ability to make a woman melt into a hot, sexually frustrated mess at his feet. And melt, I did.

Get yourself together, I order myself as I shove my key into the lock and push into my apartment. *The kiss wasn't that good,* but I know I'm just lying to myself.

My shoulders slump as I slink into my apartment. I toss my purse onto my small kitchen table and throw myself face down onto my lumpy sofa. Pounding my fists against the tattered periwinkle blue fabric, I scream in frustration.

The last time I allowed myself to desire a man, I lost my head—literally. I have to stay away from Chance. It's too dangerous. He could figure out my past with his father and discover my secret, and I can't let that happen.

I drag myself into an ice-cold shower, determined to clear my head and forget about Chance.

———

In the morning, I text Andi and tell him not to come in so early because I'm opening the studio late. I fire off the text, then turn over in bed and pull the blankets over my head to shield myself from the early morning sunshine, but that doesn't block out the sound of someone pounding on my door a half hour later.

"Come on, girl," Andi yells through the half-foot thick door, "you so need to tell me about last night."

"Go away, Andi. I'm trying to sleep," I groan and pull the blankets closer around my body, but Andi keeps knocking, determined not to stop until I get up and let him in. I throw the blankets off and sigh, "Fine, I'm coming. Jeez, keep your pants on."

Andi is bouncing on the balls of his feet when I crack the door open. I blink at him through bleary eyes as he cranes his neck to look into the apartment.

"Is he here? Did he spend the night? Did you finally get lucky?" Andi peppers me with questions.

"Whoa," I groan, "too many questions. My head is killing me."

"Girl, you have to stop drinking that lighter fluid," Andi breezes past me. "So where is he? Is he in the shower?"

"Who?" I feign ignorance.

"Mr. Lickable! Chance, duh," Andi puts his hand on his hip, looking every bit the moody model.

"Ick, no," I sneer. "What would he be doing here?"

"He went running after you when you left the bar last night," Andi points out. "Did he come back here with you? Did you hook up?"

"The jerk kissed me," I make a noise of disgust in the back of my throat, "and I think he asked me out, I don't remember."

"He kissed you?" Andi squeals. Seeing my lack of enthusiasm, he adds, "Oh, you poor thing, that's just terrible. I mean, really, to think, a good-looking man wanting to kiss you, that scoundrel."

"Don't make fun of me," I scrub my hands over my face. They come back stained with the remnants of my mascara and eyeliner. It must not have washed off in the shower last night. Great.

"You look like a demented raccoon," Andi laughs as he walks over to my kitchenette and helps himself to a box of Wheat Thins. "You know, Cora, it wouldn't be so terrible. You need a man."

"I'm doing just fine without one," I mumble defensively.

"Don't you ever get lonely?" Andi asks as he sits down on my kitchen table.

"Not really," I shrug. I have Blood to keep me company in the dark hours when I can't sleep. And Beau's always been a good friend, not as good as Irvie, but close. "I could always get a dog or something."

Andi rolls his eyes, "A dog won't give you that heat, that passion that a love affair will."

"I don't need the drama." I protest.

"What am I going to do with you?" Andi shakes his head in amusement.

"Work with me?" I suggest, raising my eyebrow, daring him to say something more about my lack of romance.

Andi sighs and dusts the crumbs from his crackers off his lime green polo shirt, "Alright, are you coming down?"

I nod, "I'll be down in ten. I need a huge cup of coffee and a change of clothes."

"You might want to wash your face too," Andi teases as he

disappears out the apartment door, narrowly missing the throw pillow I've aimed at him.

———

CHANCE

I spent the entire day sorting through some of Pop's paperwork. I found old bills, new bills, and even a drawer full of every article and story I've ever had published in publications around the world. I need to get the deeds to the house, and the shop transferred into my name and deal with some other stuff at the bank as soon as possible. I've already gotten a notice from the electric company threatening to cut off service if I don't pay Pop's past-due balance.

Despite it all, my thoughts keep flickering back to Cora. Last night was all about getting her to lower her guard toward me, but damn if I can get the memory of that kiss out of my head. The way she let herself go as our bodies molded together felt so goddamn right before she pushed me away. I swear I can still smell the sweet, spicy scent of her perfume enveloping me and taste the tangy, sharpness of the whiskey she was drinking on my lips.

I can't let myself get dragged under her spell when I take her out tonight. Last night was all about being charming and thoughtful. Tonight is about getting answers.

I set Pop's papers down on the kitchen table and Facetime Eli. I haven't heard from him in a couple of days, and I'm hoping he's uncovered something.

"Hey man," Eli's oval face and smooth chocolate-colored skin pop up on my screen, his features washed out by the fluorescent lighting over his work cubicle. He strokes the twin braids of his short beard, glancing over his shoulder nervously.

"Hey," I reply as he turns his attention back to me, "I was

wondering if you dug up any information on what we discussed the other day."

Eli sighs, "not yet, bro. It's been a shitstorm here at the office."

"Why, what's going on?" I ask.

"Dude, you haven't heard?" Eli sounds genuinely distressed.

"Heard about what?" I ask, suddenly suspicious.

"Grankowski and his wife are splitting up. She's threatening to clean him out in the divorce, but he claims he has something big to lord over her. It's big Page Six news; my boss is eating it up," Eli whispers excitedly. "Did you know they were having problems?"

"Uh, not really," I say stupidly. "I mean, how well do you insert yourself into your boss's personal life?"

Eli laughs, "Yeah, I guess you're right. I just thought maybe you knew something I could use. I'm dying to get out of the damn obituary section."

I snort.

"You know what I mean," Eli rolls his eyes.

"Yeah, yeah," I laugh. "Just try and see if you can get me that info. Any little tidbit you can dig up will help."

"I'm working on it," Eli salutes me, a jab at his military past, before clicking off.

———

At seven-fifty-five, I smooth the wrinkles out of the dark olive dress shirt I threw on, purposefully leaving the top two buttons undone because I know women love seeing a hint of my chest. I stand in front of Cora's door for a minute longer, clutching the red roses I picked up at the flower shop down the street in my hand so tightly I feel a missed thorn embed itself in my palm. I hiss back a painful curse as Cora's door swings open, revealing her on the other side.

Her eyes widen in shock as I take in her appearance. Her wavy hair is piled into a messy bun on top of her head, and she's wearing a holey, oversized T-shirt reading "Horseman's 5k, the Hessian cometh" on the front over a gray, paint-splattered pair of sweatpants.

"What are you doing here?" Cora asks breathlessly. At the same time, I snort and say, "That's what you're wearing on our date?"

"Our date?" Cora echoes as her nose wrinkles in distaste. "You were serious about that?"

"Obviously," I smirk as I wave the roses in my hand for emphasis.

"Oh," Cora says as she casts her hazel eyes over me suspiciously.

"Yep," I reply as I swallow hard, unsure what else to say. How the hell is it possible to find this girl sexy when she looks like she just crawled out of a dumpster? Composing myself, I add, "I guess when I said I'd pick you up at eight, I should have said eight-thirty. I can see you're not ready yet. Don't worry, I'll wait."

"You still want to go out?" Cora asks incredulously.

I take stock of the small apartment behind Cora, including the haphazardly thrown-together king-sized bed in the corner of the room, "Yeah, definitely, we'll go out. Grab dinner. Hang out," Anything to keep my mind from leaping to ideas of what we could do on that mattress.

"Fine," Cora frowns. Her gaze lands on the roses, "are those for me?"

"Yes, they are," I hold them out to her.

"You're crushing them," she replies flatly as she takes them from me. Looking at my hand, she sighs, "And you've cut yourself. Come in. There's a first aid kit under the sink. Help yourself. I'll just put these in some water, and then I'll get changed."

"Take your time, sweetheart," I wink as I wrap her into a

half-hug and kiss her forehead. I hear her gag in response as I move past her to retrieve the first aid kit.

I wash and clean the minor cuts as Cora disappears into a shallow closet next to her bed. As I waited, I toured the rest of the apartment, taking in the stack of dirty dishes piled up in her kitchen sink and the assorted camera equipment scattered on her small bar-style kitchen table. A mountain of books leans precariously to one side, forgotten next to the faded blue sofa like Cora had set them there after a trip to the bookstore. It reminds me of Pop's house and the store, which makes me smile. The apartment lacks a bedroom, so the king-sized bed, with its' red comforter dusting the floor, takes up most of the back wall. A pair of beat-up sneakers lay discarded in front of the nightstand beside the bed. The apartment might not be as glamorous as some of the women I knew back in the city, but it is definitely lived in, and that's what makes it all the better. It's authentic.

Ten minutes later, Cora steps out of the bathroom in the back of her apartment, and my heart stutters to a complete stop as all of the blood in my body relocates to my groin.

My eyes travel up from the black knee-length leather boots trimmed in black lace and embroidered with red roses to the distressed denim skirt whose lace underskirt brushes against her bare thighs, teasing me with glimpses of her unblemished skin. A casual blue deep V-neck shirt hugs her torso and gives me a glimpse of the lacy red bra she's wearing underneath. I gulp as I think *this girl is going to be the death of me.*

Oblivious to my drooling admiration of her body, Cora tousles her messy blonde hair back from her face before finally looking up at me through her wide, heavily lined eyes.

"What?" she demands as she catches me staring. "I didn't think you were serious about this date idea, so I wasn't expecting you. This is the best I can do on short notice."

I swallow again as I find my voice, "there's nothing wrong with the outfit. You look perfect."

She rolls her eyes and huffs out a breath, unimpressed. "So, are we going, or did you get me to change for nothing?"

"We're going out," I grin as I fight to regain my cocky indifference.

Wordlessly, Cora snatches the same bag she was carrying the night before off the tiny kitchen table and struts past me to the door. I catch up to her, placing my hand on her lower back as I open the door for her.

She wobbles on the heels of her boots, and I maintain my grip on her lower back as we descend the darkened stairwell.

"These stairs are architectural suicide," I remark as she grips the railing to keep from falling.

"You get used to it," Cora replies shortly.

"How long have you lived here?" I inquire.

"A while," is her only answer.

Outside, I lead her over to the Mustang and hold open the door so she can slip inside.

"Nice car," Cora remarks. I think she's being sarcastic until I see her run her hand over the hardtop, looking almost reverent. "What year is it?"

"It's a 1966," I reply, "You into cars?"

Cora shakes her head, "Not really. I can appreciate beauty when I see it."

"So can I," I murmur as I look at her.

Cora clears her throat uncomfortably, and the moment is broken, "So where to? I'm assuming you've thought of where we're going to go now that you've kidnapped me."

"I didn't kidnap you," I laugh as I close the car door behind her and walk around the front end to the driver's side. "Lighten up, it'll be fun. You can't stay cooped up in your apartment all the time."

"You sound like Andi," Cora mutters as she fights with the testy passenger seatbelt.

"Here, let me help," I reach over to untangle the seatbelt. A jolt of static electricity zaps me as our fingers meet.

"I've got it," Cora says, but the usual bite in her voice has softened slightly. I sit back, watching as she jerks the seatbelt a few times before clicking it into place. "So you didn't answer me. Where are we going?"

"You'll see," I reply vaguely as I pull away from the curb.

We drive in silence, Cora only once raising her eyebrows at me in question as we leave the village and head toward Tarrytown.

When we pull into the driveway of the Lyndhurst Castle, her eyes light up before she tries to smother the surprised pleasure held within. "This is where we're having dinner?" She asks, her tone hiding any hint of opinion on the matter.

I shrugged. "A friend of mine works here during the summer, and I got him to let me borrow it for the night. I called in a restaurant in town to make us dinner."

Cora grins a predatory smile, "Looks like you've really put some thought into this date."

"Of course," I grin in response, "Only the best. I may have small-town roots, but I'm a city boy now, remember."

Cora smirked, remembering our conversation in front of Beau's last night but choosing to remain silent as I parked in front of the grand entrance and ran around to open her door.

"After you," I tease as she places her hand in mine. I haul her out of the car and lead her into the brightly lit mansion, asking, "Have you ever been here before?"

Cora shakes her head wistfully, "No, never. I've always wanted to tour it, though; it just always seems stupid to tour somewhere so close to home—like I should have done it before or something."

"It's not stupid," I shake my head. "Come on, I'll show you around."

We tour the main floor before stepping out onto the veranda at the back of the mansion, where the restaurant I'd hired to cater our dinner has set up a candlelight dinner.

"Would you like something to drink?" I ask as I gesture to the wine chilling in the bucket beside the table. " Some red wine?"

"That would be great," Cora looks at the table nervously. Out of the shadows, the waiter I hired to plate the meal appears to help Cora to her seat.

I pour us each a glass of wine before sitting across from her at the table. Cora fingers the cloth napkin, a nervous habit, as she sips the wine in her other hand.

"Relax," I smile reassuringly, though my mind is already filling with the questions I need to ask her tonight. To put her at ease, I asked, "What do you think of the mansion now?"

"It's amazing," Cora breathes before giving the waiter serving us the first course one of her rare smiles. "It's even more beautiful inside than I imagined."

"Have you lived in Sleepy Hollow your entire life?" I ask as I sip my wine.

"Yes," Cora answers after a slight hesitation. She picks up her spoon and samples the soup that the restaurant prepared, a spicy Manhattan clam chowder, so she doesn't have to say anything else.

"Have you at least been to Sunnyside, then? That's even closer to home, but everyone's been there." I question as I taste my soup.

Cora's nostrils flare as she tells her soup, "Yes, I've been there."

"It's an interesting place to visit," I carry on.

"That it is," Cora concedes.

When we move on from the soup course to the fish course, I

ask, "Are you sure you didn't know my father? I could have sworn he mentioned a 'Cora Whitt' to me before. Perhaps, if not you, maybe a relative of yours; are you named after one of your relatives?"

Cora coughs violently at my question. She pounds her chest savagely before answering, "No, I'm not. And yes, I'm sure. I didn't know your father. You must have misunderstood him."

"Huh, I guess so," I reply, pretending to be disinterested. "I guess it's just one of those weird things."

Cora snorts as she stabs at her fish.

I take another sip of wine as I study her over the rim of my glass, "So, do your parents still live in the area, or did they move away?"

"My parents are dead," Cora answers sharply as her eyes connect with mine and narrow a fraction.

Guilt hits me in the gut like a soccer punch, "I'm sorry. I didn't mean to bring up bad memories."

Cora shrugs off my apology, "What's with all the questions?"

"I'm just trying to get to know my date," I say with a grin that usually has women falling at my feet, but it doesn't have much effect on Cora.

"No, you're interrogating me," Cora says bluntly. "So tell me, Chance, other than your father's death, what has you sticking around in town? I highly doubt it's as interesting as the city. What are you running from?"

"I just needed a change of pace, a little peace," I school my facial features so she doesn't know that she's struck a nerve.

"Is that right?" Cora asks smugly. "So why is a good-looking guy like you single? Don't you have a bevy of women crawling in and out of your bed back home? Why ask me out?"

"You think I'm good-looking?" I ask arrogantly.

"You own a mirror, I assume." Cora shrugs nonchalantly. "I'm sure you know you're not a hideous beast."

I laugh, "You're right. I was just fishing for a compliment.

You don't seem to give them out easily." Soberingly, I add, "Women in the city are different. You never know who's being fake, who's sincere, and who's only using you to further something in their own life."

"Careful," Cora cautions, "now you're starting to sound like me."

I laugh, "Now, we wouldn't want that."

Cora manages to crack a smile as the waiter clears away the plates from the fish course and replaces them with the steaks and sides of our main course.

"I hope you like steak," I venture.

"I love steak," Cora assures me as she cuts a piece and bites into it, letting the juices drip down her chin and the column of her neck. My pupils dilate as I think of licking the juice off her neck.

"That's a relief," I manage to sputter a little gruffly.

"You okay there, Chance?" Cora asks as she studies me carefully.

"Fine," I reply, "the wine just went down the wrong way."

"We wouldn't want you choking during our date," Cora bats her eyelashes at me knowingly.

"No, we wouldn't," I mumble as I cut into my steak. Though I keep my eyes glued to my plate, I can feel Cora's gaze piercing a hole through me.

"So, tell me, Yankees or Mets?" Cora asks as I hear her stab a carrot on her plate.

I hazard a look up at her and squint, "Did you seriously just ask me about what baseball team I prefer?"

Cora lifts one shoulder, "Well, this is a date; I assume that means we should try to get to know each other instead of you interrogating me like a suspect on *Dateline*."

I snort and flatten the glob of mashed potatoes on my plate, "I'm not that into baseball."

"A big city boy like you doesn't root for one team or the

other?" Cora sits back, looking astounded.

"Nope," I shake my head. "Besides, you're forgetting that I have small-town roots."

"Ah, so you're a football guy then," Cora concurs. I'm starting to see how my relentless questioning must have bugged her.

"I'm a reader," I declare. "Why watch a bunch of guys chase a ball around a field or a court when I can live a thousand different lives, meet tons of diverse characters, and travel to lands I can only dream about without even leaving the comfort of my apartment?"

Something softens in Cora's eyes, "Well, I can't fault you for that. Andi thinks I'm crazy, but most of the time, I want nothing more than to close up the studio at night, head up to my apartment, and lose myself in a novel. I read about places I've never been to, worlds created by authors so vividly that I begin to feel as if I have been there and smelled the fragrant spices of a Middle Eastern marketplace or spent a cold winter isolated with Dr. Zhivago, ran for my life from the Overlook Hotel with Jack Torrance on my heels. Reading is an invaluable gift."

"That it is," I confirm, then wonder, "Have you traveled much?"

Cora shakes her head sadly, "I've never been further from home than here in Tarrytown."

"You've never even been to New York City?" I ask incredulously, my hand freezing mid-air with a piece of steak skewered on my fork.

"No, never," Cora replies.

"Any particular reason?" I ask, trying not to seem nosy.

"Let's just say this area has a way of keeping me tethered to it," Cora replies vaguely, a wry smile biting at her lips.

"Well, you're young," I say slowly. "You have plenty of time to travel."

Cora nods but looks unconvinced as she finishes off her entrée.

The waiter swoops in, silent and efficient, to clear away the dinner plates and place some form of chocolatey concoction in front of us.

"You know now why I'm single, but why is a beautiful girl like you single?" I query.

"I told you. I don't trust men," Cora says.

"Not even Beau?" I ask before I can stop myself. "You seem pretty close to him."

Cora laughs, "I trust Beau, but I wouldn't date him."

"Why not?"

"Beau is like family to me. I've known his family forever," she explains as she takes a bite of her dessert. She closes her eyes and moans appreciatively, "Wow, this is delicious."

"I like a girl who can appreciate good food," I smile.

"What were you expecting, another air-headed bimbo who turns up her nose at sugar, starch, and carbohydrates?" Cora teases.

"No, I'm pretty sure I left those behind in the city," I reply slowly, "and again, you've successfully managed to evade the question."

"That's all part of my devious plan," Cora explains, "to leave you with more questions than answers."

CHAPTER NINE

CORA

"Are you going to invite me in?" Chance asks, his breath hot on my neck as he watches me unlock the apartment door.

Dinner with him wasn't as bad as I feared it would be. I figured out fairly quickly that he had asked me out to ask me questions about his father and my past, which must mean that somewhere along the line, his father must have mentioned something about me. If only I could figure out what, without alerting Chance, his suspicions, whatever they might be, were correct. I had deflected most of his personal questions readily enough, and after dinner, we strolled through the rose garden, now cut back and mulched for the approaching winter. However, the bare branches and stems and the gazebo in the center of the garden were blanketed in a layer of golden twinkling lights that gave off a romantic vibe. I almost believed we were on an actual date and that Chance was spending time with me because he was interested in me for me and not for the information I kept locked up tight.

"On our first date," I ask, pretending to be offended. "Now, what kind of girl would I be if I invited you into my apartment after our first evening out together?"

"Second, technically," Chance clarifies, "I did walk you home last night."

"Doesn't count," I counter.

"Well, you'd be the type of girl who was completely enamored by the charming, attractive man who took you out on the most amazing date you've ever been on, and now you want to thank him by inviting him in for coffee." Chance treats me to another one of his smiles that is meant to make me weak in the knees.

If that's the way he wants to play it, two can play that game.

"Fine," I murmur as I run my hand down his muscled chest, "come in for a drink or something."

"That's the spirit," Chance's voice rumbles through me as he kisses my shoulder.

I let him into my apartment, setting my keys on the hook next to the door and my purse on the floor beneath before turning and weaving my arms around his neck.

"Are you sure a drink is really what you're after?" I ask, my voice dropping into a husky whisper.

"Maybe," Chance's crooked grin tells the truth.

"Well then," I say as I trace the line of his jaw, his stubble feeling rough beneath my fingers. Chance watches me wordlessly through his heavy-lidded eyes as I stand on my tiptoes to reach him and kiss him. He makes a guttural noise in the back of his throat as his fists bunch the back of my shirt.

Kicking the door shut behind him, he backs me up to the arm of my couch without breaking the kiss, his steps light and graceful like he's leading me in a dance. I grip the back of his neck tighter as I bite down gently on his full bottom lip. Chance's hips thrust forward in response as he groans against my lips.

I open my eyes a fraction and cup him through the stiff

denim of his jeans. "Do you want to do this here, or do you prefer the bed?"

"The bed," Chance answers quickly, his words sounding slurred, intoxicated, "Definitely the bed."

"Good choice," I murmur as I pull him closer again, parting his lips with my tongue, caressing his as I edge around the couch and let him back me up to my bed. His hands explore my body as my nipples harden into stiff peaks and my core turns molten, throbbing with need.

At the foot of my bed, Chance works my shirt up my torso. I lift my arms to help him pull the shirt over my head, momentarily breaking the kiss before he throws the silky fabric to the floor and resumes his claiming of my lips.

My fingers deftly unbutton his shirt and slide the fabric down his arms, allowing it to fall to the floor as it unveils broad shoulders, corded muscular arms, and a well-defined chest covered in colorful tattoos. His abs look like they've been carved from marble until the V of his abdomen disappears into his jeans.

A huge fan of body art, I'd love nothing more than to study the ink covering him from the waist up, tracing the lines and shapes with my fingers and tongue, but Chance's fingers at the button of my skirt pull me back into the moment as he kisses and licks a path down the side of my neck to my collarbone, pressing featherlight kisses to the swell of my breasts as my skirt pools at my feet.

His pants join my skirt on the floor a moment later, and then he lowers me onto my unmade bed, nudging one knee between my thighs, creating space for him, and covering my body with his. Large, eager hands tear at the back hook of my lace bra, pulling it free as my sensitive nipples harden painfully at the chill in the room, begging for attention.

His eyes stay locked on mine, shining like unblemished copper as his lips latch onto my left nipple, licking and sucking the wanton bud as the pad of his thumb traces and strokes the other.

"Chance," I moan as I arch my back, thrusting my nipple further into his hot mouth. His eyes light up from my pleasure as he switches to give my other nipple equal attention as his hands run up and down the length of my sides, sending a shiver down my spine.

I grip the back of his head, twining my fingers in the soft strands, gasping when his expert hands rub the bundle of nerves at my core through my cotton panties.

Chance kisses a path to the top of my panties before hooking his thumbs into the sides and yanking them away in one smooth motion. Half-lost in pleasure, I watch as he lowers his lips to the bundle of nerves between my legs, kissing me there as he thrusts his middle finger into me, once, twice, as I cry out in pleasure.

He grins wickedly as his tongue and fingers work together in tandem until I feel my body constricting and exploding as I climax, screaming his name.

When I come down from my high, I find Chance watching me, a dangerous look of lust and something more serious flashing in his eyes as he shucks his soft gray boxers and sheaths himself in a condom.

"I need you inside me," I beg as I reach for him greedily.

"Don't worry, baby, I'm right here with you," Chance murmurs as he wraps his hand around his thick member, guiding himself into my entrance.

I feel his engorged head at my opening as he stares down at me, admiring my body. With one great thrust, his hard length is buried inside me, stretching me as Chance hisses in pleasure.

I pull him down to me and kiss him roughly as he begins to move inside me. As he picks up a rhythm, I wrap my legs around his waist, allowing him to drive his cock into me deeper as I dig my nails into the soft flesh of his back.

His touch and his kiss sear me, branding me as I feel my climax climbing again. His name becomes a chant upon my lips as he pounds into me, consuming me, claiming me.

I cry out in pleasure once more, and seconds later, Chance throws his head back, groaning my name as he reaches his climax.

Spent, he collapses on top of me, though careful not to crush me beneath his weight. He rolls us until I'm sprawled atop his powerful body.

I place a kiss on his chest as his fingers play with the long strands of my hair. It occurs to me as I begin to drift off that this is the first time in more than two hundred years that I have not claimed the life of a man I'd allowed in my bed. It scares me how right it felt to lay in Chance's arms.

―――

CHANCE

We wake up twice during the night and make love again. It hits me later that if being intimate is always like it is with the insatiable beauty tucked into the crook of my arm, I wouldn't care much about dating either. If she'd let me, I don't think I'd even bother leaving this bed.

In the clear light of day or the early morning, if the clock on Cora's nightstand tells true since the apartment is utterly bereft of windows, doubt claws its' way into my chest for a moment. I am supposed to be checking into her past and seeing if she has the unbelievable connection with my father that his ledgers suggest, not climbing into bed with her, but as she lies peacefully in my arms, I wondered how anyone could ever think her to be trouble. With her wavy blonde hair fanning over her bare shoulders and her heart-shaped face smoothed of the usual scowl that resides on her lips, she looks so sweet and young, so beautiful.

I blaze a trail of kisses down her shoulder to her elbow as she begins to stir. Her skin is flawless, moon-kissed, like she spends her time running around in the moonlight stark naked. Maybe that was her big secret, though it doesn't explain how my father thinks he knew her thirty years ago.

"Morning," Cora says sleepily as her hazel eyes open slowly. Her gaze sweeps over me and then over herself, lying in my arms as if she's not sure what she's seeing is correct. "You're still here."

"Were you expecting me to be gone when you woke up?" I ask.

Cora rubs one eye with the side of her loose fist, "it wouldn't surprise me. Most don't stick around."

"How many times do I have to tell you," I pause to drop a quick kiss on the lips she's just wetted, "that I'm not like most guys."

"Old habits and beliefs die hard," Cora replies sheepishly.

"Don't worry, I'll make you forget all about anyone else," I grin cockily.

Cora runs a finger down my chest, and I shiver beneath her touch, "I think you did that last night. Three times."

A laugh rumbles through my chest as I run my hand up and down her slim torso. Cora relaxes in my arms and peers at the clock over her shoulder. A frustrated groan slips past her pouting lips.

"What's wrong?" I ask as I look at the offending piece of digital plastic.

"We should get up," Cora says reluctantly. "Andi will be arriving at the studio in twenty minutes, and if I'm not down there, he'll come up here looking for you."

"Looking for me?" I ask as my forehead wrinkles in confusion.

Cora laughs, "Yes, looking for you. He's convinced I need to date more, and you're the prime candidate. He's only slightly put off that you don't bat for his team."

I laugh at Cora's serious look. I bite my lip to keep from laughing as I say, "Well, I'll have to stick around and tell him everything is going according to his plan."

"You will not," Cora protests. "Don't you have something to do? Some books to organize, maybe?"

"I could help you with your work," I tease, and Cora huffs out an irritated breath.

"You, help me? The guy that almost dropped my favorite camera," Cora accuses as she pokes me in the chest and begins to roll away to get up and get dressed.

"Fair enough," I nod along as I pull her back toward me from behind, aligning our bodies together as my cock gets the wrong idea, pressing against her backside. "I'd probably forget to take the lens cap off. Come on, let's go get cleaned up."

Cora protests all the way to the bathroom, only stopping once I've pulled her into the shower stall and buried my cock inside her while massaging her curves with the fruit-scented body wash sitting in her shower caddy.

Exactly twenty minutes later, I deposited her in front of the door that separates the stairs to her apartment and the back exit from the main space of her studio.

Gripping the back of her head with one hand and her lower back with the other, I haul her onto her tiptoes and kiss her. The minty taste of her toothpaste sends a pleasant jolt to my system.

She pulls back, looking dazed but satisfied, as she looks up at me through pleasure-hooded eyes.

"I have to run over to the bookstore and start sorting a few things out," I tell her. "Would you hate me if I came back and brought you lunch later?"

"That depends on what you bring me," Cora replies thoughtfully.

I rub my chin contemplatively, "Hmm, well, I was thinking of a garden salad with some nice, clear dressing."

I laugh as Cora swats my arm playfully, "very funny."

I kiss her again quickly as I say, "I'll see you later.

Cora shakes her head in amusement as I duck out the back door.

CHAPTER TEN

<u>CORA</u>

I try to scrub the goofy smile off my face after Chance disappears through the back door, but it won't budge. My face actually hurts from being this sickeningly happy. I feel like I'm in a cheesy romance novel.

I shake my head in distress. What is it about the men in the Jordan family that makes me feel like falling in love might not be the worst thing to happen in the world? I expected to wake up this morning with a boatload of regrets, but when I opened my eyes and saw the look on Chance's face, all I felt was peace. For once in my extended life, I didn't want to bolt, nor did I feel the need to destroy the colorful man lying in my bed.

I sigh and push through the studio door just as Andi rushes in, carrying a drink carrier full of steaming to-go cups filled with coffee and tea and a bag of pastries from Dark Brews.

"Am I late?" Andi asks worriedly as he sets his offerings down on my desk.

I glance at the clock on the wall, "no, you're right on time. Why did you bring four coffees when there are only two of us?"

"Well, partially because I overslept and thought I'd need the caffeine, not to mention a bribe in case I was late, but also because I heard some big news at Dark Brews, and you're not going to believe it," Andi gushes excitedly.

"Not going to believe what?" I ask distractedly as I grab one of the cups, sniffing it cautiously before taking a sip.

"Guess who is getting married and planning to hire us to do all of her wedding photography?" Andi bounces on the balls of his feet.

"Who?" I ask, cringing as the strong, hot liquid hits my tongue.

"Stacey Jensen," Andi looks at me expectantly, waiting for my reaction.

My forehead crinkles, "am I supposed to know who that is?"

"Um, hello, Stacey is only the most famous person from this one-horse town! She was in Chance Jordan's year in school, and she left town and became a famous model in the city. Now she's coming back home to get married to the gazillionaire she met and fell in love with while on vacay in Madrid, and she wants you to do the photographs." Andi enthusiastically explains.

"You'd think if she were that famous of a model, then she'd know plenty of photographers to do her wedding," I comment dryly, "besides, there are plenty of more famous people from here in Sleepy Hollow."

"Like who?"

"Washington Irving, obviously," I remind him.

"Old dead people don't count," Andi retorts. "So if she asks, are you going to take Stacey on as a client?"

I shrugged, "It depends on when her wedding is and if we have enough time in our workload to devote to her wedding."

"We'll bump someone if we have to," Andi exclaims, "this is big, Cora. This can make our careers."

I let him ramble on about how important this job will be and what it will do for our business, not bothering to remind him that we haven't gotten the job yet and it's my business, not "our" business. It would be no use; he's already picturing himself bumping elbows with glittering celebrities in the city.

I almost have myself convinced that I'll get through the morning without Andi, suspecting Chance spent the night in my bed when he stopped midsentence and looked at me while I booted up my computer.

"What?" I ask as Andi taps out a rhythm on his bottom lip.

"There's something different about you this morning," Andi says slowly, trying to figure out what might have changed.

"You're imagining things. Nothing is different here," I deflect as I log onto the computer.

"No, there is. You look different," Andi argues.

I laugh, "Different, how?"

"Happy," Andi replies, "you look happy."

I grin wryly, "You've never seen me happy before?"

"No offense, boss lady, but you're kind of a grump," Andi teases.

"Hey," I clutch my chest in mock offense, "that's not true."

Andi's eyes light up, "I know what it is! You had your date with Chance last night, didn't you? Ohmigod, I'm right, aren't I? He totally rocked your world last night, you naughty girl."

I can't help the laughter that escapes as I say, "What makes you think I didn't rock his world?"

"Oh, I'm sure it was a mutual world-rocking situation," Andi wiggles his eyebrows suggestively.

"You're terrible," I groan as I cover my eyes with my hands. I can picture him smirking at me behind the cover of my hands.

"Let's just get to work," I grumble.

"Whatever you say, boss lady," Andi answers sweetly.

———

CHANCE

After leaving Cora at her studio, I grab a coffee at Dark

Brews, narrowly missing Cora's assistant in the process. Andi is excited about something, so he doesn't even see me as I slip past him into the crowded coffeehouse.

The smell of freshly ground coffee beans assaults my nostrils as I get in line to place my order. After ordering a small coffee, I moved down the counter to wait. As I stand there, I feel someone's gaze burning a hole in my back, and I turn around to find the source.

My good mood fizzles as I spot my old high school crush, Stacey Jensen, waving at me from across the room.

I stroll over to where she sits with an older woman, probably her mother huddled over a bunch of magazines spread out on the too-small table. Bridal magazines, I realize belatedly.

"Hey, Stacey, I didn't see you there," I say in an attempt to be friendly.

"Well, look who it is," Stacey's eyes rove over me appreciatively. "Chance Jordan, all grown up. You look good, hun."

"It's been a while," I deflect her compliment, "how is the city treating you?"

"Fabulous," Stacey's bubbly reply would have once made me smile, but now, when I look at her, all I see is the same type of woman I left behind in New York City. "Have you heard? I'm getting married."

"Congratulations," I mumble awkwardly.

"Yeah, his name is Nick," Stacey smiles serenely, "his dad owns a bunch of luxury hotels around the world. Isn't that crazy?"

"Yeah," I agree, half-heartedly wishing I had a way out of this conversation.

"Anyway, I just called you over to say I heard about your dad's passing," Stacey continues, and my stomach churns. "I'm so sorry. It is a real shame; I know you two were close."

No, we weren't, but you wouldn't have known that, Stacey. I keep my thoughts to myself, ducking my head and saying instead, "Thanks."

Stacey reaches out to place her manicured hand over mine, "If you ever need anything, just say the word."

"I will," I tell her, trying to hide my grimace. At the counter, the barista calls my name, so I smoothly excuse myself from Stacey's attention and slip out the front door.

This is what I get for springing for the fancy, expensive coffee.

I can't help glancing in the window of Cora's studio as I pass by on the way to Hollow Books. Andi is standing in front of her desk, telling her something animatedly, and he waves his arms around enthusiastically. I shake my head. I'm sure Andi is a nice guy, but it must be annoying at times having someone so flamboyant working for you. He's like Liberace or something.

Unlocking the front door of Hollow Books, I let myself into the dark, chilly space. The smell of old paper greets me as I flick on the lights and sigh.

Transferring the house and the shop into my name was a lot easier than I'd thought it was going to be. Sometime in the past ten years, Pop had added my name to the deeds of both properties as well as onto his bank accounts, so it was only a matter of filling out a few forms, and suddenly, everything became mine. Including the bills that came with everything, although when I contacted Neil, he assured me that although probate law wasn't his expertise, he knew that since everything could be transferred to me without an estate, I wasn't liable for Pop's medical bills or any of the other debts he'd incurred other than the ones pertaining to the running of the shop or the house.

It was a big load off my shoulders. Last night, I decided that putting down roots here wouldn't be the worst thing in the world. I just had to make sure I could pull the bookstore back into the black, starting with reorganizing the shop so customers could actually find something amongst the chaos.

The overloaded bookshelves groan, and the stacks of books

piled high in untidy piles seem to taunt me as if to say *good luck with that.*

I groan as I realize how big of a project this will be while also keeping the shop open, "Oh, Pop, have you ever heard of separating by genre? Or alphabetizing?"

Of course, he had. We'd had this same argument time after time when he had me working in the shop after school in junior high and high school. Every time I suggested he move things around so that people could actually find something, he'd tell me I was being ridiculous. He had a system, and he knew where every book in his inventory was located. If a customer was looking for something specific, all they had to do was ask, and he'd be more than happy to pull it for them. Even if it were in the middle of one of these stacks, he'd pull it out if necessary.

With an exasperated sigh, I set my coffee cup down on the checkout counter and rolled up my sleeves to get to work. It was going to be a very long morning.

I lost all track of time until the bell over the door jingled, and sunlight filtered in through the opening door. A gust of wind drove a few orange and red leaves inside as Cora stepped inside.

She'd thrown on a vintage red moto jacket and a slouchy coral beanie on her head and swapped out her flats for the black boots she'd worn on our date last night. Seeing them had me flashing back to last night and how she'd kept those boots on as she wrapped her legs around my waist while I drove my cock into her over and over. I've never thought of shoes to be particularly erotic, but she could wear those boots to bed anytime she damn well wanted.

Cora clears her throat loudly, and I look up from her feet to see the mischievous look glinting in her eye. Obviously, she was also remembering our night together. Grinning, she holds up a large brown paper bag I hadn't noticed her carrying in her right hand, "Andi was driving me crazy, and I thought you could use some lunch, workaholic."

My stomach growls right on cue, "I completely lost track of time. What time is it?"

"Just past two," Cora tells me as she looks around the shop, "I see you've been busy."

I look down and find I've boxed myself in during my sorting. " Yeah, I've been trying to sort things out by genre and author, but everything is such a mess in here. I don't know how anybody finds anything."

Cora smirked as she took in the unorganized chaos and set the bag down on the floor beyond the boxes surrounding me. Stripping off her jacket and hat, she said, "I'm sure your dad knew where everything was. Chaotic people usually do. What do you plan to do with the place now? I mean, you have to return to the city sooner or later, right?"

I shake my head, "I'm not going back, actually. I'm going to try to make a go of the store, and I'm still close enough to the city that I can commute if I decide to take on a freelance job and need to meet with my editor."

"Sounds like you've thought this through," Cora comments as she begins unpacking the sandwiches she picked up at the deli down the street. I carefully climb over the boxes and sit down next to her on the floor.

"I have," I reply. "I need a break from the city, and I've already transferred the house and the shop to my name. I've even given notice at my apartment in the city."

"Wow, you've done a lot in a short time," Cora remarks as she bites into her ham sandwich. "Are you sure living in Sleepy Hollow is what you really want?"

I nod, "I think it's where I need to be right now."

Cora remains silent as we both tuck into our sandwiches. She brought me turkey on rye bread, and either she's that good at reading me, or she's a mind reader because she figured out what my favorite kind of sandwich was.

"How is your day going?" I ask her as she reaches into the bag and pulls out two bottles of soda to wash our lunches down with.

Cora shrugs, "not bad. Andi came in all excited this morning because some girl is getting married and is interested in us photographing her wedding. We haven't gotten the job yet, but Andi is already excited to bump elbows with some of the guests potentially. At least it distracted him from asking too many questions about us."

"Oh, he caught on to that, did he?" I tease her.

"Nothing gets past him," Cora groans.

"So who's the client?"

"Some girl that grew up here and went away to be a model," Cora informs me. "Supposedly, according to Andi, you went to school with her."

"You must mean Stacey Jensen," I supply her with the name.

"That sounds about right," Cora nods. "Do you know her well?"

I snort, "Stacey was *the* girl to date in high school. I knew of her, but I wouldn't say we were friends exactly. Small world, though. I ran into her at Dark Brews this morning."

"So she's the beautiful, irresistible type," Cora concludes as her lips twist into a sour frown.

"I guess some would see her that way," I say slowly. So Cora is threatened by the type of woman she thinks men are instinctively drawn to. It sounds crazy, considering I haven't been able to see anyone but her since we met, but I store that information away for future reference anyway. "But I haven't thought about her in years. She may be attractive, but she's empty inside. I'm sure Andi was just excited because he looked up to her or something."

"I'm not worried," Cora protests. Crumpling her sandwich

wrapper into a ball, she says, "I should get back to the studio. Your friend Stacey and her mother have a consultation with me in an hour. Try not to get lost in a sea of books."

I look around the bookstore and swallow hard, "I have a feeling I'll be having nightmares about these books tonight."

CHAPTER ELEVEN

<u>CORA</u>

See, this is what I hate about modern relationships; I sigh, feeling aggravated as I sit atop Blood in the hilly area behind the studio. His breath comes out in puffs of steam in the cold morning air.

Two hundred years ago, it wasn't considered appropriate for a man to come to sleep at the woman he was courting's residence. It was considered a stain against the woman's virtue.

I snort at the thought. *What virtue?* I definitely don't have any of that, but even if I did, I just moved aside when Chance came knocking at the door last night. He said he was dog-tired from sorting through all those books in his father's shop, and all he wanted was to crash. And I let him. I must be going crazy in my old age.

I'd watched as he crawled into my bed, still fully clothed, after he'd taken his shoes off and set them on the floor. He'd patted the space on the mattress beside him, and I'd sighed, crawled in beside him, and allowed him to pull me up against him. Even through the thin layer of his clothing, I could feel the hard planes of his body pressed up against my own barely clothed body. I'd had to sneak out around five to take out my frustration with myself on a ride with Blood. I felt like I was suffocating in my apartment. I needed fresh air.

From the corner of my eye, I see a figure darting through the pre-dawn light. I turn in my saddle, thinking it might be Chance coming to see where I've disappeared, only to catch a slip of darkness dart in the other direction. I turn Blood in circles, searching for the blur of motion until he neighs in protest, but the shadow figure keeps eluding me.

I'm just about to chalk it up to a trick of light or a figment of my imagination when I see it disappearing down the hill and kick Blood into a canter to follow it. I follow it all the way over to the cemetery. It figures.

The figure, nothing more than a wisp of shadow in the wind, blips in and out of my vision as I push Blood to go faster. To the back of the cemetery, I follow the figure until it stops in a spot that turns my stomach.

A foot in front of Brom's headstone, the figure solidifies. The sun has yet to rise, but I can tell without a doubt that the tall, broad-shouldered creature standing facing slightly away from me is the same one I encountered at Beau's.

Aware that he's captured my attention, he slowly lifts his head, and my heart jumps to my throat uncomfortably as I stare into those dead eyes. His mouth quirks up into a sinister grin that sends an icy chill down my spine. Movement sends my gaze leaping to the side of his face where maggots writhe in and out of an opening in his skin. My eyes jerk back to the creature's eyes, and I find him watching me in cold, calculated amusement.

"What do you want?" I yell across the distance at the Crooked One.

"We have unfinished business, Cora," the Crooked One's eerie voice purrs.

"If you're really who you resemble, then I don't owe you anything," I retort.

"You took my life," the Crooked One snarls, appearing an inch from my face in the blink of an eye. He throws me from Blood's back onto the damp grass below. Blood snorts testily as his feet stomp the ground.

On instinct, my scythe manifests in my right hand. Swinging the blade upward, I growl, "You stole mine first."

The Crooked One dodges my blade, blinking out of existence, then reappearing behind me and yanking me up by the hair. Grunting in pain, I drive my elbow into the creature's abdomen as hard as I can and spin out of his hold, throwing him to the ground.

"You're going to regret that," The Crooked One wearing Brom's skin hisses.

I jump back as he rushes forward, half flying, half leaping at the spot where I was standing. I swing my blade at his head, but he grabs the scythe with his demonic strength, sending it clattering to the ground a few feet away. I drive for it as his fist swings toward me, connecting with the corner of my mouth and the lower part of my cheek. I taste the coppery taste of my blood in my mouth as I spin out into the shadows, kicking him squarely in the ribs as the rest of my body disperses into the mist.

I land on the ground and roll over to my discarded scythe, then leap to my feet and drive the blade through the Crooked One's throat before he has the chance to get up again. His eyes glow and turn bright red as his body collapses into dust.

Satisfied that the creature was gone—for the moment—I let the scythe drop to the ground with a muffled thump and placed my hands on my knees while I tried to slow my racing heart and my ragged breath.

"That was a decent start, girl," the raspy voice of my past startles me out of my vulnerable position.

"Shit," I exhale, gripping my chest. "You scared me."

"Lesson number one, girl; always keep your guard up."

Bathsheba bares a demented smile. Her teeth look like piano keys with all the spaces where teeth once resided.

"You didn't think about hopping in and helping?" I demand. "He was stronger than he looked."

"I imagine he was," Bathsheba agrees, "but it is not my battle to wage. I've spent years fighting against and alongside Crooked Ones for good reasons and bad. It's your turn now. You left this one prone to be chosen to serve among the legions of demons and Crooked Ones. You must end him once and for all."

"And I'm guessing this isn't the end," I sigh.

"Now that would just be too easy, girl," Bathsheba laughs before disappearing into the early morning fog.

Groaning, I haul myself back onto Blood's back. My muscles scream for relief after the ass-kicking I've just gotten facing off against Brom's Crooked One, but I need to get home before Chance wakes and wonders where I've disappeared.

Blood trots home while I cling to his back, wincing at my horse's jaunty gait. When we reach the back of my studio, I shift back into my human state and jog into the building barefoot to escape the cold air seeping through the thin cotton of my nightshirt.

I race up the stairs and quietly open my apartment door just enough to peer around it and see if Chance is still asleep. I sigh in relief when I find Chance still as I left him in my bed with his chest slowly rising and falling in his sleep. I slip inside, making sure to close the door as quietly as possible before I tiptoe back to bed and slip under the blankets. I catch a glimpse at the blackened soles of my feet just as they disappear underneath the sheets. Hopefully, Chance will not be looking too closely at my feet.

Chance shifts in his sleep, rolling over onto his stomach, resting his head on my chest, and pinning me beneath him. The peaceful look on his face calms me down as I stroke his soft hair and allow myself to fall back to sleep.

———

"Morning," Chance mumbles sleepily a couple of hours later.

I crack my eyes open and quickly assess my body. I feel like I've been hit by a truck, but I don't think anything is broken. "Morning," I reply with a yawn.

Chance finally opens his eyes and jumps back in horror, "Cora, what did you do to your face?"

"What do you mean?" I ask nervously as I run my hand over my lip and the cheek that the Crooked One punched. My skin is sensitive to the touch.

"I mean, you look like someone beat you up," Chance runs his hands over my face and my bare arms worriedly. "Shit, you've got scratches on your arms too."

"These?" I look down at my scratched arms, trying to think of a good explanation for their sudden appearance. I must have scratched myself in my sleep. Sometimes, I dream that bugs are crawling over me, and I have to scratch to get them off. I do have these really long nails, see?"

Chance raises his eyebrows at my rounded nails like he doesn't believe a word I'm saying. "Do you also punch yourself in your sleep?" He asks.

I touch my cheek again in wonderment, "I don't know what happened."

"Fine, don't tell me," Chance exhales hard as he throws the blankets back. "Just let me help you get them cleaned up."

"Don't worry, I don't think they're that deep of scratches," I protest.

Chance stands at the foot of the bed, looking at me sternly. "Just shut up and let me take care of you for once, will you?"

I blush, my eyes tracking him as he strolls to the kitchen area and retrieves the first aid kit from beneath the sink.

I bury my feet in the sheets when Chance returns to sit on the edge of the bed in front of me. He spots a greenish-yellow bruise blooming on my upper thigh and shakes his head in frustration as he cleans the cuts on my arms with a wet piece of gauze, then rubs a little bit of Neosporin over them and covers them with waterproof Band-Aids.

I watch with rapt attention as he lowers his lips to the bruise on my thigh, kissing it gently. His stubble scratches the sensitive skin, and I hiss in response. His eyes flit to mine before he kisses the corner of my mouth and my cheek the same way.

"You might want to ice the bruise on your leg," Chance suggests as he places the gauze, Neosporin, and Band-Aids back into the first aid kit, "Otherwise, I think you'll be fine. Are you sure you don't want to tell me how you got these?"

"I told you," I insist, "it must have happened in my sleep."

Chance sighed, and I could see the disappointment in his eyes, even though he tried hard to mask it. "Well, I have to run home and get changed before heading over to the shop. I got about half of the inventory sorted, and I'm hoping to have everything in order by tonight."

"I understand," I nod as I rub the bruise on my thigh absently.

Chance's gaze darts from my thigh to my eyes quickly, but instead of demanding answers, he asks, "Do you want to do something tomorrow night?"

"What did you have in mind?" I ask, my curiosity getting the better of me.

"There's one of those ghost walks going on through town tomorrow night. You know, the ones that go through Sunnyside, Horseman's Bridge, the Old Dutch Church, and end up in the cemetery. We could go, and then we could get a couple of drinks after," Chance suggests.

"You're taking your chances on a second date with me?" I tease.

"Let me see. A haunted walk with a beautiful girl on my arm? That wouldn't be the worst way to spend my night. You can always squeeze my arm if you get scared in the dark," Chance jokes. It will be fun; we might even see the Headless Horseman."

"I sincerely doubt that," I laugh. Every tour plays up the local legend, but believe me, I haven't shown up for a single one of them. Now that I think about it, that sounds like an exciting idea. Maybe I'll try that on Halloween and give them all a show.

"So, are you in?" Chance asks hopefully, his rough fingers tracing circles on my inner thigh enticingly. Any higher up, he'll have me begging him to stick around and shower with me before work.

I sigh, pretending to be put out by the idea, "Yes, I'll go with you."

Chance's eyes light up, "great. I should get going; will you be alright here for now?"

I roll my eyes, "I think I can manage. I might even take a long, hot shower before heading down to work."

Chance's pupils dilate at the visual of me soaping up my naked body in the shower. I can hear the gears shifting in his mind as he tells himself he can't stay and join me. Swallowing hard, he finally says, "I'll see you later then."

"See you later," I confirm as I lean in, cupping his cheek as I kiss him. My lip stings as I press it against his. Ice. I definitely need to put some ice on these bruises—Curse Brom's Crooked One.

CHANCE

At the bookstore, I try to focus on sorting through the rest of Pop's inventory, but my thoughts keep bouncing back to the weird scratches and bruises on Cora's body. I know I was tired when I showed up at her apartment last night, but I do know those marks weren't there when she lay down beside me.

She had to have gotten up in the middle of the night and

gone somewhere. Was she meeting with someone, maybe another guy? Fiery hot rage boils through me at the thought of someone putting those scrapes and bruises on her, but it's the only explanation I can come up with. She tried to hide it from me, but I noticed the soles of her feet were nearly black from walking outside barefoot.

We haven't defined this thing between us and granted, it has only been a few days, but dammit, she should have told me if she was involved with someone else. It's the not telling me that has me pissed off. I'm not jealous. No, that can't be it.

Cora is the girl with a million secrets. I wish she'd let me in on some of them. I find myself looking at the thick exterior wall, wishing I could see through it to Cora's studio across the way. I wish I could see past the cool exterior she hides behind and the truths she locks away inside, though I fear I might not like what I find.

I can almost feel Cora erecting a new wall around her and pulling away from me by the end of the day.

I finish sorting through Pop's inventory and rearranging things earlier than I expected, so I text her to see if she wants to meet up for dinner.

> Me: Finished at the shop, and I'm starving; want to grab a bite?

> Cora: I wish I could, but Stacey has officially hired me. She's still here going over everything she wants for her wedding. Kill me now.

> Me: Remember, she's marrying rich. Charge her extra. ☺

HEADLESS

I adjust the ringer on my phone before sliding it into my pocket and locking up the bookstore for the night. As I turn, I see Cora through the vast windows of her studio, her desk the only light brightening the open-concept studio space. Three people sit in front of her desk, and I can guess that the Range Rover parked out front belongs to Stacey's fiancé, Nick. I don't envy Cora her job.

My drive home is pleasant enough, and I'm in a fairly good mood, but all that vanishes as I pull into Pop's driveway and park beside an all-too-familiar Jaguar. I'm half-tempted to back up and leave, but movement in the darkened yard stops me. Resigned, I shove the car door open and step into the night.

"Did you miss me, baby?" Carlotta steps from the shadows, and I can make out her hips swaying as she sashays forward in one of those tight pencil skirts she's so fond of. Her off-the-shoulder sweater hangs so low her tits are on display, but my eyes are immediately drawn to her mouth or, rather, the old-fashioned cigarette holder she's taking a sensual drag off. I can still remember her pulling it out and lighting up after we'd finished fucking and the burns my chest suffered when she'd flicked the hot ash from the cigarette carelessly onto me.

I used to think Carlotta was sexy and exotic, but now that I've spent some time away from her, I can see right through her. She looks every year of her age, and everything from her hair to her clothes to her makeup screams trying-too-hard. She's nothing like Cora, and the thought of her and the time I've spent with her since being back in town is like being dunked in a tub of ice water. I step back, clear-headed, and demand, "What are you doing here, Carlotta? I don't remember inviting you."

"You're not answering my calls, and I had to see you." I cringe as she closes the space between us and scratches my chest through my shirt.

"I blocked your calls," I clarify, "and I don't have anything to say to you. I've told you over and over this fucked up shit between us is over."

"Oh, now don't be that way, honey," Carlotta coos as she moves in to kiss my neck. We had some good times, you and me. I can make you feel better than anyone else."

I shove her away hard enough to send her tumbling back a few steps, "that's enough, Carlotta. You're insane, and I want you gone. Now."

"Is there someone else?" Carlotta arches one perfectly sculpted eyebrow in question.

"Doesn't matter," I shake my head. "We were over long before I ever left the city."

Clenching my fists to keep myself from physically throwing her back into her car, I brush past her and move toward the front door.

"You're seriously going to abandon me and our baby?" Carlotta's tone turns venomous as her words root me to the spot.

Spinning around, I stalk across the yard and loom over her menacingly, "What the fuck did you just say?"

A calculating grin spreads across Carlotta's red lips. "You heard me. I'm pregnant. Are you really going to walk away from our little family?"

"You've got to be fucking kidding me. I don't believe you," I scoff.

"It's true," Carlotta insists, "don't you remember in August when we all were at that boring society event at Tavern on the Green for the *New York Times*, and you followed me into the ladies' room, locked the door behind you, and bent me over the sink while my poor husband, your boss, was talking outside to some of your colleagues? I was ovulating that night."

"I don't give a damn what lies you tell, Carlotta," I snarl, "The kid isn't mine. I know I used protection." I always used protection with Carlotta, protection I provided myself, for precisely this reason.

"Hmm," Carlotta hums as her dark brown eyes glitter in the dark, "that may or may not be so, but all I have to do is tell my husband that the baby is yours, and you'll be ruined. No publication within a hundred miles will take you on."

"Get lost, Carlotta." I grab her shoulders as my tone turns hard as stone, "I want you off my property right now. I don't give a damn what happens to you, but I never want to lay eyes on you again, you crazy slut. The biggest mistake I ever made was having sex with you in the first place."

"You'll regret this!" Carlotta shrieks as she backs toward her car. "I'll ruin you, Chance Jordan. Mark my words!"

I stomp into the house without a backward glance. Slamming the door behind me, I lean against it and sink to the floor, twisting and turning the gauge in my ear angrily. I hear a car door slam, and then the low purr of the Jaguar's engine turns on and gets fainter until I can't hear it anymore.

I reach into my pocket and grab a lighter and my pack of smokes. Pulling one out and popping it into my mouth, I watch my hand quiver as I try to light up. The minute it is lit, I crush it out on the side of the pack. I repeat the motion three more times and waste three more cigarettes before I finally feel a little calmer.

What the hell was that? How could Carlotta think trying to saddle me down with a kid I know is definitely not mine would make me want to come back to her? She's obviously more desperate than I thought she was.

I sit with my back to the door, taking deep breaths and

playing with the flame of my lighter for a while—probably a half hour at least—before I finally pick myself up off the ground and grab a beer from the kitchen. I twist the cap off, discarding it in the sink on my way to my bedroom.

Grabbing the neck of my t-shirt, I pull it over my head and throw it onto the floor next to the bed before shucking off my jeans. Retrieving my phone from one of the pockets, I sit down and place it next to me on the bed. I take a long drag on my beer before firing off another text to Cora.

> Me: I just kicked an unwanted reminder of my
> past off the property. Text me when you're done
> meeting with Stacey. I'm having a hellish night,
> but you could make it all better.

I wait, hoping Cora will text me back to ask me what's wrong or invite me over, but the text never comes.

CHAPTER TWELVE

CORA

I knew I had made a mistake in ignoring Chance's text last night the minute he showed up to pick me up for our date. I just panicked. He was so tender when he cleaned up my scratches and didn't even ask how I got them or where. When he texted me when I was stuck in the middle of a verbal tennis match between my new client and her mother, I knew I was softening toward him, and it freaked me out.

I went down this road with his father. It started innocent enough—a dinner here, a walk through the park there—but before I knew it, I was spending all of my time with him. I let myself get emotionally involved even though everything about my past screamed at me that it was a horrible idea. I had to break it off.

This time, I don't want to stay away from Chance. He's not some love-struck puppy, but he's not a heartless jerk either, and I actually do like spending time with him.

I hadn't talked to him all day, so when Andi had to leave early to go to a teeth cleaning appointment, I jumped at the chance to close up the studio early and slipped upstairs to change into a pair of skinny dark wash jeans and a chunky orange off-the-shoulder sweater,

I threw on an old pair of sneakers, pulled my long hair into a messy ponytail, and grabbed a book off my coffee table before heading down to the studio to wait for Chance. It is a beautiful afternoon. The sun is shining, and the cold October temperatures have moved far north because of a hurricane brewing in the southern part of the country, so I'm content to sit on the front step of the studio and read.

Propping my feet up on the step and leaning back against the studio window, I opened my book to where I'd left off during my lunch hour. I'd been trying to branch out and expand my favorite authors, so when Amazon recommended a newer horror novel by a British author aimed at teens, I one-clicked it and gave it a try. I didn't usually delve into the young adult genre, but this author was fantastic at spinning a chilling tale.

As the sun begins to fade in the sky, a shadow falls over me, and I raise my head, my eyes meeting Chance's troubled ones.

"Hey," I spring from my seat and kiss him quickly on the cheek. I step back and admire the way his mock military jacket clings to his biceps over the soft navy blue cable knit sweater that looks soft enough to run my hands over. Tight jeans cover his legs, his knee popping through a hole in the denim as he props his right Converse-covered foot behind his left.

"Are we still on for tonight?" Chance asks uncertainly.

"Yes, of course," I nod as I reach back and tuck my book into the mailbox next to the studio door.

"I wasn't sure," Chance shoves his hands into his pockets uncomfortably as he shifts his weight from one foot to the other. You didn't text me back last night," he says.

"I'm so sorry about that," I reply, chagrined. "I was so fed up by the time I was done with Stacey and her mom and fiancé that I pretty much just crawled up to my apartment and crawled into bed with a big glass of whiskey."

"It's okay, I guess," Chance frowns. "I just wanted you to take my mind off something."

I weave my arm through his elbow, and we fall into step. "I got your text this morning. You said something about an unwanted guest. Do you want to talk about it now?"

Chance takes a deep breath. "I'm okay now. It was just a mistake from my past, but I took care of it. I don't want to ruin our night. Let's have some fun."

"Let's go," I grin enthusiastically, "I'm ready to hear all about the ghosts in this town."

"I hope you brought comfortable shoes. The tour starts at Sunnyside," Chance explains as we head south down Broadway.

"That's fine by me," I nod. I figured sensible shoes were a good idea in case we had to outrun the Headless Horseman."

Chance wraps his arm around my shoulder protectively, "Don't worry, Cora, I'll protect you."

Yes, that's exactly what I need for him to protect me from myself: the Headless Horsewoman. He doesn't need to know that.

We head away from town, and I curve into his embrace as we stroll under canopies of vibrant red, orange, and yellow leaves. I love autumn when the trees start to look like they're on fire and the chill appears in the air. It reminds me of endings, of death, and I know there won't be too many nice weekends like this before winter gets its' grip on our town, holding us all prisoner with its' icy wrath.

Sunnyside comes into view, and I get lost in a tidal wave of nostalgia. How many times had I run to this place when Irvie was alive? How many times had we sat in his parlor drinking tea and talking about books and life? Too many times to count, I'd sought refuge within these walls after a night of hunting. I'd cried on Irvie's kitchen floor one night after a brutal kill, and he'd sat beside me, stroking my hair and back and whispering soothing words to me.

In another world, if I hadn't loved him like a brother, perhaps Irvie would have been the man for me.

I banish my thoughts and tilt my head up to look at Chance in the dark, "how do these ghost walks work exactly?"

"At each location, the guide will tell us a little about the history of the place and any sort of ghostly experiences linked to them," Chance explains as we join the group in front of Irvie's house.

"Greetings," a geeky man with dark, messy hair and rimmed glasses nearly falling off his long, pointy nose raises his arms like an evangelical minister to get the group's attention. "Who's ready to learn a little history and meet a few ghosts?"

A few people in the group whoop in excitement as I arch my eyebrow at Chance skeptically.

"That's good," the guide enthuses, his nasally voice slurring his words together. "I always like to start this tour here at Sunnyside because, in my mind, the owner of this home is where the fame of this town truly began. Can anyone tell me who owned this house? Feel free to yell out if you know the answer."

When nobody immediately speaks up, I roll my eyes and shout, "Washington Irving."

"That's right," Our guide nods approvingly in my direction. "Washington Irving, as most of you will know, was America's first worldwide best-selling author and probably most notably known for his story, The Legend of Sleepy Hollow. And this," the guide gestures to the house behind him, "was Mr. Irving's residence."

"Are we going to go inside?" A young woman asks as she curls into her companion's embrace, "It's freezing out."

The guide looks taken aback by the question, "Unfortunately, the museum is closed for the evening, so we'll only be viewing the exterior and discussing the home's history before moving on to the Old Dutch Cemetery."

"This tour blows," the girl's date says.

———

The tour moves on, and Chance weaves his fingers through mine as we follow the tour through the streets, listening to the guide drone on and on about the village's history and the legend of the Horseman.

A couple of times, I catch myself opening my mouth to correct the guide, but then I realize how crazy I would sound talking about things I shouldn't have any knowledge of and shut my mouth.

"What's your take on the legend?" Chance asks as we cross Horseman's Bridge. "Are you a believer in the Headless Horseman?"

"Not exactly," I smile wryly in the dark. I believe that memories are truer ghosts than spirits from the other side. Sometimes tragic things happen repeatedly in the same place, and it leaves an imprint behind—a sad remembrance of a forgotten story."

"That's an interesting way of looking at things," Chance says slowly. Cringing at the water below the bridge, Chance mutters, "Man, I freaking hate this bridge."

"Why? Did you have a horrifying experience with a headless Hessian?" I tease, knowing that I've never terrorized anyone on this bridge or anywhere else on the cemetery grounds.

The guide raises his voice, drowning out Chance's reply. "Twelve years ago, a girl was murdered on this very spot. Locals sensitive to paranormal activity claim that they've seen the girl's ghost wandering back and forth on this bridge, waiting for the arrival of the lover that would betray her."

"That's a load of shit," Chance mutters under his breath.

I feel him tense beside me, but he wisely chooses to remain silent as the guide leads us deeper into the cemetery.

"Now there are many notable figures buried in Sleepy

Hollow Cemetery, including Washington Irving himself," the guide continues, "but I've heard tell that there's a secret section of this cemetery where the headstones are so old and lost to time that the names are no longer visible and there laid to rest are the real Katrina Van Tassel and Brom Bones."

A few people in the group ooh and ahh in interest even as I feel my spine stiffening at the mention of Trina and Brom.

"Are you okay?" Chance asks, sensing the change in my demeanor.

"I'm fine," I mumble. Suddenly, I don't want to be on this tour anymore, "Hey, do you mind if we head to Beau's early? I'm getting cold, and my feet are killing me."

It's not much of a stretch as I stand beside Chance, shivering and trying to get my teeth to stop chattering.

"Sure," Chance nods quickly, "I've been hoping you would ask me that for the past twenty minutes."

I laugh as the tour moves on, leaving us alone in the dark: "If you were bored, you should have just said something."

"I know. I didn't want to tear you away if you were having fun," I can sense Chance's rueful grin in the dark.

"Communication, the number one problem in relationships since the dawn of time," I snort as we turn back toward the main street.

"Stick close to me," Chance whispers conspiratorially, "we wouldn't want the Horseman to get you."

"Would you be my hero and save me?" I grin and bite the inside of my mouth.

"Of course," Chance puffs out his chest, "I love saving damsels in distress. They usually show me their gratitude by inviting me to their beds afterward."

I swat his chest, "smooth, very smooth."

———

CHANCE

At Beau's, I slide onto a barstool and rub my hands together to rid them of the numbness and cold as Cora excuses herself to use the ladies' room.

One of Beau's bartenders came to take my drink order, and I ordered a beer and a whiskey for Cora. Across the bar, I spot Cora pausing on her way back to me, laughing at something Beau is telling her. I see the flicker of lust in Beau's eyes as he listens to her. It's clear to anyone with eyes he desires her. Too bad I've already staked my claim on her.

"You're making a huge mistake getting involved with her, boy," a slurring voice behind me startles me, and I jump nearly out of my skin. Turning around, I find Dan watching Cora as if she were a rodent he wanted to exterminate. I shift my weight to block his view of her, and his angry eyes flash up to my own: " If you had any brains, you'd get out now why you still had the chance."

"What did she ever do to you?" I ask as I cross my arms over my chest in a silent threat.

"Nothing to me, boy," Dan mutters, "I was one of the smart ones."

He stares me down before finally throwing some cash down on the bar and taking his leave.

"What was that about?" Cora asks as she sidles up to me.

She allows me to pull her to my side and kiss her forehead as I say, "Nothing, Dan's just a lousy drunk."

Cora sighs, "Yeah, I've noticed that. I've seen him in here on more than one occasion."

The bartender puts our drinks on the bar in front of us, and Cora smiles appreciatively, "You remembered my drink."

"A man's got to appreciate a woman who would choose straight whiskey over some fruity drink with an umbrella," I wink. "It means she's a keeper."

"Is that right?" Cora's musical laugh teases my ears as she sips her whiskey.

I throw back half of my beer, trying to tamp down my sudden desire to have her alone, and bared to me right this minute.

"Are you warmer now?" I ask as I caress her bare shoulder.

"Yep," Cora nods as she shivers under my palm, from my touch, not the cold this time. Her voice lowers an octave, becoming husky. Whiskey always does the trick."

Feeling bold from the beer, I lean down and lick her lips, tasting the whiskey on her soft lips. " You're right," I smile as I pull back. "I feel warmer already."

Cora grins, tilting her head to the side in amusement. "Do you want to get out of here?"

"I thought you'd never ask."

I wrap my arm around her to keep her warm as we cross the street. As we cross the center line, a car speeds down the road, and its headlights flash angrily at us as it speeds by.

"We seem to have more trouble with cars on this road." I tease as we step onto the sidewalk.

"What do you mean?" Cora asks.

"The night I asked you out for the first time," I remind her, "you almost got hit by a car."

"I guess you're right," Cora laughs. "I guess I'm just reckless like that."

"Do you have a death wish or something?" I joke.

"Who me?" Cora asks, stepping under the streetlamp in front of her studio. The golden light shines down on her like a spotlight. "I'm invincible."

I shake my head as we reach the front door to her studio. As we weave through the inside, her equipment casts eerie shadows on the floor, illuminated only by the streetlamp.

I follow her up the stairs, watching as her hips sway alluringly with each step. Cora stops abruptly a few steps from the top and says, "That's weird."

"What?" I ask as I peer over her shoulder to see what she's looking at. A small pink box wrapped up with white and red ribbon is sitting on the floor in front of her door. "Were you expecting a package?"

"No," Cora replies warily as she crouches down to pick up the box. We step onto the landing together as Cora pulls the red bow off and tugs at the ribbon. I get an uneasy feeling in my stomach as she pulls the lid off, a small card falling to the ground in the process.

I don't get a good look at the contents of the box as Cora shrieks, letting the box and whatever horror is held inside drop to the floor as she covers her mouth and flies back against the doorjamb.

"What, what is it, babe?" I reach out to grab her arm worriedly as she points to the discarded box on the floor.

Swallowing hard, I bend down and flip the box right-side up, steeling myself as I peer inside. Sitting inside the box tied up to a small white pillow with red string is a bloody severed finger and a skeletal finger twined together.

"What the hell," I exclaim as I fight the bile working its way up my throat. "Who would send something like this?"

Behind me, Cora shakes her head wordlessly as she nervously fingers the chain of the necklace she never takes off, but I've never paid too close attention to.

Shaking my head in disgust, I reached for the note that fell away when Cora opened the box. Ripping it out of the envelope, I read the two words scrawled on blank white paper: *You're next.*

"Oh my god," Cora gags as she covers her eyes and faces the wall.

"We have to call the police," I say, pulling my phone from my pocket.

"What if it was some sick Halloween prank?" Cora asks.

"Either way, we have to call them," I reply. Then I think, "Did you lock all of the exterior doors before we left this afternoon?"

Cora thinks back, "Um, yeah, yeah, I definitely did. I usually keep the back door locked, and I locked up the front door before I sat down to read on the front step."

"Does anyone have a spare key?" I ask.

"Of course not," Cora shakes her head. "Wait, well, Andi does, but he wouldn't do this. I can't even get him to take the garbage out."

"I'm definitely calling the cops," I tell her as I reach out my hand to her. "Come on, we'll go downstairs and wait for them there."

After flipping the lights on in the studio and settling Cora into her desk chair, I flipped the coffee maker on to make Cora something hot to drink and dial 911.

"911, please state your emergency?" The dispatcher asks when the call connects.

"My girlfriend and I were out, and when we arrived back at her apartment, someone had left a severed finger on her doormat," I tell the dispatcher.

"What is your location?" The dispatcher asks after a long, uncomfortable pause.

"We're at the Sleepless in Love Photography Studio on Broadway," I tell the dispatcher, "my girlfriend lives upstairs."

"Alright," the dispatcher replies in a calm tone, which all dispatchers are trained to use. I've got the police on the way. Did you notice any signs of a break-in?"

I look over at Cora, who shrugs, "We didn't look too close, but she said she locked the place up before we left earlier."

"Okay, what I want you to do is take your girlfriend and wait outside until the police come in case whoever left the… package is still inside." The dispatcher instructs.

"Okay, we will," I reply as I prop the phone between my ear and my shoulder and gesture for Cora to get up and come with me. I wrap my arm around her, squeezing her so tight she gasps a little.

As Cora and I step outside, the cops are already arriving, so I disengage with the dispatcher and lead Cora over to meet with Chief Devries.

"Chance," Devries says stiffly in greeting before focusing on Cora. His expression softens as he says, "Can you tell me what happened while my deputies go and check things out?"

"We were coming home from Beau's," Cora gestures vaguely across the street where a small crowd is already beginning to form, "and there was a little box on my doorstep. I opened it and – and there was a bloody finger inside," Cora's voice breaks as she buries her face in my chest.

"It's alright," Devries pats her shoulder awkwardly, "it was probably just a prank."

"I don't think so, Chief," I pipe up. "There was a note with the box—it said she was next."

Cora shudders against me as Devries's mouth thins into a hard, grim line. Turning to one of his men, he shouts, "I want a forensic team here now."

"Yes sir," the officer replies, then says something on his CB radio.

"Why don't you come to the station," Devries suggests as he looks from Cora to me, all traces of his usual grit and sarcasm gone.

"Come on, babe," I urge Cora toward Devries's car. "You don't want to be here while the police are doing their thing."

Cora nods numbly as she allows me to lead her to Devries's cruiser.

––––––––

Two hours later, Devries took our formal statements and questioned Cora about whether she knew of anyone who would send her something like that. I held her close as she told him she didn't know anyone who would, but I could see a darkness pass over her face that suggested maybe she did know somebody who would.

Devries's men and the forensics team had processed the scene and bagged the box and its contents for testing and evidence before clearing the scene, but I still insisted that Cora come home with me.

"I have to go back to my apartment and check on things," Cora protests.

"The person who left that package is still out there," I remind her. "What if they come back?"

"I can take care of myself," Cora bristles.

"I'm sure you can," I agree. "I would just feel better if I knew you were with me and safe."

"As much as it pains me to say this," Chief Devries chimes in, "I think it would be for the best if you accompanied Mr. Jordan to his residence. I'll have a squad parked outside your apartment in case the person who left the package comes back. In cases like these, the perpetrator usually likes to come back and see the reaction, insert himself into things, and such. You don't want to be home alone if he comes back."

"But you just said you'd have an officer parked outside," Cora challenges.

"Yes, outside." Devries draws the words out slowly. "Not inside."

"Fine," Cora exhales angrily. Turning to look at me, she says, "I'll come home with you."

Sighing in relief, I take off my coat and put it on Cora's shoulders to warm her up. I step back as Chief Devries shakes her hand and assures her that he will let her know after they process the evidence if they find anything.

We drive in silence, and I can tell that Cora is really shaken up, so I reach across the center console and squeeze her hand reassuringly. She smiles faintly before leaning against the window and staring out into the night. We pull into Pop's driveway, and I make quick work of bundling her up and letting her into the house. Flipping the lights on, I show her my room and the adjoining bathroom, where she excuses herself, telling me she needs a hot shower.

I nod solemnly and tell her to let me know if she needs anything before settling onto my bed and waiting for her to come out.

I hear the water turn on in the bathroom and finger the fabric of the quilt on my bed as I replay the scene at Cora's apartment. Maybe Pop was wrong all this time; maybe Cora isn't a threat; perhaps she's a target.

CHAPTER THIRTEEN

I sink into a crouch at the bottom of the narrow shower stall and grab my head, my fingers weaving through the wet strands like a web.

Every time I blink, I see those fingers staring up at me from inside the box. Having killed over and over again for centuries, I've developed a strong stomach, but something about seeing that bloody severed finger in the box unnerved me.

I wish Chance hadn't called the police. How exactly was I supposed to explain that I'm pretty sure a demonic creature that's wearing the skin of the man who I loved and died at the hands of centuries ago sent me that package to taunt me? I'm sure it was his way of telling me our encounter in the cemetery would not be our last.

Banishing the image of the severed finger from my thoughts, I rise into a standing position, briefly rubbing the petrified eye around my neck before pouring a quarter-sized amount of Chance's shampoo into my palm and lathering it into my hair.

The more I think about it, I realize Chance is right; I couldn't face going back into my apartment just yet, but I wish

I'd had the forethought to have someone run up to grab some clean clothes and a few of my toiletries.

I wash up quickly and then wrap myself in the fluffy brown towel draped over the towel rack before towel drying my hair using the hand towel lying discarded on the bathroom counter.

"Hey," I murmur as I step out of the bathroom, still wrapped in the towel.

"Hey," Chance replies softly with a tone laced with the last thing in the world I want – sympathy. "How are you feeling?"

"I'm alright," I shrug, "Just processing."

"I found you some old sweats of mine," Chance grabs a stack of clothing off the bed and hands it to me, "You can sleep in them if you want."

"Thanks," I tell him as I hand him back the sweatpants and slide the old gray t-shirt over my head, letting the towel drop to the floor. The shirt falls to my knees as I read what's printed on the front: Property of Sleepy Hollow High School Athletics Department; Home of the Headless Horseman. The bold block lettering arcs above and below a silhouette of the Headless Horseman. I fight the urge to roll my eyes. This town is crazy about Irvie's story.

I pull the eyeball necklace from under the shirt's neckline, finger it subconsciously, and then pull my hair off my neck.

"Is that an eyeball around your neck?" Chance asks. His face pales as he looks at the charm I wear around my neck.

"It's not real," I lie as I circle the pupil with the tip of my index finger.

"Is that an Ouija planchette you've embedded it in?" Chance leans forward for a closer look.

"Yeah," I reply calmly. It's my interpretation of the Arabic hamsa hand to protect against people who wish to harm me."

"I'm not sure it's working." Chance raises his eyes to look at me. "Now, come here," he orders as he climbs under the covers and pats the bed for me to join him.

"Bossy tonight," I comment as I return the towel to the bathroom and crawl onto the soft mattress beside him. Chance reaches around me to flip off the lamp beside the bed.

"After tonight, I want you near me so I know that you're safe," Chance's voice is muffled as he kisses my neck and tucks my body up against his.

"I'm fine, Chance," I insist. "It was probably a stupid prank."

"We don't know that yet," Chance counters. He smooths down the soft cotton t-shirt covering my body, and his hand brushes innocently against my sex, igniting a fire within me. I hiss out a shallow moan, but Chance doesn't hear me as he says, "And until Devries decides to get us some answers, I'm not taking any chances."

I harrumph when I realize that Chance isn't planning on satisfying either of our bodies tonight and adjust the pillow under my head. I begin to close my eyes when something Chance said earlier tonight smacks the forefront of my consciousness. "Wait; while you were talking to the dispatcher tonight, did you call me your girlfriend?"

Chance yawns, "Huh, yeah, I guess I did. Do you have a problem with that?"

"I guess not," I spit out reluctantly. Only my tone admits my inner distress.

"Good," Chance says as he kisses my shoulder, missing the unspoken feelings in my tone altogether.

I lie there, suddenly wide awake, even as Chance's breathing evens out and he grips me tighter in his sleep. How could I be such an idiot? I'm right back where I don't want to be, getting close to a man, allowing him to take me on dates and develop feelings for me.

I'm not meant to be with anyone. Tonight cemented that in my mind. If I don't hurt him, there's a chance that some other part of my past will. I should be distancing myself; I should be running as fast as I can in the opposite direction, just like I did with Chance's father. I'm just not sure it will be as easy this time.

———

I woke up alone in Chance's bed the next morning, and much to my dismay, I felt disappointed instead of relieved. *Get yourself together, Cora. He's just a man. You're too twisted to fall in love. Remember what happened last time?*

I rub the sleep out of my eyes and set my bare feet on the hardwood floor, instantly regretting it as the soles of my feet touch the cold wood.

I hop across the room and pull the door open, stepping onto the soft hall carpeting as the scent of bacon wafts over to me from the kitchen down the hall.

Following the inviting scent to the kitchen, I find Chance standing with his back to me, frying bacon and eggs on the stove. His bare shoulders are hunched as he scrambles the eggs, and I admire the lines of the long tattoo that covers his entire back, which disappears into the waistband of his striped blue boxers.

"That smells really good," I say, breaking his silent concentration.

"Hey, I didn't hear you get up," Chance says over his shoulder as he turns the bacon. Wiping the grease from his hands on a kitchen towel, he turns to face me, bracing both of his hands on the kitchen island. "How did you sleep?"

"Fine," I shrug, "about the same as I always do. Is there any coffee?"

"Over there, next to the fridge," Chance points his thumb over his shoulder to show me. He watches as I pick up one of the mugs next to the coffee maker and fill it to the top with piping-hot liquid. I take a tentative sip and cringe at the strength of the coffee. Chance chuckles, "Sorry about that. As a journalist, I'm up late a lot working on a deadline, so I like it strong."

"There's strong, and then there's eye-opening," I smirk as I set the mug back down on the counter.

"Are you going to work today?" Chance asks as he turns back to the stove.

"No," I shake my head. "It's Saturday, and I don't have a wedding booked, and I don't have to open the studio. I should check in with my editor at the Gazette, though. He called me a couple of days ago because he wants me to photograph a few events for next week's special Halloween edition."

"So you freelance for the Gazette?" Chance asks, sounding surprised.

"Yeah," I nod enthusiastically, "the editor contracts me out when his normal photographer needs some help. I photograph the events he sends me to, and they integrate it with their reporter's piece."

"What sort of pieces?" Chance inquires.

"Whatever they need me to photograph," I shrug one shoulder, "sporting events, community events, local news, that sort of thing."

"Have you ever considered freelancing with a larger publication or even traveling as a photojournalist?" Chance wants to know as he plates our breakfast.

"I wish," I reply honestly. The whole I-can't-leave-the-area thing puts a little bit of a damper on that, but I don't tell Chance that. "I don't have the time, though. I keep pretty busy with bookings for weddings and special events locally."

"You should think about it," Chance suggests. "I spent a couple of years traveling and picking up freelance work for publications all over the world, and I loved it. It was a great experience."

"Do you miss it?" I ask cautiously as I grab a fork and bring my plate around to eat on the other side of the kitchen island.

"Sometimes," Chance admits, "but I decided it was time I put down roots somewhere. Act like a responsible twenty-eight-year-old and all that."

"Well, you are getting kind of old," I tease, and Chance glowers at me. Imagine how shocked he'd be if he found out how old I really am. The thought sours my mood as I take a bite of the crispy bacon in my hand.

"After you meet with the editor, what are your plans for the day?" Chance asks, and I can tell there's something he wants to ask me.

"I'm not sure yet," I chew on my lower lip. "Maybe I should go back to my apartment and hang out or something."

"I have an idea, but I'm not sure you're going to like it," Chance says as beads of nervous sweat appear on his forehead.

"Okay…" I draw the word out as I wait for him to continue.

"I was thinking we could check into a B&B for the night," Chance traces random shapes on the countertop, not wanting to risk seeing my reaction. "It would give us a chance to get away and relax after everything."

"Are you sure that's a good idea?" I ask, "I mean, we've only been hanging out for a couple of weeks now, maybe not even that long."

"And yet we've been on two dates, had sex once, and slept together twice," Chance's lip curls up into a crooked grin. "Isn't this what people starting a relationship do? Go away for a weekend together?" I open my mouth to protest, but Chance cuts me off, "And it's not even really a whole weekend, just one night."

Something about the shy way he's asking me and the hopeful look on his face has me changing my mind from the quick refusal I was about to give him, "I guess it wouldn't be so terrible."

"That's my girl," Chance laughs, "I'm going to drive the commitment-phobe out of you yet."

I snort, "I wouldn't go that far."

"Finish up your breakfast," Chance throws his paper napkin onto his plate. I realize I've been picking at my food while Chance has eaten enough to feed three people. I'll jump in the shower and pack a bag, then I'll take you wherever you need to go to meet with your editor."

"Sounds good," I nod as I dig into my untouched eggs.

I finished my breakfast and washed the dishes in the kitchen sink before returning to Chance's room to put on the clothing I was wearing yesterday. I'd have to run back to my apartment and change before going to meet with my editor anyway, so I texted him and explained that I'd be meeting him a little later than usual.

As I return the earrings I removed from my ears before going to bed last night, I knock one of the small posts off the nightstand and kneel to retrieve it. I feel around under the bed when my hand brushes against something leather.

Curiosity has me pulling the object out, a thick leather-bound book. I turned it over in my hand, but I found no title, so I flipped open the pages. My stomach instantly plummets along with my mood.

Inside the book, I find page after page of handwritten names and dates, both of which are too familiar to me. Thinking it can't possibly get worse, I keep flipping to the end, and then it gets worse. The last page is a note to Chance from his father explaining the names in the book to him, and he mentions me. *Shit. Shit. Shit. Shit.* Has Chance read this book?

I hear the bedroom door opening, but I don't have enough time to return the book under the bed, so I flip to one of the first pages and look up as Chance steps out of the bathroom. Warm steam filters out of the room as he wraps a towel around his waist. He looks up and sees me sitting on the bed, the smile on his lips dimming a little.

"Hey, I found this under the bed when I dropped my

earring," I say calmly, even as my heart thunders like angry hoofbeats against my chest. "What is it?"

"Oh, that," Chance replies just as disinterestedly, "my father has been keeping track of deaths he considers strange here in the Hollow for years. I guess it was a bit of a hobby for him."

"That's strange," I laugh, even though I feel like I'm going to throw up the breakfast Chance made for me. Trying to sound casual, I ask, "Have you read the whole thing?"

Chance shrugs, "a little here and there," scrunching up his nose, he adds, "To be honest, it doesn't really interest me."

"Oh," I breathe as the vise gripping my heart loosens slightly.

"Yeah," Chance nods, "well, let me get dressed and throw some clothes in my overnight bag, and we'll be good to go meet with your editor."

"Sounds good," I smile, thankful that he's changing the subject and only somewhat surprised that he still wants to go away with me for the night. This book and its contents came a little too close for my comfort. "I should probably drop by my apartment before I meet with my editor so I can change. These clothes smell like stale donuts and bad coffee."

Chance laughs, "That's the precinct smell. I've known it myself."

"Really, you do?" I arch my eyebrow as I ask, "Why?"

Chance scratches at the stubble on his chin, "I was the one that found my dad, so at first before they ruled it as natural causes, Chief Devries and the department thought I might have killed my father."

"Are you serious?" I ask incredulously. "Oh wait, I think I read about that in the Gazette."

"Yeah," Chance frowns, "it wasn't my finest hour. But enough of that, I'll get ready."

———

Chance insists on entering my building first and sweeping to make sure nobody else has left me any new packages. Even when we enter my apartment, he insists on giving it a good once-over to make sure nobody has broken in. Instead of annoying me like it would on any other occasion, I find Chance's concern endearing.

He sits on the couch while I change out of my dirty clothes, throw them into the overflowing hamper in my bathroom, and put on a clean pair of vintage stonewash jeans and a baggy green sweater.

I throw a few things into a backpack I find on the floor of my small closet, glancing over once, and I see Chance flipping through one of the books on my coffee table.

"I'm not taking that long," I joke as I zip up the bag and grab my purse and my travel camera bag. I don't like to be unprepared in case I see something I want to photograph.

"Huh?" Chance pulls himself from the book, looking slightly confused. Understanding dawns on him as he smiles sheepishly, "No, it's not that; I just haven't read this book before. It looks interesting."

He holds up the new Ted Dekkar novel I just bought online, and I nod, "Yeah, it's new. I just got it myself."

"Are you ready to go?" Chance asks, putting the book down and standing up to help me with my bags. His eyebrows shoot up, and he sees my backpack, camera bag, and purse. "You're bringing all of this? We're only going overnight."

I pat the camera bag, "I never know when I might spot something worth capturing. You understand, right? You're a writer; you must carry around paper and pens everywhere."

"Paper and pens are a little more compact than a bag of equipment," Chance teases.

I laugh, "Oh, shut up. Come on, I told my editor I'd meet him at Dark Brews in five minutes."

Downstairs, I wait while Chance puts my bags into the trunk

of his car. I force myself to act naturally and not jerk my hand away when he slips his hand into mine as we walk down to Dark Brews. Part of me still fights the normalcy of whatever is brewing between Chance and me after years of telling myself never to trust a man again.

As we approach the coffeehouse's entrance, I spy something strange peeking around the side of the red brick building. Squinting to get a better look, I freeze as my whole body goes taut.

Peering around the side of Dark Brew's façade is Brom's decaying Crooked One form. His black, soulless eyes glitter with malice as he smiles at me, looking particularly twisted and deranged. Seeing that he has gotten my attention, he pulls back the sleeve of his black tunic, revealing a skeletal arm with its ring finger missing. The arm rises toward his mouth, a sliver of silver hitting the morning light. A sickle, I realize as he raises it to his mouth and taps it against his lips to taunt me. I blink rapidly, willing the apparition to disperse.

Chance tugs at my hand, then stops and cocks his head at me when he realizes I've stopped walking in the middle of the sidewalk. "Are you alright?"

The words come to me slowly, as if fighting their way through thick, gelatinous air to reach my ears. "What?" I try to focus on his voice to bring me back to my senses.

"I asked if you're alright," Chance repeats, looking concerned.

"Oh, yeah," I nod vigorously. "I just thought I saw someone that I used to know."

"Are you sure you're up for the meeting? I'm sure your editor wouldn't mind if you rescheduled," Chance comments. "I know you've had a stressful twenty-four hours."

"No, I'll be fine," I force a smile.

"Okay then," Chance nods, still not looking convinced.

———

CHANCE

Cora's meeting with the Sleepy Hollow Gazette editor, David, goes pretty well. Younger than I expected, David is a stocky man, probably in his early thirties, with a shock of fire-engine red hair and a slightly darker goatee. Square, chunky-framed glasses magnify his large green eyes, and combined with his other facial features, he looks somewhat like an anime character.

While making small talk with Cora and sipping at a mug of coffee that smells strongly of pumpkin, David outlines the Halloween events he wants her to cover for the paper. She diligently takes notes and works the events into her schedule, periodically asking questions about specific shots that David is looking for.

When David learns that I'm a journalist, he asks if I'd be interested in writing freelance articles for the Gazette.

"I decided to stick around in town to run my father's bookstore now that he's passed," I tell him, "but I wouldn't mind doing a few pieces here and there."

"Great," David replies, sounding pleased by my answer. He handed me his notepad, and he said, "Write down your contact info, and I'll call you when I have something for you."

I write down my name and number, trying to make my handwriting as legible as possible, but it still comes out looking like chicken scratch. David looks at my info and nods, then slips me his card and tells Cora to send in her photos after she's attended the events.

I excuse myself while Cora wraps up her meeting with David, stepping out in front of the building and leaning against the cast iron frame that outlines the summer patio. As I watch people shopping and strolling down the street alone or with friends or family, my thoughts keep wandering back to who might have left that box on Cora's doorstep. I'm convinced that she knows whoever it is, but who in her life would be so sick or hate her that much? She's a loner, after all.

I can rule out Andi because he's like an annoying kid brother to her; he looks up to her so much. What would his reasoning be? Beau is also out because he's her friend, and I can tell he also has strong feelings for her. So, who else does Cora know in town? She hasn't mentioned anyone else she knew from school or anything, which suddenly strikes me as odd. Her past is one big mysterious void Cora avoids talking about as much as possible.

As I stand there debating possible stalkers, I spot Fall-Down Dan leaning against the shop next to Dark Brews, glaring at the coffee shop through the front window to where Cora sits talking to David. The malice in his eyes is unmistakable. Dan could have done it; he definitely has a strange fixation on Cora.

That's reason enough for me to close the gap between us, getting right up in his face and demanding, "Was it you? Did you put that severed finger on Cora's doorstep, you sick freak?"

"I don't know what the hell you're talking about," Dan sneers at me before popping a toothpick between his lips.

"I think you do," I accuse as I jab him in the chest with my index finger. "I've seen you watching her, and I know you've got some weird ass grudge against her, but you've crossed the line this time."

His eyes turn hard, and flinty and spittle flies out of his mouth. He says, "I wouldn't go near that monster if she were the last woman in the world. I sure as hell didn't leave any severed finger on her doorstep. If I thought scaring her out of town would work, I could think of a lot of better ways to do it."

"Just stay the fuck away from her," I snarl as he begins to walk away, "or next time, I won't be just warning you off."

He doesn't even bother turning around, continuing down

the street away from Dark Brews like he doesn't have a care in the world.

My chest is still heaving when Cora steps out of the coffee-house and weaves her arms around my waist in a rare case of public affection. I kiss the top of her head and force myself to calm down.

"That meeting went well, I think," I comment, trying to forget about the confrontation with Dan so Cora and I can enjoy the rest of our weekend. Cora and I walk down the block to my car while David comes out of the coffeehouse and waves to us before getting into his vehicle.

"Yeah, I think you'll like David," Cora replies distractedly as she scans the street like she's looking for someone or something. "He's great to work for."

"He seems so," I reply. Her jumpiness hasn't gone unnoticed by me. I know part of it is from last night's nightmare package, but it's more than that.

I knew when I came out of the bathroom this morning that she knew I knew more about the names in Pop's ledger than I was letting on. She'd flipped back to one of the older entries quickly, but it hadn't slipped past me that she'd seen Pop's note about her. I know there's something she's hiding, but it doesn't make any sense. The dates in Pop's ledger go back decades, and the only logical explanation that could tie her to them isn't rational at all. I don't believe in ghosts or vampires or anything else supernatural, but I can't think of any other reasonable explanation of how Pop could have known her thirty years ago. And Eli still hasn't gotten back to me. Not that I've checked in with him recently.

Another thing bothering me is Cora's strange actions on our way to Dark Brews earlier. She'd stopped dead in her tracks, her face turning pale and ashen as if she'd just seen a ghost. Something had frightened her, but when I asked her about it, she clammed up quickly. Thinking back, I wonder if she had seen

Dan glaring at her, and the knot of worry in my chest loosens a little. I don't think Dan will be a problem anymore.

Regardless, it seems like the more I learn about Cora, the more complex she becomes.

"Are we going far?" Cora asks when we get into the car.

"Not too far," I shake my head. "We're taking a staycation getaway."

Cora laughs, "I've read about those in Cosmopolitan magazine; very economical."

I snort and look over at her, "You read Cosmopolitan?"

"Sure, why not?" Cora challenges.

"Isn't that magazine geared toward giving women relationship advice?" I ask. "You, the girl who hates commitment and romance, read that because…?"

"Maybe I just read the magazine for the sex tips," Cora deadpans.

My cock jumps to attention and strains against my zipper, and I white-knuckle the steering wheel as the car swerves a little. An oncoming car honks the horn angrily as I return to my lane.

"You okay there, Chance?" Cora looks like she's trying not to laugh.

"Just peachy," I grind out. "I wouldn't worry, though; you're pretty damn good in that department."

"Just what a woman loves to hear," Cora smirks, "not that she's beautiful or smart or talented, just that she's good in bed."

"You're all of the above," I amend.

Cora rolls her eyes at me and stares out the window the rest of the drive to the bed and breakfast I booked us a room at.

"Wow," Cora breathes as we pull into the circular driveway of the cozy Victorian bed and breakfast I'd found online.

"I thought you might like it," I wink at her as we get out of the car. Cora wanders over to the wraparound porch as I grab our bags from the trunk.

Running her hand over the smooth wood of the porch and smiled at me over her shoulder, "It's beautiful; I forgot this place was here."

"Are you happy we came?" I ask, feeling slightly nervous as I follow her inside.

"So far," Cora beams.

The front door spills into the warm lobby, and my eyes quickly adjust to the change in lighting. A large, colorful rag rug covers most of the floor, and to the left of the door, a comfortable-looking sofa faces an inviting fireplace. Magazines and brochures of local interests are stacked neatly on the coffee table in front of the couch, and on the other wall, a solid oak table holds a large bouquet of fragrant blooms.

Above the table, the wall is covered in old photographs, and Cora moves toward them automatically. Setting the bags down at our feet, I wrap my arm around her waist and snuggle her against me as we look through the framed photos of the area's history.

Most of the photos show progress and change in Tarrytown, Sleepy Hollow, and the other area villages and towns from about the mid-eighteen hundreds onward, while others show parties and memories captured in time.

Something catches my eye in one of the photos, and I lean in to take a closer look. The handwritten note beneath the photograph reads Halloween 1899. Sitting in the middle of a table full of people with a champagne flute raised in a toast is a girl who looks remarkably close to Cora.

"Hey, the girl in this photo looks a lot like you," I point out the photo to her. When she doesn't reply, I look down at her face and notice that Cora has turned considerably pale and exceptionally still. Something is definitely going on with her today. She's so jumpy.

I shake her shoulder a little, and she looks up at me, her face blank but looking faintly ill. "Are you alright? You look like you've seen a ghost."

Cora opens her mouth to respond, but before she can answer, an elderly voice asks, "Are you checking in?"

Cora and I jump, spinning around guiltily to face an older woman who looks and dresses like she might have been here when this home was built more than a century ago.

"Yes, ma'am," I reply as I grab our bags and steer Cora to the front desk. "We have a reservation under Jordan."

The woman types something into the computer on the desk, squinting at the screen before pulling her glasses up to her eyes from where they dangle on a cord around her neck. She nods as she reads whatever she has pulled up. "Yes, I have it right here. One night stay for a Chance Jordan and Cora Whitt." Looking at us over the top of our glasses, she adds, "I'm presuming the two of you aren't married."

"No, ma'am," I reply apologetically.

"In my day, a man married a woman before he shared a bed with her," the woman replies sternly. Glancing at Cora, she frowns and asks, "Are you alright, dear?"

"Yes," Cora smiles faintly, "I'm fine, thank you for your concern."

"It's been a long couple of days," I smile at the innkeeper. "I thought it was best to take a night away from home so we could relax and recharge."

The elderly innkeeper nods, understanding, "That's a wise idea. Everyone needs a break sometimes. Will you need one key or two?"

I look down at Cora, who shrugs; turning back to the innkeeper, I say, "One should be fine, I think."

"Alright," the woman nods, "well if I can get you to fill out this registration form, I'll get you all checked in."

At the top of the stairs and to our left, I let Cora into our guest room. A beautifully carved four-poster bed faces a floor-to-ceiling window that showcases a stunning view of the Hudson and the colorful trees in the distance. The rest of the room is sparsely furnished with quality recreations of a nineteenth-century bedroom set; the only sign that we haven't stepped back in time is the sleek flat-screen television mounted to the wall. Through a door, the room connects to the adjoining bathroom, but I don't bother to investigate.

Sweeping Cora into my arms, I tilt my head and place a kiss on her lips. "Alone at last," I grin down at her, "no phones, no work, no distractions, no–"

Three sharp knocks on the door interrupted me mid-sentence. Cora laughs and pulls out of my embrace to answer the door.

The elderly innkeeper eyes us sternly as she hands Cora a stack of towels, "I brought you some fresh towels, and I forgot to tell you I serve dinner in the dining room at five sharp. If you don't feel like coming down, there is a menu next to the bed so that you can call down with your order, and I'll bring it right up to you."

"Thank you," Cora tells her from behind the mountain of towels. "We appreciate it."

The innkeeper sighs as she looks at me warily, "I'll leave you to it."

The elderly innkeeper pulls the door shut behind her, and I wait a heartbeat or two as I strain to hear her footsteps as she descends the staircase. I then turn to grab the towels from Cora's arms and place them on top of the dresser.

I crack up when I see Cora's embarrassed flush as I pull her back into my arms. " Where was I exactly?"

Cora licks her lips seductively as she pulls me down to her level, "Right about here, I think."

"Mmm," I hum, pressing her to me as I set fire to our bodies, brushing her lips with mine and stroking her tongue with my own when she opens for me.

CHAPTER FOURTEEN

CONTRARY TO THE innkeeper's assumption, Cora and I don't christen the bed right away. Instead, we kick off our shoes and lie down on the bed, where I hug her close to my body and stroke her back soothingly, urging her to unwind.

Eventually, Cora nods off as I feel the stress lifting from her body. I stroke her hair while she sleeps, trying to puzzle out her strange behavior over the past twelve hours and her mysterious history. Pop said that nothing in the Hollow was as it seemed. Did that include Cora? More than once today, she seemed afraid and worried, staring off into the distance and jumping at something that always appeared just out of my line of vision.

Whatever Cora is, it's becoming too late. I'm already in too deep with her and I'm beginning not to care what she's done or who or what she is. But her fear concerns me. Is she in some sort of trouble? Is somebody stalking her, hunting her like a wild animal? The thought of someone hurting her makes me furious, and my free hand balls into a fist involuntarily. What-ever she's done, whatever she's hiding, I'll fight to protect this mysterious woman lying in my arms. Of that, I swear.

Cora sleeps peacefully for an hour or two before blinking up at me as the sun begins to set outside our window.

"Did you sleep well?" I ask, brushing a kiss across her forehead and dropping another on her cheek.

Cora's cheeks flush bright pink as she says, "I can't believe I fell asleep. I'm so sorry; you must have been really bored just laying here while I slept."

"Nah," I shake my head, "it wasn't so bad. I was studying your sleeping habits."

"That's only moderately creepy," Cora laughs as she sits up. Her stomach growls loudly, like it has just woken up from a nap, too. Cora's hand falls to her stomach. "Oh god, that was embarrassing."

"Want to order something for up here?" I ask as I reach around her for the menu on the nightstand. "You'll need your energy for later, anyway."

"I like the sound of that," Cora says, her voice turning that low, sexy, husky sound it becomes when she's thinking about sex.

I scan the menu, which turns out only to be a list of what the innkeeper is preparing for dinner, my eyes lifting to meet Cora's as I teasingly ask, "So do you want the Beef Wellington or the Beef Wellington?"

Cora grabs the menu out of my hand and scans the list, "So much for room service."

"Oh, I think she'll bring it up to the room," I tell her, "I just don't think she's going to deviate from what she was planning to make."

I point to the small script type at the bottom of the "menu" that reads, "No substitutions, take it or leave it."

Cora laughs and shakes her head, "Alright, phone it in downstairs. I'm going to go freshen up."

An hour later, Cora and I sat cross-legged on the bed while we finished up the remains of the meal the innkeeper grudgingly delivered to us.

"So, books, I know you love them, but do you ever read anything besides horror?" I ask as I drag the end of my dinner roll through a puddle of gravy.

"I like a good murder mystery," Cora answers after a minute of thought. "Even the obvious, easy-to-figure-out ones. They're my guilty pleasure."

"You have a strange fixation on death," I observe as I reach out to wipe away a drop of gravy that's managed to escape the corner of her mouth. I'm learning quickly that, for a woman, Cora is a really messy eater.

Cora smirks, "I watch a lot of *Dateline* too. Does that scare you at all?"

"Not in the least," I answer her challenging stare head-on. "I actually find everything about you, even your weird quirks, completely sexy."

"Is that so?" Cora asks, her eyes sparkling in the lamplight.

"Definitely," I murmur as I lean in and kiss her, increasing the intensity of the kisses each time as my hunger for her builds. I grip the back of her head, pulling her closer as a moan forms in the back of her throat.

Pulling back but careful not to break contact with her, I slide off the bed and place our empty plates on the floor in the hallway before returning to the bed and covering her body with mine. If I weren't hard enough already, my body responds instantly as her soft body molds to mine. My erection strains against the front of my pants as I stroke her silky hair and coax her mouth open with the tip of my tongue and mimic the joining our bodies are both screaming for.

Cora's eager hands tug at the back of my t-shirt, pulling it up and over my head. A shiver runs through me as her hands explore my back. I pull aside the neckline of her baggy sweater as my lips graze the bare skin of her shoulder and collarbone. I dust her skin with kisses as her hands find their way into my hair, tugging lightly as her back arches upward to meet my hot mouth.

My hands move lower, going under her sweater to skim her soft skin as I slide her shirt up tantalizingly slowly. I can see Cora's desire for me building in her eyes just from my touch. I toss her sweater onto the floor and pull down the cups of her black lace bra, drawing one taut nipple into my mouth before moving on to the other. As I lick and suck on her hardened peaks, my hands reach behind her, flicking open the closure of her bra and dropping it to the floor with her sweater, then moving on to remove her jeans and panties.

My name sounds like a prayer on her lips as I kiss a path down her torso to her panty line.

She stops me, looking down at me through heavy-lidded eyes, and says, "No, I want to taste you."

I groan in want and allow her to push me over onto my back as she pulls her jeans and panties the rest of the way off, then pops the button on my jeans. Sliding them and my boxers to my ankles, I kick them off as she takes my hard length into her small hand and licks the head of my cock while maintaining eye contact with me.

My hips thrust upward as she takes me into her mouth, and I exhale a string of curse words as she begins bobbing her head up and down on my cock.

Her pace increases as I feel her tongue stroking the sensitive underside of my length. This girl very well might be the devil, but her mouth feels like heaven wrapped in velvet. I grow harder and larger in her mouth, throbbing as her expert mouth drives me to the edge of my sanity.

Gripping the back of Cora's head, I force her to take more of me and nearly lose it on the spot as I feel her cup my sack. My eyes roll back into my head, and a guttural sound bounces around in the back of my throat as I grunt out, "fuck babe, that's it."

Spurred on by my words, Cora begins to stroke my shaft as she sucks on my length. Unable to hold back anymore, my balls draw up, and I explode in her mouth. Satisfied for the moment, I sink back against the pillows as Cora wipes a drop of my come from the corner of her mouth and does something sexy and completely unexpected, which has me instantly growing hard again; she licks it off her fingertip.

"Come here," I say hoarsely as I grab Cora around the waist and lower her on top of me. My erection teases her entrance, not quite entering her yet as I grab the back of her head, lowering her face to mine and claiming her lips possessively. We become a tangle of lips, teeth, and tongues as my thumbs trace tiny circles around her hardened nipples.

Cora bites my lip, and I groan against her lips and tug on her nipples gently. She leans back to look at me as her hands rub my chest, sending slivers of pleasure through me.

My cock pulses with need, and I manage to hiss, "Ride me, babe."

Cora smiles, ever the seductress, as she guides my erection to her entrances and begins sliding down my length inch by inch, the pace so agonizingly slow I can't help myself from gripping her hips as my hips thrust upward, driving myself into her until she's full.

I wait for her to adjust to the fullness as her body stretches to accommodate me. Cora drops her head back, a look of ecstasy on her face.

Slowly, she begins to move and rock against me, finding a rhythm as she bites her lip sexily.

Quickening her pace, Cora balances her hands on my chest, scratching my skin lightly. I place my hands on her hips to guide her movement. Leaning down, Cora traces the lines of the tattoos covering my chest and shoulders with her tongue, and my eyes roll back into my head at the sensation.

Her long, wavy hair fans out over her round, perfect breasts as she takes me into her body over and over again, changing pace to grind her hot core against my base, and I grip her hips tighter.

My hips thrust up to meet her body as our movement becomes more frenzied, our breaths more labored, until I see her crest the wave of pleasure she's been riding, reaching her climax as she screams my name loud enough to wake everyone in the bed and breakfast.

Watching as she broke apart around me, coming undone, pushes me over the edge, and I follow her into the orgasmic abyss.

When I come down from my high, I pull Cora down into my arms, holding her close, our bodies still joined as one. She smiles at me, no doubt feeling as sated and relaxed as I do at this moment.

Kissing her lips and the hollow of her neck, my thumb grazes her arm soothingly as we lay there together. Her fingers play with my hair as her eyes flutter shut. We don't say a word, but after what we've just shared, we don't have to.

"Why are you so afraid of relationships?" I ask to break the silence after a while.

Cora tenses in my arms, the relaxed cloud around us bursting. "I told you before, I don't trust men."

"Why not?" I ask, and then I think, "Do you trust me?"

Cora shrugs, "I was hurt once, very badly, by a man I thought loved me. He spoiled things for all other relationships. In a way, I became someone else after that."

"What did he do?" I prompt her to explain further.

Unconsciously, Cora reaches up to her throat and clasps it, her eyes widening as she becomes swept away in a memory. When I clear my throat to get her attention, she blinks rapidly before meeting my gaze, and she looks ashamed. "I don't want to talk about it."

"Okay, I can respect that," I acknowledge. "Just tell me, do you think that person could be responsible for leaving that package on your doorstep."

The green tinge of nausea on Cora's face gives me her answer even though her mouth remains closed. Her eyes silently plead with me to let it go, so I sigh and hold her tighter.

"I won't let anyone hurt you," I murmur into her hair, "nobody will harm you ever again."

"What if I'm a harm to myself?" Cora's voice is muffled from where she presses her face into my chest, and I'm not sure I've heard her correctly. I'm about to ask her to repeat herself when she asks, "Why aren't you in a relationship? As far as I can tell, you're not a jerk."

I laugh at that, "Thanks, sweetheart." Sighing, I admit my truth, "I got myself into a mess back in the city."

"What kind of mess?" Cora asks, pushing up so she can look me in the eye.

I exhale hard, frustrated with myself, "I told you that I traveled around the world for a while, right?" She nods, so I continue, "When I got bored with traveling and living out of hostels and hotels all the time, I decided to put down roots in the city. It's been my dream for years to land a job at the New York Times. It turns out I didn't get hired there, but I did find a great job at the Post. My boss was excellent, and he pretty much ran with anything I wanted to work on. Anyway, just after I got hired, he invited me to a big Fourth of July party he throws every year. I went, and I was having a good time when I saw this woman step into the yard. She was slightly older than me but beautiful – an exotic beauty like you see in those stupid ads in fashion magazines. I didn't know who she was at the time; I just knew that I wanted her, so when she crooked her finger at me and gestured for me to follow her into the pool house on the other side of the yard, I thought I had scored.

Long story short, we had sex and then rejoined the party separately. I wasn't under any notion that this was the beginning of a relationship. I didn't want that. I didn't want to be tied down to anyone, really. It was just a quickie in my boss's pool house, you know? Anyway, I went to grab another beer from the cooler when my boss called me over because he wanted me to meet his wife."

"Oh shit," Cora's eyes widen in horror, "I see where this is going."

"Yep," I nod cryptically. "It turns out the woman I'd just screwed in the pool house was none other than my boss's trophy wife, Carlotta."

"No wonder you've sworn off relationships," Cora murmurs sympathetically.

"I wish that was where it ended," I grimace. "After that, Carlotta cornered me on my way out. She told me that her husband thought the world of me, but if she told him I'd just fucked her in their pool house, he would have no problem blackballing me with every publication, major and minor, in the country. I couldn't have that with my dreams of working for the *New York Times* on the line, so I asked her what she wanted for her silence. She demanded that I come over to their house on Long Island four times a week on the nights that her husband worked late or had social obligations in the city and screw her. I was to be completely at her disposal any time she wanted me. Apparently, her husband was too old for her taste, and she needed someone young and attractive to rut with."

"Oh, Chance," Cora's eyes well up with unshed emotion. "I'm so sorry you went through that."

I swallow hard, forcing down the emotions rising inside me from Cora's sympathy. I was expecting her to be judgmental like any other woman would be. I didn't expect this reaction. "It went on for three years. I think the final straw for me was when she forced me to do her in a public restroom at an event we attended this past August. I felt dirty, and I've never been more disgusted with myself. I genuinely liked my boss, and I couldn't believe I'd been betraying his trust like that for so long. So I ended things between Carlotta and me that night, and I began plotting my escape.

Then, about a week before my father died, I got a letter from him asking me to come home. It was the perfect opportunity. I quit my job, once again reiterated to Carlotta that things were over between us, and quickly found a new renter for my apartment."

"You did the right thing," Cora stroked my hair, and I began to relax. The tight coil I'd let build in my stomach was unwinding slightly.

"Unfortunately, nowhere is far enough away from Carlotta," I say bitterly. "The night you had to work late and meet with Stacey and her fiancé? Carlotta showed up at my father's house demanding that I take her back and using her usual threats. She'd been calling me since I returned home, but I'd blocked her calls, and she decided to show up. I told her I didn't care who she told. I never wanted to see her again."

"Good for you," Cora nods approvingly.

I smile sadly, "So I guess we're both screwed up by relationships."

Cora laughs, the sound coming out just as bitter as I feel, "I guess so."

"At least we have each other," I murmur, kissing her forehead tenderly.

"Mmhmm," Cora replies wordlessly as she burrows further into my chest. Her hair tickles my nose, and I fight the urge to sneeze.

I'm just about to drift off when a frightening thought occurs to me, "shit."

"What, what's wrong?" Cora sits up sharply.

"I just realized," I say slowly and cringe at what I have to tell her, "Before, when we were together, we didn't use protection."

Cora's eyes pop open wide as she stares down at me. Tamping down her emotions, her face turns into a blank mask as she mumbles, "S'okay, we should be fine."

I watch as she forces herself to relax, her body language turning cold and detached as she rolls off of me and turns to face the wall. I run my hand down her back in a silent apology for being so careless, and though her body shudders and reacts eagerly to my touch, Cora doesn't say another word.

Curling myself around her, I drag her back into my arms from behind, wondering why I'm not freaking out as much as I should be. I've never taken a woman without using protection, not wanting to risk the consequences, even if the woman I was with told me she was on birth control. But with Cora, the thought of the consequences doesn't scare me at all. I'm sunk.

CORA

I lay awake for hours, the past twenty-four hours replaying in my mind over and over like a bad movie. I've had two run-ins with Brom's Crooked One, and judging by the severed finger and the sickle he held to his mouth, things are only going to get worse until I figure out how to put a stop to him.

Then there's the mess I'm in with Chance. I'm getting too comfortable, in too deep with him. For crying out loud, we got so caught up in the moment we forgot to use protection when we had sex. I know better than that, but I'm not sure it even matters. I'm a two-hundred-thirty-year-old ghost monster; it's not like I'm even capable of getting pregnant. The problem is no matter how normal this feels between us, I have to be realistic.

Nothing can come from this. He'll grow older and move on with his life just like his father did.

I just wish my damn heart didn't seize up every time I think about what he confessed to me tonight. Our lives aren't so different after all.

I should end this right now. I should get up, get dressed, and leave, or better yet, I could lose hold of my human self and disappear into thin air. I shift my body slightly to test Chance's reaction. As I scoot away from him, Chance's grip on my waist tightens and pulls me back against his hard body.

"Don't go," Chance whispers huskily in my ear.

"I didn't realize you were still awake," I murmur without turning to face him. "I was just wiggling my toes. They're getting numb."

Chance's feet brush against mine in response, "better?"

"Mmm," I reply. I guess Chance isn't a heavy sleeper if he was really ever sleeping at all. I close my eyes and order myself to fall asleep. I'll figure something else out in the morning.

———

I wake up to bright sunlight streaming through the massive windows. Among other things, Chance and I forgot to shut the drapes before falling into bed last night. Groaning, I yank the heavy quilt over my head to block out the light. Early mornings suck unless I'm just coming home from being out all night.

Beside me, Chance shifts and sits up. I hear a sharp intake of breath, then, "Damn. Cora, are you awake?"

"Yes," I mumble, my voice muffled by the quilt.

"Just," Chance pauses, unsure of what to say. "Stay under the blankets for a minute."

"What, why should I do that?" I laugh at the absurdity of his request as I sit up and throw the quilt back.

I gasp, covering my mouth to fend off a sudden wave of

nausea. A set of eyes, a nose, and a jack-o-lantern mouth have been painted on the window in blood. The words "always watching" are scrawled underneath in jagged letters.

"Oh my god," I groan and then dash for the bathroom, almost not making it before heaving myself over the bowl and throwing up all of last night's dinner.

"Shhh," Chance says soothingly as he crouches down behind me and gathers my hair away from my face. With his free hand, he rubs circles on my back. "I'm sorry you had to see that. Stay in here while I talk to the innkeeper and get our things packed. I'll shut the curtain so you don't have to look at it again. I don't know what the hell is going on, but I'll figure it out."

I nod, not quite capable of speech yet, as I rip off a strip of toilet paper and wipe my mouth. Chance hugs me to him protectively for a moment and then gets up and stalks out of the bathroom. It's only then that I realize we're both still naked. If I weren't so repulsed by Brom's latest show of force, I'd think our undressed state was humorous.

Twenty minutes later, Chance told off the innkeeper as if she were personally responsible for the display on our window, demanding a full refund. Then he stomps back into our room and throws our things into whichever bag is closest before striding purposefully into the bathroom and deciding he needs to dress me.

I feel like a small child as he throws a sundress I don't remember packing over my head and then layering last night's sweater on top of it. Wordlessly, I allow him to slide my boots on and lace them up before pulling me to my feet.

"It's okay, Chance," I force him to look me in the eye. "You keep treating me like I'm going to break at any moment, and I'm not, okay?"

"Some sicko is targeting you," Chance spats, "and I'm supposed to be calm about the whole thing? Fuck that! This shit is increasing in frequency, and I swear that when I get my hands on whoever is doing this, they're going to wish they'd never laid eyes on either one of us."

"There's nothing you can do," I shake my head.

"What do you mean there's nothing I can do?" Chance asks angrily. "There damn well is! There are a lot of things I can do, starting with contacting the police when we get back to my house."

"Your house?" I wrinkle up my nose.

"Yes, my house," Chance confirms, "Until this all blows over, you're staying with me. I want you where I can see you at all times."

"Why don't you just stick me in a cage while you're at it," I glare at him, crossing my arms over my chest like a sulky teenager. "You sound like some cheesy male character in a romance novel, and you know how much I hate those."

"Don't you see? This isn't some damn novel. This is real life. Someone is threatening you! I'm doing this for your well-being," Chance's expression softens a fraction as he taps the side of his leg anxiously.

"I'm not a child, Chance," I remind him. "I can take care of myself. I have been for a long time."

"Obviously not very well," Chance snaps, his eyes blazing hot with anger.

My mouth drops open in disbelief, but I quickly shut it and push past him out of the bathroom. Our weekend getaway is thoroughly ruined; I sling my overnight bag over my shoulder and grab my other two bags, stopping only to say, "I'll be in the car."

"Cora," Chance sighs, "I didn't mean to say that. Come back. I'm not sure it's safe to walk to the car on your own."

I shake my head incredulously before throwing the door to our room open, startling the innkeeper, who pauses mid-knock on the other side. I push past her down the stairs.

I'm going home. I don't care what he says. He doesn't know a thing about me or what's really stalking me. I have it handled.

I can't believe that I was just last night trying to think of a way for us to work. Even if I weren't a monster, our personalities would constantly clash, and I don't want to live out the rest of my life like that.

CHAPTER FIFTEEN

"TAKE ME BACK TO MY APARTMENT," I demand when Chance climbs into the car.

A muscle in Chance's jaw jumps angrily, but wisely, he doesn't say anything. In fact, we don't say a word to each other the entire drive back to my apartment.

Without waiting for Chance, I leap out of the car the minute he puts it into park and grabs my bags from the backseat. Twirling my keys around one finger, I ignore Chance as he turns the car off, grabs his bag, and follows me to the door.

I'm unlocking my door, somewhat successfully ignoring the insufferable male hovering over my shoulder, when a police cruiser pulls up beside Chance's Mustang. My key misses the lock as I watch Chief Devries heft his portly body out of the cruiser and amble the ten feet across the gravel parking lot.

"I've been trying to get ahold of y'all since yesterday," Chief Devries drawls, tipping his head to stare us down and trying to look authoritative even as he yanks up his too-loose pants.

"We decided it would be best if we went away for the night," Chance explains.

"And your phones didn't work on that little getaway?" Chief Devries narrows his eyes at Chance.

"Do you have any news about the, um, package?" I ask, cutting in.

Chief Devries gives Chance another long look and then turns to me and removes his obnoxious cowboy hat. "Yes, that's why I've been tryin' to track you down, Ms. Whitt. I think it's best if we discuss this inside."

"Alright," I blink, feeling suddenly queasy at what the Chief has found out. I know who the skeletal finger belonged to, but the other one is a mystery.

Pulling the door open, I lead Chief Devries into the dark hallway and then into the empty studio space. Chance trails behind us, closing the doors and then coming to stand behind me as I sink into my office chair.

We watch as the police chief wheels Andi's chair over to the front of my desk and lowers himself onto the ergonomic memory foam cushion. The chair groans in protest under his weight.

"We found out that the bloody finger someone sent you belonged to the body of a Jane Doe we found earlier Friday afternoon. She'd been dead since late Thursday evening, and it took us until this morning to identify her. Now," Chief Devries pauses to pull something out of his pocket, "I'm going to show you a picture, and I need you to tell me if you've ever seen the person in the photograph. Can you do that?"

"Yes, sir," I nod around the thumbnail that's magically worked its' way between my teeth. I bite down as Chief Devries flips the photograph over and places it face up on my desk. Chance sucks in a startled breath, but I push away all sound as I try to figure out where I've seen the woman in the photo before.

The woman appears to be in her late thirties, but she looks like she takes great care to appear younger. Her skin is tanned, her eyes mocha brown, and her hair a silky black sheet, probably hinting at a Spanish heritage. My forehead crinkles as I think hard. I know I've seen her recently, but where?

"That's it," I say, snapping my fingers. "I saw her on Thursday when I went out to get something for lunch. She was sitting outside Dark Brews arguing with someone on her cell phone. It got heated, and more than one person was staring."

"And you didn't know her before that time?" Chief Devries asks.

I shake my head, "No, I'd never seen her before. I didn't talk to her or anything. I just saw her in passing."

"And you didn't see her after that?" Chief Devries inquires as he types a note onto his smartphone.

"No, not after I went into the deli to pick up lunch. Is she… was she murdered?" I ask, already fearing the answer.

"It looks that way," Chief Devries confirms my suspicions.

"How did she die?" I ask carefully and clasp my throat subconsciously.

"The cause of death has been determined to be a deep throat wound," Chief Devries replies grimly. "Her throat was cut from ear to ear, and then she was dismembered. That's why it took some time to determine it was her finger that was sent to you."

Chance's fingers dig into the back of my chair tighter, his knuckles turning white. A glance up at his face tells me something is very wrong. Chance's handsome face is shuttered, utterly devoid of emotion.

"What about you, Chance?" Chief Devries asks when he notices Chance's expression, "Do you know this woman?"

I wait for Chance's response, seeing him swallow hard before answering, "She's my former boss's wife."

I gape at him, but Chief Devries nods like he knew all along, and Chance is merely confirming what he already knows.

"Did you know that she was in town?" Devries asks, "To see you, perhaps?"

Chance narrows his eyes and then feigns ignorance, saying,

"Why would she have been coming to see me? I barely knew her."

"Is that so?" Devries doesn't sound like he believes Chance.

"I didn't have any interaction with her outside of functions she threw and attended with her husband, my boss," Chance lies.

"Did you know that Mrs. Grankowski had recently filed for divorce from her husband?" Devries wants to know.

Chance scratches his chin disinterestedly. "I guess I heard something through the grapevine."

"Yessiree, she was leaving her husband, going after half of everything he owned," Chief Devries relays almost gleefully. "Our M.E. also discovered that Mrs. Grankowski was pregnant when she died. Now, son, do you really expect me to believe that a woman leaves her wealthy husband and shows up in the hometown of her husband's former employee—an employee who quit abruptly and left town—and that it's all just one big coincidence?"

"Look, I don't know why she was in town, but it didn't have anything to do with me. I quit my job at the paper because my father needed me to come home and run the store for him," Chance snaps, getting agitated.

I swallow hard and turn back to meet Chief Devries's gaze. "If all you said about this woman leaving her husband, wanting his money, and being pregnant is true, then I think the person you ought to be talking to is her husband. Not going around making slanderous accusations toward Chance."

"Whoa, little lady," Chief Devries raises his hands defensively, "now nobody is accusing anyone of anything. Chance and I are just having a little chat, aren't we, son?"

"Guess so," Chance mumbles.

"Well, thank you for updating us," I stand up, putting an end to the conversation. "I take it that you haven't found out who killed this woman or put her severed finger in a box and left the box on my doorstep."

"I, ah, no, we haven't," Chief Devries fumbles for words, obviously not used to being dismissed so abruptly.

"Well, I trust that you'll let us know when you know more," I state as I move to open the back studio door leading into the hallway and stare at the bumbling police chief until he gets the message.

"That I will," Devries assures me as he replaces his cowboy hat on top of his head. Glancing back at Chance, he adds, "I'll be in touch."

———

Once I hear Chief Devries exit through the back door and poke my head out to double-check, I spin around to face Chance. "That's Carlotta?"

"Yeah," Chance replies, looking faintly ill. He lowers himself into my desk chair, cradles his head in his hands, and groans.

"She came to see you on Thursday night, didn't she?" I ask.

Raising his head to look at me incredulously, he asks, "What, do you think I had something to do with her death, too?"

"Of course not," I retort. I know he didn't because it reeks of Brom and his cursed Crooked One's dirty work. It's a message. He's telling me he knows what I did to Trina, but I can't tell Chance that. "I do, however, think there are a few things you and I should discuss. Starting with whether you knew Carlotta was pregnant."

Chance twists the gauge in his left ear, a flash of guilt flitting across his features.

"You did know," I accuse.

He sighs, coming forward with arms raised like he's prepared to stop me from running away. "When she showed up at Pop's, she told me she was pregnant. Carlotta claimed that if I didn't come back to her, she'd ruin my career and tell everyone, especially her husband, that the kid was mine."

"Was it?" I ask, backing out of his reach.

Chance shakes his head, "No, definitely not. I'm not that stupid. I always use protection."

I cock my eyebrow and say, "You forgot to use a condom just last night."

"That was different," Chance protests, doing that finger-thigh tapping thing again.

"How was that different?" I ask, crossing my arms over my chest.

"When I'm with you, I lose my mind. I forget everything that's important and what I should be doing. All I can see is you." Chance's expression turns pleading. "I was never that interested in Carlotta that every other stray thought faded away. In the beginning, she was just an easy lay, but then she turned into a nightmare. I would have never been so careless at the end to forget something so important."

I roll my eyes, "you're heading back into romance novel guy territory again."

"Are you always such a goddamned cynic?" Chance demands angrily. "Do you really not have any feelings at all? Or have you just kept those damn walls stacked high around yourself for so long that you're afraid to let anyone love you?"

I snort, looking away, "Love is nothing but an illusion."

"Do you know where that attitude is going to get you?" Chance asks. When I don't reply, he says, "Alone, completely and utterly alone."

My eyes meet his, "Maybe that's the way I should be."

"You can't honestly believe that," Chance looks incredulous.

I shrug, "Who knows, maybe. I think you should leave. I don't need you hanging around acting like a knight in shining armor, ready to swoop in and save the princess. I'm not a damsel in distress."

Chance shakes his head glumly, "Fine, keep on thinking that way. You know where to find me when you change your mind."

"I won't," I promise.

———

CHANCE

Walking away from Cora was the hardest thing I've ever done. With each step, every part of me rebelled, demanding that I turn around and make her see that she was being unreasonable.

I know she's lashing out right now. Someone is after her, maybe the ex-boyfriend who hurt her. I'm sure remembering the outcome of that situation has her wary of allowing herself to try again with someone new. I can accept that. Something tells me she'll come around and stop acting so frustratingly hot and cold all the time.

It just infuriates me that every time I begin to gain ground with Cora, she decides to push me away again. I've never had to work this hard for a girl before, not even Stacey back in high school.

And then there is the Carlotta issue. Fuck. I can't believe she went and got herself killed. Correction, she went and got herself dismembered, and now Chief Devries thinks I did it. I just got off his goddamned radar, and he's already back to looking at me through those beady eyes of his like I'm a serial killer. Just because it turns out she wasn't lying about being pregnant, it doesn't mean that I was the father or that I killed her. Sure, I didn't like her, but why would I ruin my life over someone like her?

I drive back to Pop's house a little too fast as I run through the possibilities of who might have killed her. I doubt her husband would have killed her. My former boss was too even-tempered for that, and even if he did find out we'd been screwing behind his back, I think he'd be more likely to be emotionally destroyed by it and drink himself into oblivion than to kill her.

I contemplated the possibility that she was meeting with someone besides me and then quickly dismissed it. No guy, after spending any length of time with Carlotta, would get so jealous that he'd kill her because he wasn't her one and only. They'd be thankful to have some of the pressure that came with Carlotta's possessive attention taken off them.

So who, then, a random stranger? No, it has to have something to do with Cora. Why else would someone have sent her Carlotta's severed finger? It may very well be that Carlotta was an innocent bystander in all of this. In that case, in a way, maybe it is my fault. If she hadn't come here looking for me, she might still be alive in the city, scheming to find her next boy toy.

When I get back to Pop's, I grab yesterday's mail and throw it on the table in the hall, delete a bunch of messages from Pop's answering machine, and drag myself down the hall to my room.

I throw my duffel bag on the floor and shuck my clothes into a heap, careful to toss my phone onto the bedside table before striding into the bathroom and turning on the shower.

I'll give Cora a day or two to calm down and see that she overreacted and that what's brewing between us can work. She'll be back.

———

When I wake up on Monday morning, I feel optimistic. I spent the rest of Sunday forcing myself not to think about Cora, choosing instead to build a website for Hollow Books and link it to new social media business accounts.

I set up a section on the website dedicated to in-store events, starting with a Legend of Sleepy Hollow-inspired party on Halloween night. Brainstorming some ideas on a fresh piece of notebook paper, I begin taking notes about contacting Dark Brews to concoct themed coffee and tea drinks because what do book lovers like more with their books than coffee and tea? I also make a note to discuss a few signature pastries. I detail a rough draft of a display that customers will see when they walk into the door and some simple yet spooky decoration ideas to spice up the shop. Maybe if Cora and I are speaking by next weekend, she'll help me set things up.

I can plan a drop-in from the guy who has dressed up as the Horseman my entire life and have him entertain my customers, maybe read the legend holding the book high in one of his hands, a jack-o-lantern in the other and reciting it in that deep, booming voice he uses to scare kids out trick-or-treating.

I stopped for dinner around six, then went back to my computer and looked into stocking the books of independent authors from the tri-state area in the shop. I even contacted a few that I'd heard of through social media and sent out some feelers.

I woke up this morning feeling like I'd accomplished something, so I decided to go for a run before breakfast. I've never been much of an athlete, preferring books over football, basketball, or baseball, but for a while in high school, I was a member of the track team.

A little out of shape, I run halfway through town before turning back to fill up on coffee and take a shower at home.

I'm standing in the kitchen in my boxers, drinking my coffee when my phone rings. Seeing Eli's work number, I swiped to accept the call.

"Hey man, what's up?" I answer casually as I refill my coffee mug.

"Exactly what have you stepped in out there in the boonies?" Eli asks without preamble.

"Is this about Grankowski again? Because seriously, Eli, I wasn't—" I manage to say before Eli cuts me off.

"No, this isn't about your boss, but believe me, we'll get to that in a minute," Eli says quickly. "This is all about Cordelia Whitt."

"Have you finally found something on her?" I ask eagerly, my coffee mug forgotten on the kitchen counter, as I walk around the island to grab a pen and a pad of paper.

"Well, that depends," Eli says wryly. "It depends on who exactly you've been talking to because, by all accounts, this 'Cordelia' person appears and disappears through time like a freaking ghost."

"What do you mean?" I ask as I scratch my skin.

"There has only been one Cordelia Whitt who has lived in New York State or anywhere else in the country since the country's founding, and by all accounts, she died in 1804 at the age of twenty-one. Since that time, however, a woman resembling Cordelia Whitt around the same age has popped up off and on throughout the years."

"Popped up how?" I ask my gut churning so hard I'm not sure I want to know.

"Mainly in photographs and mentions in the local paper out there. A photograph in the paper about being the town's first female photographer, a mention of her in 1899 ringing in the century at some local pub, another photograph of her at an underground speakeasy during the 1920s, on and on – here's a photo of her protesting the Vietnam war in the sixties. Hell, now that I look closer, I think even your famous local author, Washington Irving's obituary, was written by someone writing under the name 'Cord Whitt.' And each time she's appeared over the years has one thing in common."

"What's that?" I'm nearly afraid to ask.

"There's been a higher mortality rate among young males in the area." Eli relays grimly, "And there's something else."

"Do I want to know?"

"I found a photo in the paper covering some local wedding

back in 1987, some society bigwig, anyway, and in the corner of the photo nearly invisible to the naked eye, but confirmed by a caption under the picture, is this woman – now calling herself 'Cora Whitt' – and your father if I'm not right. His name was Chancellor Jordan, wasn't it?" Eli asks. His voice sounds like it's coming through a long, patchy tunnel. When I don't respond right away, Eli says my name worriedly, "Chance?"

I swallow hard, my voice coming out thick and scratchy as I request, "Can you email me everything you've found?"

"Yeah, sure, man," Eli replies, sounding surprised and concerned. "Are you sure you're alright?"

"Um, yeah, it's just been a busy morning." I clear my throat. "Thanks for your help, Eli. I'll have to call you back later."

Eli starts to say something else, but I cut him off and end the call. I walk to Pop's office feeling like a heavy weight has just been dumped onto my shoulders as I sink into the cushioned desk chair and log into my email account.

Eli's email comes in a minute later with a note attached saying that he's worried about me and suggesting that he come out for a few days.

Ignoring Eli's heartfelt concern, I scroll to the bottom of the email and download all of the attachments Eli has forwarded to me. It turns out there are quite a few. Rubbing the space between my eyes, I click on the first photo dating back more than one hundred fifty years. This is going to be a long morning.

CHAPTER SIXTEEN

<u>CORA</u>

After a fretful night's sleep, I was in no mood for Andi's usual antics, nor was I prepared for the worried, furtive glance he kept sneaking in my direction. Obviously, someone told him about the finger-in-the-box situation, and it didn't take me long to find out who when I pulled up the main page of the Gazette's website.

The top article's headline reads: **Local Business and Freelance Photographic Journalist Finds Severed Finger on Doorstep. Is Sleepy Hollow Drawing in Dangerous New Residents?**

I cringe at the headline and shut down my web browser. I look up and catch Andi watching me again, his smooth skin creased and wrinkled in worriment.

"Oh, for Pete's sake, I'm alright," I roll my eyes and slam my palms down on the desk.

"How can you stand to be here after what you found?" Andi comes over to sit on the corner of my desk.

"It was probably just some stupid prank," I insist to calm Andi down even though I know better.

"I heard it belonged to a woman they found dismembered in the cemetery," Andi shivered, his knowledge stunning me into silence. Just how much of the story did the Gazette report? Usually, in a murder investigation, the police like to keep some information under wraps so they can nail their killer.

"Well," I start and then pause, having nothing else to add. Frowning up at him, I say, "Don't you have some work to do?"

Realizing I'm not playing around, Andi scurries back to his desk and shuffles some papers around, looking for the proofs I put him in charge of for one of our clients.

The rest of the day is fruitless. Neither Andi nor I can concentrate on our work; Andi because he keeps watching me, waiting for me to break, and me because his staring is driving me insane.

Finally, I say, "Alright, we're not getting anything done today, so why don't you just head home early?"

Andi's eyes bulge wide, "are you sure you're okay alone here? Maybe you should call Chance."

"Chance and I are no longer together," I replied stiffly as I shut down my computer.

"Because of the incident?" Andi asks, his voice a whisper.

I shake my head, "No, not because of that."

"I can stay if you want to hang out and talk," Andi offers.

"I'm fine," I insist, smiling to prove my point.

Andi purses his lips, not believing me for a minute. I stare him down until he finally begins gathering his things. I get up and put my back to him, searching my bookshelves for a new book to read as I hear his footsteps move toward the door.

"Thank goodness," Andi breathes as someone steps inside the studio, "maybe you can talk some sense into her."

Whoever has entered grunts in response, and then the sound of the chime over the door tells me Andi has left for the day.

I turn and find Chance standing in the entryway to my

studio. I sigh, putting my hands on my hips as I say, "I told you I didn't want to see you."

"We need to talk," Chance says roughly, his tone lacking any trace of warmth and affection.

This is it, he knows, I realize as I feel all the blood rush from my face.

"Talk about what?" I ask, avoiding his gaze as I trace imperfect circles on my leg with my fingertip.

"About this," Chance strides forward and slaps a thick book down on the desk in front of me.

"What is this?" I ask, even though I recognize it to be his father's ledger.

"Pop's ledger, I'm sure the names inside look familiar to you if you even bothered to learn the names of all the men you killed," Chance says venomously.

My stomach clenches, filling me with dread and guilt for the first time since Bathsheba brought me back to life. "You don't understand."

"Then help me understand how you could have killed all of these men. Explain to me how you can be decades older than me, hell, maybe even centuries older, and yet look like you're younger than I am. What are you? Who are you? Tell me the fucking *truth*," Chance snarls, "unless you just want to keep lying to me."

"I'm the *Headless Horsewoman*," I say quietly.

Chance snorts in disbelief, "Unbelievable. I thought maybe if I confronted you, you would tell me the truth, but this is ridiculous."

"I'm not lying," I insist, scratching at the corners of my eyes, which are itchy and swollen from unshed tears.

Chance crosses his arms over his chest, and I force myself not to get distracted by the sexy tattooed muscles peeking out of the sleeve of his shirt. "Explain yourself."

I sigh and sink into my desk chair, dropping my head into

my hands and weaving my fingers through my messy locks. Speaking to the floor, I begin, "The legend that this town thrives on is wrong. It is true, but it is written with a twist to protect me. Washington Irving, or Irvie as I called him, was my best friend growing up. I was born Cordelia Whitt on March 18, 1783, the bastard daughter of a married local merchant and a housemaid. My mother died when I was eleven, and my father refused to take me in, so I followed in my mother's footsteps and became a maid.

When I was sixteen, I met a boy a couple of years older than me in the market. His name was Brom Bones," I pause when Chance raises his eyebrows dubiously, "Yes, the same one from the story. Anyway, for me, it was love at first sight. He was attractive, funny, and charming. We became lovers, and I started sneaking out to meet him in the barn of the property he told me would someday be ours when he made me his wife. For five years, we screwed like rabbits in the hay loft, and Brom whispered sweet nothings about the future in my ear as we lay there tangled up and covered in hay. It turns out that's all they were: pretty little lies.

When I was twenty-one, I found out that Brom had no intention to marry me. Instead, he had proposed marriage to the town sweetheart, Katrina Van Tassel." I swallow hard and force myself to continue, "You see, Trina, although beautiful, was a cold, calculating, vindictive bitch. She really wanted to marry Ichabod Crane, the school teacher all the women swooned over, but when he didn't immediately want to marry her, she decided to marry Brom instead. I met with Brom to plead with him not to marry her, but he betrayed me, calling me nothing but a whore, and then Trina stepped out of the shadows and told him to get rid of me. I was so angry I didn't have time to see it coming."

"See what coming?" Chance asks cautiously, and I realize he's come to sit on the other side of my desk.

"The sickle, you know, one of those curved blades used to cut wheat?" I describe it as my vision clouds over, taking me back to that horrible night. "He swung, and I didn't have a chance to duck or move away. It took my head clean off. I didn't realize I was dead at first. My mind was conscious, but there was nothing but darkness."

"So you're a ghost?" Chance asks.

I shrug, "In a way, I guess. In that dark, in-between place, a raspy-voiced woman came to me, offering me a chance to live again. She provided me immortality and a chance to get revenge on Brom. It can't come as much of a shock that I took her up on her offer. I returned to the land of the living and killed Brom. The necklace I keep around my neck is Brom's petrified eyeball, a trophy of my first kill. By that time, he'd married Trina, and she was expecting his baby and the minute the child was born, I slaughtered Trina where she lay.

After that, I made it my mission to remove all traces of Brom's family line from the world. Generation after generation of men, I seduced to my bed until they were all dead. But I still wasn't satisfied. So, I moved on to killing men who cheated on their wives or girlfriends. Those are the names in your father's book."

"And the legend?" Chance prompts.

I sighed, "As I said, Irvie was my best friend. After my first kill, I learned that killing gave me the ability to become corporeal again, solid. I showed up at Irvie's house, and he accepted me on the spot, helping me control what I am. When I don't look like this," I sweep my arm down my body, "I look like a headless female rider. Irvie was always a jokester and a storyteller, and he was dying to tell my story. Only to protect me, he changed the story. He made the headless creature a horseman, a Hessian who lost his head in battle, a ghost who may or may not have existed. He left it ambiguous, telling the story of Brom, Trina, and Ichabod – who was really only an innocent bystander who got frightened when he saw me resurrected in my true form."

"So you've been killing for more than two centuries?" Chance asks, looking disgusted with me.

I nod, "I lived with Irvie the rest of his life, and I killed more frequently in the beginning, luring men to my bed and slashing their throats with an invisible blade when they reached their climax. Over time, I struck out on my own, taking odd jobs here and there and isolating myself. The only people I've allowed myself to stay close to have been Irvie's descendants, the youngest of whom is my friend Beau. My killing rate has dropped dramatically over the past half-century, with only two men per year to keep my body sustained. I appear as human and alive as anyone else; I still eat, sleep, and have to keep up with proper hygiene."

"How do you justify the killings?" Chance asks, his tone is unforgiving.

Rubbing the bridge of my nose, I explain, "While you may consider it murder, I see men who aren't worthy of the life they've been given. Men who are willing to throw away women who love them and families they've created to have sex with a shiny, young bimbo – the bimbo being me. Because of what Brom did to me, I can't stand cheaters, so in a way, I'm doling out punishment the only way I know how to."

"But it's still killing," Chance argues. Flatly, he adds, "So you're like a succubus?"

"A what?" I scrunch up my nose in confusion.

"A sex demon," Chance explains, actually looking sheepish. "I watch Ghost Adventures."

"Um, no, I only kill the men during climax because they're distracted and don't have time to stop what I'm about to do," I explain.

"Oh." Chance frowns. "How does my father fit into this?"

"He was a mistake," I mumble.

"How so?" Chance asks.

"I met your father in the late eighties pretty much by accident. He asked me out, but I turned him down," I smile at the memory. "Your father was a lot like you; he was persistent, and finally, I ended up going out with him. We started spending a lot of time together, and for the first time in a long time, I allowed myself to be carefree and happy. Then I started realizing your father was getting too attached, wanting to build a future with me, marry me, the whole deal."

Looking into Chance's eyes, I urge him to understand. "It never would have worked out. I'm immortal, forever frozen at twenty-one. I'll never physically age or be able to have a child. I can't die, I can't get sick, I haven't even had a menstrual cycle in more than two hundred years. And I have to kill to survive; otherwise, I'll wither and turn into a monstrous thing. A creature no man could ever love."

"So you broke his heart," Chance concludes.

I nod sadly, "I dropped out of sight, and we never saw each other again."

"So let me get this straight, thirty years ago, you screwed my dad, and now you're screwing me," Chance points to himself. "Do you realize how sick that sounds? What, do you compare the two of us while you're with me?"

"I never slept with your father," I shake my head violently.

"Oh yeah, right," Chance rolls his eyes.

"I didn't, I swear," I urge Chance to believe me. "I cared about your father, that's true. We went out a few times, but although there were feelings on both our parts, it never went past kissing. It was never like it's been between you and me."

"So if I'm to believe you, why wasn't it like that? Why didn't you tell him what you're telling me?" Chance wonders.

"You practically had to force the truth out of me. I've never let anyone get close enough to me to know my secret. Besides, the way things ended was for the best. I hate being suffocated by men. I love my freedom, which is why it's probably a good thing I am what I am. I'm not the marrying type or the girl you bring home to meet Mom."

"I don't have one of those anymore." Chance flashes a sad smile. Turning serious, he asks, "Did you know her? My mom, I mean?"

I shake my head, "In the beginning, after I pulled away, I watched your father from afar. I wanted your dad to be happy, and I watched as he met and fell in love with your mom. It was painful but necessary. But to answer your question, no, I never met her face to face."

"What's happening now, who's behind it? I assume you didn't send yourself a severed finger," Chance questions me.

I shake my head, opening my mouth to explain. The front door to my studio bursts open, and Chief Devries and two other officers barge in.

Stalking across the room, Chief Devries yanks Chance to his feet, grabbing his arm and twisting it behind his back, "Chancellor Jordan the Third, you are under arrest for the murder of Carlotta Grankowski and felony stalking. You have the right to remain silent. Anything you say can and will be used against you in a court of law. You have the right to an attorney; if you cannot afford an attorney, one will be provided to you. Do you understand these rights as I've read them?"

CHAPTER SEVENTEEN

"YOU'VE GOTTA BE FUCKING KIDDING me," Chance struggles in Chief Devries's stronghold.

"Do you want to add disorderly conduct, attacking a police officer, and resisting arrest to your charges, boy?" Chief Devries demands as I hear him yank Chance's shoulder out of its' socket as he clamps the handcuffs onto his wrists.

"Stop, you're making a big mistake," I cry, "Chance didn't do anything."

"We have a mountain of evidence against him, little missy," Chief Devries argues. "I bet your boyfriend here didn't tell you he was having an affair with the deceased."

"Chance wouldn't kill anyone," I protest. "I know he's innocent."

"Love is blind, little girl," Chief Devries's expression hardens as he hauls a still-struggling Chance out of my studio. Chance's face lights up with pure rage, his eyes narrowing at me suspiciously as I watch the officers force him into the back of Chief Devries's cruiser.

I have to fix this for him. I can't let him go down for a murder that I know Brom's Crooked One committed. I'll get him out of this mess, even if he will never forgive me for what I am and what I've done.

———

CHANCE

"So here we are again," Chief Devries slaps a file onto the interrogation room table and slowly lowers himself into the cheap folding chair. I bet he was chomping at the bit to get the chance to rip into me as I was booked and processed. Crossing his beefy arms over his chest smugly, Devries says, "I've finally got something on you that I can make stick. Tell me, boy, why'd you kill her?"

I lean forward like I'm going to confide my darkest secrets to him and very slowly enunciate, "I. Want. My. Lawyer."

Devries frowns, his irritation written clearly across his face. "You sure you don't want to confess? I know a psychopath like you is probably dying to share all the gruesome details."

I snort, "Just get me, my lawyer. Do you think you can handle that?"

Devries glared daggers at me as he shoved back from the table and exited the overheated shoebox, which he called an interrogation room. The door slams with a bang, rattling the plastic shades in his wake.

I lean back, tipping my chair back onto its' back legs, and prop my still-handcuffed hands behind my head, settling in to wait for Neil to arrive from the city.

Either Devries purposefully sat on my request for my lawyer, or Neil had to be dragged away from something back in the city because it's three hours before he arrives and joins Devries and me in the sweltering interrogation room. My stomach growls as Neil sits down beside me, smelling strongly of steak, reminding me that I haven't had anything to eat since this morning.

"Your case is circumstantial at best," Neil addresses Devries as he sets his briefcase on the flimsy table.

"Nah, I don't think so," Devries drawls as he chews on a toothpick. "You see, I've got means, motive, and opportunity."

"Hmm, I don't remember hearing that you'd found a murder weapon anywhere, let alone anywhere near my client's person or residence," Neil replies swiftly, "and as for motive, whether or not my client was sleeping with the deceased, having an affair does not mean he committed murder; furthermore, as for your opportunity I have multiple witnesses that will testify that not only was my client out with his girlfriend at the time of death but he was with a group of people at the time also."

Devries narrows into angry slits, "Tell me, boy, are you going to let this suit talk for you? Or are you going to tell me why you did it? Did your boss find out you were boning his wife and fire you? Or did you lose it when she told you she was carrying your child? I doubt your new girlfriend would have been very accepting of that, even in our new progressive society."

"Don't say a word," Neil advises me.

"Wasn't going to," I reply as I sit back.

"I guess we'll let the court decide his fate," Devries gets up, opens the door, and says to someone, "Take him to a cell."

"What?" I ask, looking wide-eyed at Neil.

Apologetically, Neil says, "I'm sorry, Chance, you're charged with second-degree murder. I can't get you out of here until your arraignment in the morning, at least. You're stuck here for the night."

I shake my head, looking down at the table, "this cannot be happening."

"We'll figure this out," Neil promises as a jailer enters the suffocating room and yanks me to my feet.

"I didn't do this, I swear," I tell Neil.

"I know," Neil nods, "I believe you. Just hang in there until the morning."

The jailer drags me through the hall from the police station to the jail. Shoving me into another small, windowless room, he thrusts an orange jumpsuit into my hands, "Strip down and put this on."

"Do you get off on this?" I smart off as he removes the handcuffs. "I bet you do, watching guys strip down to their underwear. I bet it gets you nice and stiff."

Without warning, the jailer shoves me face-first into the brick wall, "Yeah, I do get off on seeing sick fucks like you get what you deserve."

"What happened to 'innocent until proven guilty'?" I retort.

"What if I don't believe you are innocent?" The jailer hisses in my ear.

"This is excessive force, you know," I point out. "You're violating my rights."

"Strip down before I shut you up," the jailer demands, releasing his death grip on me.

Without breaking eye contact and not giving him the satisfaction of watching me squirm, I strip down completely and shrug on the prison-issued boxers, white t-shirt, and orange jumpsuit. Years of working out and changing in locker rooms taught me to be confident about my body. I know I have a better body and a bigger cock than most guys, and that knowledge has afforded me a bit of cockiness.

I smirk in satisfaction when the jailer's eyes widen at my boldness, confirming my assumption about his preference. "Get a good look, perv?"

The jailer's eyes snap to me and harden as he grabs my arm a little too hard and snaps the handcuffs back onto my wrists before leading me back into the hall and down to an empty cell.

It isn't until the cell door clangs into place with a disturbing finality and I'm left alone in the dark that my arrogance drains out of me like a machine running out of steam.

How could this happen to me? I didn't kill Carlotta, dammit!

It's just my rotten luck that she had to get herself killed in my hometown, where the bumbling police chief already has it out for me. I cannot spend the rest of my life in prison for a murder that someone else committed.

My head is admittedly spinning after everything that I've learned today. The woman I've been falling for isn't even human, and now I've been accused of murder. This has to be some bizarre dream or prank, and I'm just waiting for someone to jump out and say, "Gotcha!" but it doesn't happen.

I can't change anything about the Carlotta thing right now, so I guess it will be one long night to think about everything Cora told me. I guess Pop wasn't kidding when he said that not everything in this town was as it seemed.

I just wasn't expecting *this*.

Hours pass until night eventually turns into day. My eyes are bloodshot and itchy, and I didn't sleep a wink last night. In my current predicament, I was too afraid to close my eyes and get some rest, and the sounds of the other inmates shifting and making noise in their cells kept me on edge.

Finally, a nondescript jailer collects me from my cell and watches as I shower in the communal shower and hurry into the suit that Neil brought for me to wear to court.

I'm shuffled into a gray van with shackles on my wrists and ankles and transported to the courthouse in White Plains. The entire ride over, my mind keeps begging; don't send me back to that jail cell.

Neil meets me inside, looking professional in his three-thousand-dollar Armani suit, and leads me into a conference room.

"This hearing is for your arraignment," Neil explains, "That means that the charges against you will be read in front of the court, and you will enter a plea. After we enter your plea, it will be determined whether you are eligible for bail or if you have to remain in jail. I'm hoping to get you out on a cash bond because, in this type of case, a signature bond is pretty unlikely. The court will then decide the amount for bail. Hopefully, we can show that you're not a flight risk and you don't need a ridiculously high bail. Like I told that idiot police chief last night, the case against you is circumstantial. They have no real proof that you did anything. They just decided you were the killer and were too lazy to chase any other leads. In the best-case scenario, I can get this whole thing dropped for insufficient evidence; in the worst-case scenario, we'll have to go to trial, but we won't know that until after the arraignment hearing. Do you understand?"

I nod numbly. Even if I'm allowed bail, after Pop's bills, I don't have anything left unless I put both the house and the shop up as collateral.

By the time I'm led into the courtroom, all traces of cockiness or arrogance have abandoned me, and I'm embarrassed to say I'm actually shaking. I stand beside Neil as the judge shuffles to his bench. By all accounts, the judge shouldn't be an intimidating man. He's short and balding with a thick mustache and wire-rimmed glasses. He looks like the type of guy I'd hire to do my taxes, and he stumbles over his long black robe as he reaches his chair. In any other situation, I wouldn't be afraid of him, but because my fate rests in his hands, I've never been more scared of anyone in my entire life.

Once the judge is seated, I'm allowed to sit down. Beads of sweat dot my forehead as I wait anxiously while the judge sorts through some papers in front of him, details of the case most likely.

"Will the defendant please rise," the judge's voice is high-pitched and congested. Neil elbows me to stand with him, and my knees quake, threatening to give out as I force myself to stand. "Chancellor Jordan the Third, you are hereby charged with two counts of murder in the second degree and one count of stalking with malicious intent. How do you plead?"

"Not guilty," I answer through parched lips.

The judge instructs the court reporter, "Let the record reflect that the defendant has entered a plea of not guilty."

"The defense asks that the defendant be allowed out on bail," Neil addresses the judge. "The defendant is not a flight risk, and he has ties to the community."

"The state requests that bail be set at two million dollars and that the defendant turn over his passport." The prosecutor, a slightly pimply face man not long out of law school, stutters his request.

"I believe two million dollars bail is a bit excessive," the judge says, looking down at the prosecutor through the top of his spectacles. Given the state's case against the defendant being what it is, do you even have enough evidence to proceed?"

"We believe we do your honor," the prosecutor assures the judge.

"Well, let's make sure of that first," the judge replies, "We do not want a repeat of last time."

I look at Neil, confused, but he shrugs his shoulders, as out of the loop as I am.

"Of course not, your honor," the prosecutor stutters.

"I am ordering an evidentiary hearing in two weeks' time," the judge bangs his gavel. In the meantime, bail is set at five hundred thousand dollars."

The prosecutor pales as the judge leaves the bench and retreats to his chambers. Neil turns to me, looking relieved. "That went better than I expected. I think the judge may already be swayed to our side."

"Yeah, but he set bail at five hundred thousand dollars," I say miserably.

"I thought it was fair," Neil comments. "It could have been

worse; he could have ordered the two million dollars bail and forced you to wear an ankle monitor."

"It might as well have been the two million dollars," I groan, "I don't have access to that kind of money."

"I've got it covered," Cora says, appearing behind the defense table. "I'll post bail and get you out of here."

"And you are?" Neil asks, staring Cora up and down as he rises from his seat.

"Cordelia Whitt," Cora offers her hand for Neil to shake, "but please, everyone calls me Cora."

"You're the new girlfriend?" Neil asks her. "Aren't you awfully young?"

"I'm older than I look," Cora says wryly, and my stomach turns. I remember exactly how old she really is despite how she looks.

"If you say so," Neil replies, allowing himself to be charmed by Cora.

"I'll go take care of the bail, and I'll meet you back at the police station if that's how it works," Cora turns to me shyly.

Neil nods, "Chance will have to be processed for release, but you'll be able to take him home from the police station."

"I'll see you soon," Cora murmurs as she kisses my cheek awkwardly.

Neil promises he'll be waiting with Cora at the police station back in Sleepy Hollow as the guards shove me back into the transport van.

Leaning my head back against the van's wall, the ride back to the station passes quickly. My mind keeps circling back to the fact that I might be getting out on bail, but that doesn't mean that this nightmare is going away just yet.

The jailer from last night is waiting to process me out,

manhandling me roughly throughout the whole process. I hope I don't ever see him again, but guys like him could very well become my reality if Neil can't get me out of this.

Back in my sweater and jeans, I rub my raw wrists as I meet Neil and Cora in the lobby of the police station. Cora looks relieved that I'm out but decides to keep a safe distance away when she sees the look on my face. I don't know how to feel about her right now, but the last thing I need is her making things worse.

"I've cleared my caseload, and I'll be checking into a hotel in Tarrytown to work from," Neil informs me as we walk outside. "I'll want to meet with you tomorrow to go over the case, but for right now, I think it's best if you go home with Cora and get some rest."

I open my mouth to protest, but Cora swoops in, smiling gratefully and saying, "Thank you, Neil, for everything that you're doing for Chance."

"It's my pleasure," Neil smiles faintly at me. "I know this guy well enough to know he's getting a raw deal, and I'm going to do whatever it takes to get him off."

"Thanks, man," I pat him awkwardly on the back before Cora ushers me to her car. Or rather, my car, I realize as I slide into the passenger side of my Mustang.

"Do you even have a driver's license?" I ask Cora once we're alone.

Cora snorts, "Of course I do; what kind of question is that?"

"Well, since you're not alive or human or whatever," I comment.

Cora frowns, "There are ways of obtaining forms and such. I have to have some documentation so I can own property and have a bank account. I just have to create new ones every couple of decades."

"Speaking of bank accounts," I shoot her a wary look, "do I even want to know how you got the money to bail me out?"

Cora shrugs, "I've been alive for over two hundred years, Chance. Even though in the beginning things were a little tough financially, I've worked odd jobs here and there throughout my entire life. I haven't splurged on much other than my Hasselblad and the building where my studio and apartment are situated, so over time, I've created quite a large nest egg."

"And you have nothing better to do with it than waste it on my bail?" I ask, feeling bitter for no reason.

Cora looks at me, eyebrows raised, "Would you rather that I'd left you in there to suffer?"

I hesitate, then reluctantly say, "No."

"Then quit complaining," Cora says.

"Did you kill Carlotta?" I ask bluntly. I've been wondering that since I was arrested.

Cora slams on the brakes in the middle of the road, the Mustang fishtailing at the sudden loss of momentum, and looks at me like I've lost my mind, "Of course not. I didn't even know Carlotta."

"I just figured with your history," I say.

"Let's get one thing straight, Chance," Cora's eyes are alight with fiery rage, "I kill men that cheat on their women. I've only killed one woman in my entire life, and that was Trina, and I think I had a goddamned good reason for that. I'd never set eyes on Carlotta before seeing her outside of Dark Brews last Thursday, and even then, I didn't know who she was until after she was dead. I may be a monster in your eyes and the eyes of anyone who would find out what I am and pass judgment, but I'm a monster with morals."

"A monster with morals," I snort. "You've killed what, at least four hundred men in your life? And you think you have morals?"

"I didn't say I was perfect," Cora retorts as she grips the steering wheel tightly.

"So, who killed Carlotta?" I ask, "And don't tell me that it doesn't have anything to do with her finger ending up on your doorstep or the jumpy way you've been acting. Not to mention, the morning I woke up, and you were covered in dirt and bruises and wouldn't tell me how you'd gotten them."

"Brom is back from the dead," Cora sighs angrily, "well, sort of anyway. Of course, he wants revenge because I killed him, but it's more than that. He came back more twisted than he was in life. I can only assume that he's the one who killed Carlotta, though his motive is a mystery to me. I know he's the one that sent the finger, though; it was his skeletal finger wrapped around Carlotta's. I was out trying to kill him the morning that I came back with bruises. Sometimes, I like to go riding on my horse, Blood, in the early mornings, and on that particular morning, he was there waiting to ambush me. I drove him back for the time being, but it wasn't enough to destroy him. And yes, I'm jumpy because I keep seeing him around town, watching me, leaving me psychotic gifts and threatening messages."

"So, the bloody message on the window of the bed and breakfast?" I ask, already knowing the answer.

"Yep, that was Brom's handiwork," Cora confirms.

"How can he be back from the dead? You killed him, right?" I watch her carefully as she resumes driving.

Cora laughs bitterly, "he killed me, and yet I'm here, aren't I?"

"So you're saying he's like you?"

"No," Cora shakes her head, "he's a Crooked One, a soulless demon that kills without morals or conscience that handed over its' humanity for another shot at wreaking havoc. Whatever keeps him going, he's nothing of the man he once was. He's an empty shell masquerading as the man I used to love."

Cora goes silent, and I look up and realize we're already pulling into Pop's driveway. The gears screech as Cora puts the car into park and gets out.

"I get it, though," Cora spouts as I shove open my door and

get out, "you can't forgive me. I'm too horrible of a person, and you don't want to be around me. I knew this was coming, and that's why I tried to break things off multiple times to save us both from this mess. But you wouldn't take no for an answer, and here we are. Don't worry; you won't have to see me ever again. I just thought I was doing something nice for you."

"Cora," her name slips from my lips like an exhausted plea. I don't know why I'm calling her back. Everything she's said is true. I can't deal with her right now when I've got all this other shit to face.

Seeing the look on my face Cora shakes her head smiling regretfully, "I should have known better, but dammit, the men in your family are like quicksand."

She turns to go, but a weird thought occurs to me, bubbling to the surface: " Hey," Cora turns back to me, a strange look on her face as she waits for what the reason I've halted her. " Does Beau know what you are?"

Cora's face turns blank, "of course he does. Everyone in his family does. The real story of *The Legend of Sleepy Hollow* has been passed down from generation to generation. Irvie used to tell his nephews about me. It was their favorite scary story."

"Oh."

Cora nods, a look of finality in her eyes, as she shocks me by transforming before my very eyes, a cloud of smoke obstructing my view. When she comes back into sight, she's different; she's nothing more than a slightly translucent, headless woman atop the back of a massive stallion. The horse rears up, and the horse and rider gallop away, disappearing.

It's only after Cora is wholly gone that I identify the strange look on her face. It looked startlingly like hope.

CHAPTER EIGHTEEN

<u>CORA</u>

I shouldn't have shown Chance my true form. It's not like it matters; I know I'll probably never see him again. I couldn't help myself from glancing back at him to see his reaction before I disappeared into thin air. I could tell by the look on his face that, until that moment, he didn't entirely believe my story. I supposed it wasn't easy to see the woman he'd been lying in bed with only days earlier fading into near translucence astride a demonic horse with nothing but air where my neck and head should be.

A part of him, I'm sure, was curious, dying to ask if I could see, hear, and taste when in my spectral form. I don't have any answer for how I can do those things, just that I can. Though I'm missing my head, it's like a phantom limb that still functions as it ought to.

I spend the rest of the week acting like a shut-in. I attend the events my Gazette editor, David, asked me to photograph and submit my work to him, but I spend the rest of my time skulking around the studio. Realizing I'm in a foul mood, Andi gives me a wide berth.

Outside, the world gears up for my favorite holiday, Halloween. Halloween in Sleepy Hollow is unlike anywhere else in the world, except perhaps up in Salem, Massachusetts. Weeks before Halloween, the entire town transforms into a spooky getaway; the businesses put out festive-themed displays in their windows while residents deck their front lawns with witches, cauldrons, cobwebs, and silhouettes of the horseman that made the town famous while each window box is lined with gruesomely carved jack-o-lanterns to spook the children and scare away dark spirits.

Then, each year, on Halloween night, children trick or treat while adults gather at Sunnyside for the Horseman's Ball. At the ball, one local man is named Horseman for the night, and he gets to ride through town, visiting some of the local haunts before choosing a woman to swoop up onto his horse and "kidnap" for the night. I've never attended the event, but I have been known to watch through the windows like an uninvited observer.

It's been five days since I last saw or spoke to Chance. I should be relieved, but I miss him in the same phantom way I miss my head when I'm in my spectral form. This is ridiculous. We only spent three weeks together. How did I let a man—especially one as frustrating as Chance—become such a fixture in my life?

I'm alone and wallowing in my apartment, drowning my feelings in whiskey, when someone comes banging at my door. Andi knows better, and I doubt Chance has changed his mind. He's busy preparing for the Halloween in the Hollow event he scheduled at Hollow Books for tomorrow night anyway. There was a big ad in the Gazette about it yesterday. I wonder how many people are just going so they can gawk at the murder suspect.

"Go away," I yell at whoever is still stupid enough to be banging at my door.

"I'm worried about you, Cora," Beau's gruff, disembodied voice filters through the door.

"I'm not in the mood to talk, Beau," I reply tiredly as I refill my glass.

"You're acting like a teenage girl," Beau rumbles as his voice becomes louder and clearer. I look up and see him standing just inside the doorway.

I raise one of my freshly plucked eyebrows, "I'm pretty sure I locked that door."

"I can pick a lock in under ten seconds," Beau lifts one shoulder and then lets it drop.

"That's an interesting skill to have," I remark as I throw back my entire glass of whiskey in one gulp and savor the taste.

"Just because you can't physically feel intoxicated doesn't mean you should drown your liver in alcohol," Beau observes as he pulls out the stool next to me and sits down, drumming his fingers distractedly against the cheap Formica island countertop.

"Why not?" I ask.

Beau purses his lips, unable to come up with a good enough answer.

"I thought you'd be busy helping your family set up for the Horseman's Ball," I comment as I get up and retrieve another rocks glass from the cabinet and fill it with two fingers of whiskey before handing it to Beau.

The town may organize and plan the Horseman's Ball, but Beau's family still holds the deed to Sunnyside and is always a vital part of the event.

"I got off easy," Beau says, "I'm in charge of supplying the booze, and I don't have to deliver that until tomorrow morning."

"Lucky you," I mumble.

"You could come, you know," Beau suggests. This isn't the first time he's asked. I say no every year. "It's open to the public, and you're a local business owner; it might be a good idea."

"I'm not a people person," I remind him. Looking darkly into my empty glass before reaching clumsily for the bottle, I mutter, "Especially this year."

"I've never seen you this bent out of shape by a guy before," Beau says, and I hear genuine concern in his voice.

"Who is bent out of shape?" I laugh a little too loudly. Adjusting my volume, I say, "I'm just in a dark mood. Everyone goes through one of those now and then, even a monster like me."

"You're not a monster, Cora," Beau says sharply. "Did he say that to you?"

I'm surprised at the heat in Beau's tone. Meeting his gaze with my watery one, I shake my head slightly, "He didn't have to. I know what I am. I'm a monster, a killer, a destroyer of lives. Nobody could accept someone like me."

"You're a girl that was betrayed by someone you trusted who made a rushed decision to get revenge," Beau observes. "You're not a monster. You may act tough, and you may kill to survive, but you're not a horrible person. You're beautiful and smart, and even if you didn't have that otherworldly ability to draw men in, you would still have men lining up, dying to spend time with you. So don't listen to anything Chance or anyone else says to the contrary."

"That's the problem," I laugh bitterly, "guys are dying because they've been with me."

"Cora," my name rushes out with a sigh, just like it did the last time Chance said my name, but this time it's different.

I look into his eyes, seeing the scorching heat sizzling there as he angles his head toward mine and kisses me, pulling my bottom lip between his as he grips the back of my head with thick, wide-spread fingers.

Even though it feels wrong, even though Beau is just a good

friend and nothing more, I do what I do best; I grab his hand and lead him over to my untidy bed, allowing him to lay me down and touch my bare body in the dark.

———

I wake up alone in the morning, not that I expected Beau to stay. Whatever last night was, it wasn't a romantic 'let's get together' kind of thing. How do you handle it when you've just crossed the line between friends and something else with someone you value more than most in your life?

I'm going to pretend it didn't happen. After all, Beau and I were just two people who drank too much whiskey and needed a release, just two writhing bodies in the dark.

I yawn and stretch as the thin yellow sheet covering my naked body slips away. Getting out of bed, I tug the sheets free, ball them up, and shove them in the laundry hamper. Making a mental note to throw a load of laundry into the washer, I step into the bathroom as the soles of my feet slap against the linoleum.

Reaching in to turn the water on, I lean against the glass shower door and close my eyes. I don't know why I thought sleeping with Beau would make me forget the messy turn my life was taking. Chance knows what I am, and who knows what he'll do with that knowledge now. Maybe he'll turn me over to the cops, telling them that I killed Carlotta even though I didn't, and I'll just wither away into a brainless hag in a jail cell somewhere. It's just as bad as trying to figure out what to do about Brom's Crooked One.

I've done research, but I can't find a single mention of Crooked Ones or Gatekeepers on any mythology or paranormal website. A few sites mention demonic possessions, but that usually involves the person being alive. A doppelganger sounds plausible, but again, they are apparitions of living people. Hell, even Stephen King doesn't have a literary explanation of how Brom's lookalike was created and is now walking the Earth.

Though she wasn't much help last time, another talk with Bathsheba might be the only way to find out how to get rid of Brom once and for all. I just hope I can find her again.

Showered, dressed, and transformed into the headless horsewoman, I nudge Blood into a canter as we search the cemetery for Bathsheba. After three rotations throughout the acreage, I finally find Bathsheba sitting in the middle of Horseman's Bridge.

"I never did understand why they named this Horseman's Bridge," Bathsheba comments, reading my mind as she cocks her head to listen to the raging water running below the bowing wooden planks at our feet.

"Because of Irvie's story," I roll my eyes and dismount before joining her to sit on those creaky wooden planks. "He wrote that Brom, or 'the horseman,' chased Ichabod over the bridge and threw the flaming pumpkin at him. I did scare Ichabod accidentally when I returned to the land of the living, but I didn't throw any stupid pumpkin at him. That was just a bit of storytelling on Irvie's part. He had an odd sense of humor."

"You miss him," Bathsheba observes.

"Yes," I admit.

"Have you dealt with the Brom issue yet?" Bathsheba inquires.

I shake my head, "I keep seeing him around, and he keeps making threats. He even killed a woman last week, yet he hasn't come right up and approached me since the last time we fought each other. I don't know how to send him back to where he belongs."

"I'm more concerned about your heart, girl," Bathsheba murmurs.

"My heart?" I echo in confusion. I thought she wanted me to banish Brom.

"You're losing your humanity, Cordelia," Bathsheba says bluntly. I've always liked how straightforward she is, but this sudden change of topic gives me whiplash.

"I haven't killed recently," I say defensively. "It's been almost a month since my last, and I don't plan to kill again until spring."

Bathsheba shakes her head firmly, "you're not allowing anyone into your life either, girl."

"What life?" I snort. "I'm only half-alive as it is. Besides, you, of all people, know that nobody would accept what I am."

"You haven't given anyone the chance to," Bathsheba counters.

"That's not true," I argue. "I've tried, but it never works out."

"You don't give it a chance to work out," Bathsheba comments. "The man whose father you also loved—you pushed them both away. And what about Master Irving's great-great-great-nephew, Beau? You didn't give him a chance either."

"Beau and I are just friends," I mumble, "and Chance has made it very clear that he wants nothing further to do with me."

"You need someone, Cordelia," Bathsheba urges me to understand. "Embracing life and relationships, feeling positive instead of angry and bitter maintains your humanity. Your humanity is what makes you different than the Crooked One. Your humanity is your true power. It will be what allows you to end the Crooked One once and for all. Without embracing your humanity, you'll become just a shell of a human, a mindless killing machine like Brom. I don't want that to happen to you. You need to forget the pain of the past and realize that you do have a future, and only when you realize that will you be able to defeat the Crooked One."

I turn to argue my point with her but find that Bathsheba has already faded away in that mysterious, unnerving way of hers.

―――――

CHANCE

All week, I've been forcing myself not to think about Cora. I'm better off, or so I keep telling myself. What Cora's done and what she's been doing for more than two hundred years is murder, no matter what she says, and how can I ever allow something like that? Allow her to leave my bed and seduce another man to his death. How would that make her any better than the cheaters whose lives she steals? Where's the justice in all of it? She should be the one facing a murder rap, not me.

Not that those beliefs stop me from reaching for my phone to call her or setting aside old first-edition copies of Stephen King novels that I find in Pop's inventory before I remind myself that I have no plans to intentionally see Cora again so I'll never have the opportunity to present her with my treasures.

On my way to the shop, I keep telling myself not to look across the street and to avoid the festively decorated windows of her studio altogether, but even so, I can't stop myself. I let her get under my skin.

This morning, my heart stalled when I saw Beau coming out of Cora's apartment too early to drop by for a quick chat. I guess it didn't take her long to go out and fuck someone else. I guess it means that I really didn't mean anything to her. I don't know why I'm surprised or why I even allow myself to get upset, but I do.

Just thinking of Beau, the guy I'd once thought of as a friend, strolling out of her place looking pleased with himself, has me involuntarily curling my hands into fists as they itch with the desire to knock his teeth out. I have to force myself not to march down to the bar and start a fight. The entire police department has been watching me like a hawk this week, just waiting for me to slip up and give them a chance to throw me behind bars again. Unfortunately for them, I'm able to restrain myself. I won't give them the satisfaction of returning me to that dark, dank cell.

It was bad enough on Wednesday when I had to stand back and watch Chief Devries and his minions ransack my house and the shop with the excuse of a search warrant.

Neil insisted that they had no grounds to search my property now that I've been formally charged. The fact that they've completely dropped the ball in collecting evidence shows that they don't have a leg to stand on in court.

As we stood by watching helplessly as they turned the house over, Neil read me the coroner's report, "According to the coroner's findings, the body was dismembered with such sharp precision that the murder weapon is likely some sort of archaic farming tool and not, no matter what anyone thinks," Neil pauses and looks at Chief Devries out of the corner of his eye, "anything like a normal household knife or saw. In fact, the blade was most likely some sort of heated metal because the wounds where the limbs were severed from the body were cauterized."

"That is just one opinion," Chief Devries grumbles.

"Well, they won't find anything like that here," I tell Neil. "Pop wasn't into farming or gourmet cooking, and the biggest knife he owned was probably a paring knife or a steak knife. I don't remember Pop ever owning a saw of any type."

"Hmph," Chief Devries hems and haws, "just because we're not finding anything doesn't mean that you didn't do it. It just means that you had plenty of time to dispose of the murder weapon in the Hudson."

"Then drag the river and find out," Neil retorts confidently.

"The D.A. wouldn't authorize that," Chief Devries frowns.

Neil smiles smugly as we watch the police department and the forensic team pack up, their shoulders slumped in disappointment.

"Chance?" A perky female voice calls my name, pulling me out of my thoughts.

I blink and find Stacey Jensen standing in front of me, trying to get my attention. I ran into her earlier this week at Dark Brews. She'd heard about my situation and told me she knew I couldn't have killed anyone, even going as far as to offer to have her fiancé find me the best criminal defense attorney in the country.

When Stacey heard about the event I'd scheduled for tonight before this mess took off, she insisted on helping me with it. She's been amazing dealing with vendors and consulting with a design friend on how to maximize the theme for tonight with decorations and displays for the shop.

"Yeah, sorry I zoned out for a minute," I shake my head and focus on Stacey. "What were you saying?"

"I was asking if you had anything else you wanted me to set up before I go to change for tonight," Stacey replies as her eyes sweep over the shop.

I can't believe how different the shop looks. Stacey raided every craft store she could find, and the results definitely paid off. When guests walk in the front door, they'll be met by a life-sized wooden silhouette of the headless horseman. At the horseman's feet are four ghoulishly carved faux pumpkins, one of which has a butcher knife thrust through the eye hole, spurting fake blood into a trough underneath the display.

"Everything looks amazing, Stacey," I tell her honestly. "I can't thank you enough."

"What are friends for?" Stacey smiles warmly, then slings her purse over her shoulder and promises to be back an hour before the event starts.

As the door shuts behind her, I cross the room to view the massive dollhouse Stacey and her decorator friend overhauled to look like a replica of Dracula's mansion. Next to the dollhouse sits a bookcase built in the shape of a coffin, complete with red silk trimming the shelves. I managed to dig up some old but not outrageously valuable editions of *Dracula, Carmilla,* and Anne Rice's *Interview with a Vampire* that adorn the shelves along with ancient tomes about vampire lore.

The back of the shop is divided into Dr. Frankenstein's lab and a section devoted to *The Mysteries of Udolpho.* Dr. Frankenstein's lab holds a metal operating table set with horror novels and plastic knives and scalpels. Displays of bubbling beakers filled with food coloring and dry ice cast the corner in an eerie green glow while the other corner is decorated in the things that bring on nightmares and go bump in the night. Somehow, Stacey managed to dig up the scariest-looking skeletons, and all of the props look like they've come straight from a movie set.

The rest of the shop is swathed in black fabrics, with ravens whose eyes follow you around the room, fake cob-webbing, and dimmed lights to make the whole place look sinister. Later, when the shop owner from Dark Brews arrives with the specialty drinks and pastries Stacey helped me order, we'll set up a table next to the register for easy access to the Bat's Blood coffee, Pumpkinhead's Revenge lattes, and Brain cookies.

When the event is in full swing, the "Headless Horseman" will make an appearance to spook the guests and read a section of the legend aloud.

Planning this event with Stacey has gotten my mind off the murder charges and Cora's deadly confession, and I just hope I can keep it together while the fake horseman is in the shop.

I wonder briefly what Cora will be doing tonight. Does she celebrate Halloween at all? Will she be accompanying Beau to the Horseman's Ball at Sunnyside? As a descendant of Washington Irving, Beau's presence is all but mandatory at the annual event.

Shoving all thoughts of Cora to the back of my mind, I step out of the shop to retrieve the costume I rented for the occasion from my car.

With my rotten timing, Beau is stepping out of his bar, pushing a dolly of boxes filled with beer and other alcoholic beverages toward a large white van in front of his property.

A moment of awkwardness locks us in our place, staring at each other without knowing what to say to the other.

"Chance," Beau finally manages stiffly.

"Beau," I tip my chin at him as my tone comes out cold as ice.

Uncomfortable silence stretches out between us, gripping us both by the throat in a viselike grip. Finally, Beau shakes his head, breaking the spell, and begins shuffling across the sidewalk to the van.

I don't know what makes me say it, but before I can stop myself, I say, "Don't hurt her. If you're what she wants, treat her right."

Beau sneers at me, "You're one to talk. What do you care?"

"I don't," I say.

"Then leave her alone," Beau replies. "That's what you should have done from the beginning."

"You really care about her, don't you," I noticed the way he looked at her before, but this is more than just a case of lust.

"I do," Beau nods slowly. "I guess I just understand her more than everyone else, and I can see the side of her that she tries to hide. But you wouldn't know anything about that; you just see the world in shades of black and white, right and wrong. I see the gray areas and find that the people worth knowing are the people that live within those gray areas."

Beau wheels the dolly into the truck and slams the doors, then hops in the driver's seat, leaving me standing there speechless.

I guess Cora told him that she told me what she was.

———

Two hours later, Hollow Books is full of customers and friends browsing the shelves, viewing the Halloween displays, and mingling over coffee and pastries.

"Chance," Stacey calls my name as she weaves through the crowd, dragging a man who can only be her fiancé in her wake. The man is in his early thirties, with short black curls and olive skin hinting at a Greek or perhaps Italian heritage. His light brown eyes crinkle in the corners as he smiles down at his enthusiastic bride-to-be. "I'd like you to meet Nicolai, my fiancé."

"It's nice to meet you," I shake the man's hand, and as he accepts my handshake, he looks around the room, looking over-whelmed.

"Please, call me Nick," he replies as he runs his free hand through his hair. "Is it always this busy?"

"Hardly," I admit. "I'm not sure if it's because of the event or if the town just wants an up-close and personal look at a poten-tial murder suspect."

Nick frowns, "Yes, Stacey has told me of your misfortune. I hope you know that if you ever need anything, all you need to do is say the word. Any friend of Stacey's is a friend of mine."

"I really appreciate that," I feel the tips of my ears turn red with embarrassment. "Stacey has been a huge help pulling this all together these past few days. You're a lucky man."

"Someone needed to steer you in the right direction," Stacey pipes up. Turning to her fiancé, she whisper-shouts, "He was actually thinking of decorating the place with paper pumpkins cut out of orange construction paper."

"Oh, the horror," Nick grins wryly at me.

"I'm a man," I groan, "I'm not good at decorating stuff."

"That's why you need to find a good woman," Stacey insists, "so you have someone to help you pull off events like this."

"Is that why people get married?" I ask jokingly, and Stacey punches me in the arm, though not hard enough to even hurt.

"Hilarious, Chance," Stacey shakes her head and then glares at her fiancé, who is trying not to laugh.

In the front of the store, the shop door opens and slams against the outer wall with a bang loud enough to silence everyone inside the bookstore. A headless person wearing a black riding cloak, brown riding boots, baggy black pants, and a loose-fitting white shirt saunters inside, tossing a lit pumpkin back and forth in his hands.

"Right on cue," I grin appreciatively as the actor playing the headless horseman steps further into the shop. Near the entrance, an older woman gasps and faints into her companion's arms.

A few small children run up to take a better look at the horseman, and he crouches down and presents them with a handful of candy he pulls from inside his cloak. As he's crouched down, I notice something odd. The guy that usually plays this part in town is relatively tall, probably six-foot-three or four, and solidly built, but the person at the front of the shop can't be much more than five-foot-four and skinny as a whip. Did the wires get crossed, and the guy selected to ride to the Horseman's Ball show up instead? It would explain why the costume is so baggy on him.

The partygoers give him a wide berth as he stalks through the store and steps onto the platform Stacey and I placed in front of the door to my office. Still holding the pumpkin in his right hand, he reaches into his cloak and retrieves a tattered copy of *The Legend of Sleepy Hollow*.

The horseman clears his throat a couple of times, then begins thumbing through the dog-eared pages. I didn't give him direct instructions as to what part of the story he should read, giving him the opportunity to read whichever passages he preferred.

Finally, he stops paging through the book and begins to read. His voice sounds strangely hollow and eerie as he reads, *"All the stories of ghosts and goblins that he had heard in the afternoon now came crowding upon his recollection. The night grew darker and darker..."*

The actor playing the Horseman's voice becomes deeper and more sinister as he reads the last section of Washington Irving's iconic story. Tension fills the room as the crowd listens raptly to the reader's every word, frozen in terror as the story is painted vividly in their heads.

As I listen to the end of the story with fresh ears, I think of Cora's story and how her friend had changed the story of her life into something completely different. For the first time, I wondered what Washington Irving was really like. Did he care for Cora? Was he bothered by what happened to her? Was his ambiguous ending of the story meant to destroy the family name of the Van Tassels and Bones, who might have still been living in the area when the story was published? As a friend, it could have been his way of getting revenge for the girl he couldn't help in any other way.

The room bursts into applause, and I blink rapidly, realizing that the horseman has finished his story and is leaving into the starry night.

On his way out, playing on my distracted thoughts, he'd left a note beside the cash register, a note I wouldn't find or read until it was too late.

CHAPTER NINETEEN

Chance was so wrapped up in his thoughts that he didn't hear me finish reading the section of Irvie's story I'd been bewitching the assembled crowd with. I had to use one of those voice-changing apps to disguise my voice, so Chance wouldn't figure out that I'd switched places with the actor who usually ran around town playing the horseman. The actor, who was currently down the street at Beau's, passed out from drinking too much at the bar.

After I finished reading, I walked to the back of the store and thanked Stacey for having me. It was a strategic move, so nobody would catch on that I wasn't who I was supposed to be. I'd seen her helping Chance out earlier today and felt intense pangs of jealousy as she helped him carry in decorations.

Watching them together, even though I know that Stacey is crazy in love with her gorgeous foreign fiancé, finally made me see that Bathsheba was right. I need Chance in my life, and if I want any future with him, I have to send Brom's Crooked One doppelgänger back to the dark depths where he belongs.

I've spent the entire afternoon setting out my plan. But first,

I'm going to have one last night out to enjoy myself in case I never have another chance to live.

Before I left Hollow Books, I left a letter addressed to Chance next to the cash register.

Now, back in my apartment, I'm getting the last of my affairs in order before Beau comes to take me to the Horseman's Ball.

Sitting down at my kitchen table, the one that has one leg shorter than the other three, I open the folder I keep on my desk downstairs, pull out a piece of the fancy stationery I splurged on a few months ago, and jot down a note to Andi telling him that I'm going away for a while and that I want nothing more from him than to pursue his real dreams. I fold the letter and stick it in a matching envelope with something to get him started, then shoot him a text.

> Me: I have to take a little trip. There'll be an envelope in the top drawer of my desk for you on Monday morning. Let yourself in to get it.

> Andi: Is everything okay?

> Me: Fine, just a little out-of-town business.

Standing, I move over to my closet and pull out the long, glimmering gold gown I keep shoved at the very back. I hesitate as the silky fabric cascades through my fingers, and I wonder briefly if the dress is too flashy. Before I can talk myself out of it, I lay the dress on my bed and slip off the baggy horseman costume, allowing the scratchy discarded clothing to pool at my feet.

Slipping the gown off the hanger, I bunch it up and slip it over my head. The fabric kisses my body as the skirt falls to the floor. Smoothing the gown down, I turn in front of the full-length mirror on the back of my closet. Thick straps hold the dress in place before crisscrossing my back and dipping into the low cut in the back of the dress. A sweetheart neckline accentuates my bustline, and the bodice hugs my torso a little too tightly before the skirt flows out from the waist. I bought this dress on a whim because it made me look like an actress on the red carpet, but I haven't had the guts to put it on until tonight.

I quickly twist my strawberry blonde waves into a braided chignon and secure it at the nape of my neck before sticking simple gold drop earrings into my ears.

Satisfied with my appearance, I sit down on my bed, reaching underneath blindly to retrieve the waterproof lockbox I've kept hidden under every bed I've slept on for the past century.

From my nightstand, I retrieve the tiny silver key I keep taped to the bottom of the drawer and pause before opening the box. I haven't looked at the contents of this box in a very long time.

Dusting off the top of the box with my palm, I take a deep breath and stick the key into the lock. The lock opens with a click, and I reveal the box's hidden treasure.

Before Irvie wrote *The Legend of Sleepy Hollow*, he wrote something else, something a lot less fictional.

Irvie's first draft of *The Legend of Sleepy Hollow* was something completely different. It's a story about our childhood – about a mischievous young storyteller who secretly loved the bastard daughter of a local merchant, how he admired her silently as they ran wild together until the day that the girl fell in love. It's a story about my relationship with Brom, all of the gory details he was able to pry out of me about how I fell in love and was later betrayed by Brom after my death on a cold evening when I joined him by his warm fireplace. It's about how Irvie still loved me after my death even though I thought of myself as a monster, spending nights weeping dry tears after I'd killed someone.

Despite what Chance thought, I do have remorse. Even if I think the men I've killed are cheating scumbags, it's still a dark stain on my soul, and the chilling thoughts of how I've just ended a life forever often make me so sick the morning after that I spend the day retching.

I knew that Irvie loved me. It was obvious enough. I just saw him as my family, my only family for a time. To me, no matter how he looked as he aged, I'll always remember him as the gangly teen he'd been with his jaggedly shorn shoulder-length brown hair and bright eyes that lit up like he was always up to no good.

Though I never loved him the way that he loved me, Irvie never turned his back on me. He gave me a place to stay and things to occupy my time. When he traveled abroad, he always brought me some trinkets to make me smile. He saw me at my darkest, and he accepted me just the same.

I brush away an errant tear as I carefully remove the manuscript from the lockbox and pull back the yellowing cotton rag I'd wrapped it in to protect it from the elements. Irvie's last letter to me drifts to the floor as I place the manuscript on the bed.

Scooping the letter up, I unfold it gently. A bit of the ancient paper crumbles at my touch as I reread Irvie's words.

Cordelia,

I know that our time together is coming to an end. Soon, I will be dust upon the wind, and you will be left with just the memory of the years we spent together to keep you company. Accompanying this letter is my most prized possession, the first and true draft of The Legend of Sleepy Hollow. I know I promised that I would change the story to protect you, but I had to write this version. This is your story, our story. It's not as dark or haunting as the published version, and I'm not sure how eager a publisher will be to take it on once I'm gone; I want you to have it. Do what you wish with it, keep it, lock it away, have it published - it's up to you.

Never doubt that I love you, my darling. You were my best friend and my muse, and I treasured every moment we shared. Know that you will never be alone in this world as long as my family line lives on. As you know, I have told my nephews your story, and by this time, it's a memorized bedtime story that they shall pass on to their children, and their children will hand it down through the generations. My family will know you on sight and welcome you no matter what you think of yourself. Think of it as me continuing to live on with you forever.

Don't cry for me, darling, for this is not the end. It is only the beginning.

Yours,

Irvie

———

A soft knock brings me back to the present. I wrapped the manuscript back up in the rag I kept it in and dropped it into a large brown envelope to give to Beau, along with another letter just for him.

"Come in," I call as I stand up and anxiously smooth the imaginary wrinkles from my dress.

Beau lets himself in, a bouquet of roses in his hand, as he adjusts the collar of his early nineteenth-century tunic. For the Horseman's Ball, it's customary to dress for the era of The Legend of Sleepy Hollow, and I'm taking a considerable risk wearing the gown I've selected.

Beau's mouth drops open when he lays eyes on me, and for a moment, he looks just like his famous relative. "You look stunning," Beau breathes, his voice coming out tight as he crosses the room. He sets the bouquet on my kitchen table on his way to wrap me in a decidedly unfriend-like hug.

"Thanks," I blush at his compliment.

"Are you ready to go?" Beau asks as he pulls back to study my face.

"Actually, can we talk for a few minutes first?" I request. "I want to talk to you about something."

"Uh-oh, that doesn't sound good," Beau frowns.

"It's nothing bad," I assure him, "at least, I don't think so."

"Okay," Beau replies reluctantly as he moves back to sit on the arm of my couch.

Grabbing the envelope with the manuscript, I place it on the coffee table in front of Beau.

Tapping the envelope against my open palm nervously, I start to speak: "Tomorrow, I have to go away for a little while, but I have something I need you to do for me."

"Is everything alright?" Beau asks worriedly.

"Yes," I nod, "there is just something I have to take care of."

"I didn't think you could leave the area," Beau says.

"I can't," I sigh, "where I'm going is here but not here."

Beau's forehead crinkles and he begins to ask me to explain, but I cut him off.

"What I need you to do is very important, so listen carefully."

I wait to make sure he's listening before I continue. "On Monday, I need you to go to Sunnyside. If anyone asks, tell them that you have to pick up leftover beverages from tonight's ball. I want you to go to the basement, then after twenty minutes, come back upstairs and say that you've just discovered what is in this envelope. Obviously, take it out of the brown envelope first, but be very careful because it's very old and very valuable."

"What is it?" Beau asks.

I sigh, about to tell one of the biggest secrets I've ever kept, "It's the first draft of *The Legend of Sleepy Hollow*. It's the true story, my story."

"Shit," Beau's eyes widen at the significance. "You've had that this entire time?"

"Yes," I confirm. "Irvie left it to me to do with what I wanted. Recent events have told me that I need to stop being so afraid to let myself live. That's why I have to go away, to clean up a mess I've created, but I need you to pretend to find this manuscript at Sunnyside. Show it to Sunnyside's historians and make sure that they have it authenticated. Once it's authenticated, please make sure this story is published. Explain to your family that this is what needs to happen, for my sake. You guys, of course, will get the full proceeds."

"That's not fair," Beau argues. It's your story; you deserve it more than we do."

"No, I don't," I shake my head. "One last thing: when this story is discovered, I want you to give the Gazette the exclusive interview about the manuscript and the story behind it. You need to make sure everyone knows this story is true."

"Of course, anything for you, Cora," Beau assures me as he grabs the envelope and places it on the couch beside him so he can grasp my hands tightly. "As long as this is what you really want."

"It is," I nod.

"How long will you be gone?" Beau asks as he studies our linked hands.

"I don't know," I say honestly.

"But you'll be careful, right?" Beau asks.

"I'll try my best," I grin. "Come on, cheer up. We have a ball to get to. Help me enjoy my last night here."

Beau forces a grin, "It'll be the best damn night out you've ever had."

"That's what I want to hear," I laugh as I allow him to pull me to my feet. Grabbing the ornate gold Venetian mask I found at the local costume shop this afternoon, I fasten it to my face and let Beau take my hand. "Let's go shock some locals."

Beau's laugh echoes in the enclosed hallway as he helps me down the stairs. I'm going to enjoy my last hurrah, dancing and partying until my feet hurt and I've drunk too much for my own good. Tomorrow, I'll be gone, and who knows if I'll make it back.

Early the next morning, I transformed into my spectral self and mounted Blood, nudging him toward the cemetery in the early morning mist.

Last night, Beau made sure I had a fantastic time, and I could tell he was disappointed when I didn't invite him to spend the night with me. It's better this way, especially when he reads my letter and knows how I truly feel for him.

I leave the life I've worked hard to build behind without a backward glance as Blood carries me where I need to go.

When I get to the cemetery, Bathsheba is waiting for me on Horseman's Bridge. I expect that she knew I'd be coming, whether today or two weeks from now; she doesn't look surprised to see me.

"You've decided to do the right thing, girl?" She asks, her voice sounding raspier than usual.

"I've decided to fight for what I want for the first time in centuries," I explain.

"Good girl," Bathsheba murmurs, a hint of pride shining in her eyes.

"I suspect I know where I'll find him," I comment as I look toward the part of the cemetery that conceals Brom and Trina's forgotten graves.

"Of that, you can be certain," Bathsheba nods. Coming closer and gripping the leather of Blood's harness, she says, "Good luck, Cora. I'll see you on the other side."

"Thank you, Bathsheba," I whisper, "for helping me to see what I should do."

She backs away as Blood and I trot on over the bridge and further into the cemetery.

I feel Blood go tense beneath me as I urge her toward Brom and Trina's graves. He shakes his head and snorts in agitation, so I dismount and stroke his neck lovingly. This might be the last time I see Blood, and the thought brings tears to my eyes. Burying my face in his silky mane, I say goodbye to the one constant in my life for so very long.

"Goodbye, boy," I murmur, "I'll try to come back for you. I love you so much; you've been so loyal and trusting all these years."

Blood neighs like he understands what I've said and isn't ready to say goodbye, but there isn't any other way. He won't continue forward, and I can't stay.

I pet him one last time before stepping away. Blood's a ghost horse, so there's no need to loop his reins around the branch of a tree. He's free to roam where he wishes or return to Bathsheba if I should not return.

Each step forward feels like I'm walking on shards of glass, and my entire body is taut with anticipation as I reach Brom's grave. Unsurprisingly, his Crooked One is already there waiting. Twin sickles glisten in the morning light as he sharpens them against each other to appear menacing.

"Are you ready to surrender?" Brom's Crooked One taunts.

"Surrendering means admitting that I've done something wrong," I counter. "I'm here to send you back where you belong."

"You don't think you've done anything wrong?" the Crooked One's voice rises in disbelief. "You killed my wife and children."

I smirk, "Yeah, it took me a while to track them all down; how very ambitious of you to get so many girls pregnant around the same time."

"You're just sore because you weren't one of them," the Crooked One retorts. "It must hurt, knowing that out of all the whores I took to bed, you weren't even worth making a child with."

"I see it as being lucky," I say calmly as I brandish my scythe ever so slowly, "especially considering your true nature. And to say that I'm a killer when all I wanted was revenge. You killed me and the girl you threw from the bridge, and most recently, you killed that woman from the city."

"You mean the woman that your lover was also seeing?" the Crooked One sneers and advances on me. "I thought I'd do you a favor and maybe frame you for murder at the same time."

"How nice of you," I narrow my eyes as I jump out of the path of his blades, "you shouldn't have."

"I'm going to enjoy killing you again," the Crooked One huffs as the blade of one of his sickles slices through the air and narrowly misses my neck.

I retreat, parrying his onslaught of attempts to slice me to bits, our blades clashing musically in the still morning. Even the wildlife has run from our encounter. I have no intention to walk away from this fight with my life. I want to wear Brom's Crooked One down enough to take him with me when I go.

Sometimes in life, you have to make sacrifices for the people you care about. I'm sacrificing my life and my immortality so that Chance will have a chance to live his life in peace. I don't want him to develop the same obsession with the deaths that I've caused that his father fixated on, so it's best that I go away forever.

"I've got you," the Crooked One announces as he goes for his kill shot.

I gasp as the sickles slice an "x" across my chest, tearing me open. My eyes water, and I see the blackness of the in-between world shimmering at the periphery of my vision. With my last ounce of strength, I reach forth and grab Brom's Crooked One by the throat.

"And I've got you," I gasp and tighten my grip on him as the void swallows us whole. The Crooked One looks shocked as his Brom skin peels away, and he claws at me, trying to careen himself back to safety, but it's no use. I've got him, and I'm not letting go.

THE LETTERS

October 31, 2018

Dear Andi,

I have to go away for a while, so I won't need you at the studio anymore. Don't worry; I have a friend watching over the place while I'm gone. This past year, you've been a stellar employee and a wonderful friend. I don't know what I would have done without your help in those initial first months.

Andi, you and I both know that you're meant to be in front of a camera instead of behind it. Don't pretend that you're not secretly reading Vogue online when you're supposed to be helping me with proofs for the clients.

You deserve more than this little town. Believe me when I say it's best to get out of here at the first opportunity, and I'm here to give you that opportunity. Enclosed, you'll find a check for twenty thousand dollars. Take it and start your life over in New York City. Be a model or an actor wherever the wind blows you. And before you even start, don't worry—I can afford it.

Just promise me that you'll go and live your life, and someday, when you have the chance to pay it forward, you'll bestow some kindness on a soul as worthy as you are.

Always,

Cora

October 31, 2018

Chance,

By the time you find this letter, I'll be gone. I just wanted to say how truly sorry I am for all the trouble I've brought to your life recently. It was not intentional.

I'm going away to make things easier and fix things for you. I've already started a few things that should help clear up some of the mess.

I know you didn't kill Carlotta, but I hope you know that I didn't kill her either. I know who did, though, whether you choose to believe me or not. Brom did come back from the dead as something dark and unnatural. Why he waited so long to strike out against me, I don't know, but you should know that Carlotta was not his first kill.

Twelve years ago, a girl was murdered in town. You probably went to school with her, probably knew her, and saw her regularly. I didn't realize at the time. I was too busy drowning my feelings in whiskey and flirting with out-of-towners until Beau, who was only eighteen at the time, had to carry me home. When news hit me of the murder and, subsequently, her boyfriend being arrested for the crime, something just didn't seem right to me. I brushed off the odd feeling at the time, but now I know. It was Brom's calling card. He was telling me he was back, and I wasn't in a good enough place to realize the signs.

Why he lay dormant for so long after that killing, I don't know. I know that he's escalating, and he won't stop until he destroys me.

I'm going to let him. I have a plan to drag him with me to the other side. I've taken steps to ensure that Brom's crimes come to light and you go free. I know you can never forgive me. I just ask that you put this blip in time behind you and find happiness, love, and someone who deserves you, whether you stay in this town or move on to somewhere with less painful memories.

I realized recently that when I was with you, allowing myself to feel and love didn't seem like such a scary concept anymore. Maybe if I wasn't the monster that I am, we could have really had something. I guess I'll never know.

Goodbye, Chance, go on and grab the life you deserve. I'll be rooting for you from wherever I end up.

Cora

———

October 31, 2018

Dear Beau,

I want to start by saying thank you for being my constant friend, for not judging me, and for sticking by me despite knowing the truth about me. You remind me so much of Irvie in that regard, and it almost feels as if his spirit is alive again within you.

I trust you to fulfill the last tasks I've left you with; I know I can count on you. Look, I don't want what happened between us the other night to screw up our friendship. I was hurting and lonely, but I shouldn't have allowed it to happen. I need you in my life too much to make things awkward between us, so maybe my going away for a while is for the best.

I know my leaving doesn't make much sense to you, but the cliff notes version is that Brom is back from the dead. He's killed twice that I know of, and he wants nothing more than to eradicate me. I have to stop him before he can destroy any more lives, even if it means killing myself, too. Don't be sad for me if I don't come back. I've lived my life, and if it's my time to pay for what I've done, then I welcome my end with open arms.

Just know that you mean so much to me, and I'm grateful to have been able to call you a friend.

'til we meet again,

Cora

CHAPTER TWENTY

CHANCE

It's been two weeks since Cora disappeared from town, leaving only a note behind, a haunting note that sent a chill down my spine when I read it.

I remember that night twelve years ago. I was only sixteen, and Gil and I had snuck a couple of six-packs of beer out of the fridge at Pop's, and we ended up at the cemetery getting wasted with a couple of other guys from school just beyond Headless Horseman's Bridge.

We were halfway through the second six-pack when we heard two sets of footsteps coming across the bridge. A girl giggled, and Gil, the other guys, and I ducked into the tree cover, thinking we were going to luck out and have a private porno acted out for us in the middle of the cemetery.

That's when we saw them. Her name was Jenna, and she was in our class. I didn't know much about her other than she was quiet, but not because she was shy or bookish. No, Jenna was silent in a way that told you to stay away because she'd seen or done things that made her too damaged to deal with the rest of the world. Rumor had it she was dating some older guy from

Tarrytown who had dropped out of school and played in a local band.

The guy who emerged from the covered bridge with Jenna was definitely older, though exactly how much older I couldn't tell in the dark. He was tall and lean, but the way he carried himself told me that he wasn't entirely comfortable in his skin. There was just something off about him, but at the time, I couldn't put my finger on what.

We hid and watched them kiss in the half-moon light, and the way he groped her was a little too rough. They climbed onto the girder like we'd all done a time or two. It was a routine dare and a rite of passage growing up, but Jenna struggled as her companion pulled her along with him.

She cried out that he was hurting her, but he ignored her. Our friends got uncomfortable and scattered back through the woods, but Gil and I exchanged an uneasy look and got to our feet, about to reveal ourselves and step in when it happened.

Gil and I watched in frozen horror as Jenna screamed, her arms windmilling as she fell backward into the rushing water below. Jenna didn't just fall. Jenna had been pushed, and the guy that had pushed her watched from the girder, looking strangely calm.

I wanted to do something, go after the guy, or maybe see if Jenna could be helped, but Gil grabbed my arm and asked me if I was insane. Jenna was dead, and there wasn't anything we could do about it, but we needed to get the hell out of there before her killer realized he'd had an audience.

Jenna's boyfriend was eventually arrested, tried, and convicted for Jenna's murder. There was just one slight hitch. The guy that they'd arrested, Jenna's real boyfriend, was not the guy that had been at the bridge and thrown her off.

I wanted to speak up, but Gil made me promise that we would never talk about that night again. It was better that way, he'd insisted at the time. The killer was still out there, and if he found out that we saw him, he'd come after us. So I took off, left town, and the memory of the night that haunted me like a ghost as far behind me as I could. Unfortunately, the ghosts of your past have a way of finding you no matter how far or fast you run.

I'd had nightmares about that night and hallucinated Jenna standing at the foot of my bed, dripping wet and pleading for help in every apartment in every city I'd lived in all over the world. For a time, I thought the best way of driving the nightmares away was to drink myself into oblivion.

Maybe it is fitting that I'm now facing murder charges for a crime I didn't commit. The worst part is that the monster that killed Jenna is Cora's Brom. I don't doubt now that Cora was telling the truth. I could feel the helplessness she felt about Jenna's death, a girl she didn't even know. It's the same helplessness and guilt I feel every time I allow memories of that night to surface.

And Cora decided to confront Brom head-on. The startling finality in her letter scares me, and I know that she's going to allow him to destroy her. Fuck, she could already be gone. I'd thrown up after I read her letter the morning after Halloween, then high-tailed it to her studio and apartment, but she was already gone.

I had no idea where she left for or where this in-between place Cora talked of was. My next stop had been to ask Beau if he could tell me. He had to know Cora had to be stopped, but for whatever reason, he'd pursed his lips and refused to say.

Now, two weeks later, I sit in a courtroom next to Neil, waiting for the evidentiary hearing to begin. Neil is confident that after today, this mess will all be over, but he won't say why he's so confident.

The judge arrives, takes the bench, and asks the same nervous prosecutor if he is ready to proceed.

"Y-y-yes, your honor," the prosecutor stutters, and I wonder if he's really nervous or if he actually has a speech impediment.

"Your honor, the defense asks that the charges be dropped due to insufficient evidence," Neil stands and interrupts as he buttons the jacket of his expensive suit.

"I'm listening," the judge stares at Neil over the top of his glasses.

"The defense believes that the prosecution jumped the gun by charging the defendant based on a small-town police chief's dislike of the defendant. There was no evidence linking my client to the crime before the time of arrest, and when the police did search my client's property after he had already been arraigned, there was no evidence linking him to the crime either. My client also has a solid alibi for the time of the murder. I believe that the police chief was upset that the defendant could not be charged with the unfortunate, natural death of his father, so he was determined to pin this murder on him without even considering other suspects, such as the deceased's husband or the possibility that this was a murder committed by an unknown third party. Finally, there is this," Neil holds up a slim DVD case, "Your honor, I present a sworn deposition that the prosecutor himself sat in on from a friend of the defendant who will not only corroborate that everything I've said is true but prove that the victim was merely a case of wrong place, wrong time."

"I'd like to see that," the judge says as he gestures for the bailiff to retrieve the DVD.

"But, your honor," the prosecutor cuts in.

The judge silences him with a harsh look, "You did sit in on this deposition, am I correct?"

"Well, yes, your honor," the prosecutor admits reluctantly.

"And you had the chance to question this witness, I assume," the judge continues.

"Yes, your honor," the prosecutor sits back down in defeat.

It takes a minute to wheel a television into the courtroom, during which time I look at Neil questioningly. Who is this friend, and why didn't Neil tell me?

I don't have to wait long as the DVD starts to play, the screen filling with Cora sitting at a conference table across from Neil, the prosecutor, and a mousy, young court reporter.

"Thank you for taking time out of what I'm sure is a busy schedule to sit down with us. Will you please state your name for the record?" Neil asks Cora on the screen.

"Cordelia Whitt," Cora answers loud enough to be heard on the tape.

"Do you promise to tell the truth, the whole truth as far as you know, and nothing except that truth under penalty of perjury?" Neil asks Cora as she is sworn in for the deposition.

"I promise," Cora vows.

"What is your relationship to the defendant, Chancellor Jordan Junior?" Neil asks Cora.

"We're friends," Cora asks after a slight delay.

"You and the defendants are friends and nothing else? Remember, you are under oath, Ms. Whitt," Neil reminds her.

"We went out a few times and have spent significant time together over the past month, but we are not in a relationship," Cora clarifies.

"I see," Neil scribbles something on a pad of paper on the tape, "but you do not believe that the defendant is guilty of the charges brought against him."

"I know he's not guilty," Cora replies confidently.

"How do you know that for sure?" Neil asks her.

"Well, for starters, he was with me on the night of the murder. We went on a ghost tour around town, then went for drinks at the bar across the street from my photography studio and apartment. When we returned to my apartment, we found a threatening package on my doorstep, and we spent most of the rest of the night in the company of the police before returning to Chance's home." Cora explains, "And before you ask, plenty of people saw us out together. We weren't alone until after we had been with the police."

"Do you know who might have sent you that package or who might have killed the victim?" Neil asks Cora.

"Objection," the prosecutor argues in the courtroom, and the DVD is paused while the judge listens to the objection. "This question calls for speculation."

"Your honor, as this witness was sent the package in question, a crime that my client is also charged with, the witness may very well know who sent it and who killed the deceased."

"I'll allow it," the judge decides, and the tape starts up again.

Cora begins speaking on the tape again, grasping her neck as she says, "I know who sent me the package, and I suspect he also killed the deceased as well as committed another murder about twelve years back."

"Tell me what you suspect," Neil asks her on the tape. The courtroom is eerily quiet, hanging on Cora's every word.

"I have this… ex-boyfriend, I guess you could say. The relationship ended badly some time ago, and for a while, he completely dropped off the radar. Lately, though, I've been seeing him everywhere, and he's been acting threatening toward me. I believe the finger in the box was a message for me, especially along with the note that said that I was next." Cora begins shaking, and at first, I think it's an act, but then I realize her eyes are slightly glazed, lost in a memory that truly frightens her.

"And you think that this ex-boyfriend of yours is capable of murder and that he may have killed as long ago as twelve years ago?" Neil asks skeptically. "Forgive me, but you don't look old enough to have had a boyfriend twelve years ago."

"I know he's capable; he killed–" Cora cuts off, catching herself, "I mean, he attempted to kill me, which caused the breakup. He was a great deal older than me, and I found out that he had been involved with a girl who was murdered in Sleepy

Hollow twelve years ago. That is the reason why when you wanted to subpoena me, I requested this taped deposition. I'm about to leave town for my safety."

Cora's fabricated story is woven so convincingly, even I believe it. The basis is factual: Brom was her boyfriend, and it looks like he is a psychotic killer, but if anyone did any digging, they wouldn't find any trace of him between the early eighteen hundreds and about twelve years ago.

"Thank you for your honesty," Neil tells her, his voice softening sympathetically. "I have no further questions."

"Do you really expect the court to believe this story, Ms. Whitt?" the prosecutor asks sharply, his voice devoid of the stuttering mess I've become accustomed to in court. "Isn't it true that you're just making this all up to save your boyfriend from getting a life sentence?"

"It's not a story," Cora bristles, staring the prosecutor down on the tape. He squirms under her intense gaze and shuffles some papers in front of himself as Cora says, "And as I previously mentioned, Chance is not my boyfriend. I'm not some starry-eyed kid who would lie for some guy in court. I filed stalking charges against my ex-boyfriend two years ago; they are well documented with the police department and the court."

I wonder how Cora managed to pull that one off.

"I think I've heard enough," the judge announces, turning the taped deposition off. Turning to the prosecutor, he asks, "Do you have anything new to add, some compelling evidence that you haven't just wasted the taxpayers' money by charging the wrong man with this murder?"

The prosecutor shrinks in his seat, "After extensive searching, the state has no new evidence against the defendant."

The judge sighs, "I was afraid this would happen again. Very well, I have no choice but to dismiss the charges against the defendant for lack of evidence. Next time you step foot in my court, make sure you have a solid case before you attempt to charge anyone with a crime." Banging his gavel on his desk, he says, "Mr. Jordan, you are free to go with this court's sincerest apologies."

"What the hell just happened?" I ask Neil after the judge has exited the courtroom.

"I believe the legal term would be that your girlfriend's deposition just saved your ass," Neil cracks his knuckles. "What happened between you two anyway? Are you sure you can't give her another chance? It's obvious that Cora is in love with you."

"I don't think Cora is capable of loving anyone," I murmur, although I'm not sure I believe that anymore.

"Then you're blind or an idiot," Neil chuckles, slapping me on the back as he gets up and shoves the case file into his briefcase.

I fall silent as I think about what Cora just did for me. She promised she'd fix things, and she did.

"Excuse me," a voice from my past clears his throat and steps in front of the defense table. "Chance, could we please talk for a moment?"

I pale as I face my former boss. I hesitate as Neil says, "I'm not sure that's a good idea."

"Please," Mr. Grankowski insists, "it will only take a minute."

"Sure," I reluctantly get up and follow Grankowski a few paces away. "Look, Mr. Grankowski, I'm sorry about what went on between your wife and me. When I first saw her at that first party, I didn't know that she was your wife, and by the time I did, she was threatening to ruin my career if I didn't keep seeing her. That's why I quit. I couldn't deal with it anymore. You have to believe that I didn't kill her, though. I'm not that kind of person."

"I believe you," Mr. Grankowski says softly. I see the pain I've inflicted on him etched in his eyes, and it makes me think of Cora and her lifestyle. Mr. Grankowski clears his throat again uncomfortably, "I wish I could say that you were the first of my employees that Carlotta blackmailed into having an affair with her, but you weren't. You probably wouldn't have been the last, either. Carlotta didn't marry me for love. She only wanted my money. It took me a while to realize that – or maybe I did realize it, but I didn't want to believe it. I know you didn't kill Carlotta. I never believed that for a second. I'm glad that the court realized that too. There's just one thing I need to know."

"What's that?" I ask cautiously.

"The child Carlotta was carrying," Mr. Grankowski blushes, looking embarrassed, "was it yours?"

"No," I shake my head vehemently. "She tried to tell me it was, but I know without a doubt that it wasn't."

My former boss relaxed, and I could see the relief on his face. "Thank you."

I nod, "I hope they catch whoever killed your wife." Even though I know that they won't.

"Thank you, Chance," Mr. Grankowski retrieves a handkerchief from his pocket and blows his nose. I just want you to know that I don't harbor any ill feelings toward you. If you ever want to come back to the Post, there will be a job waiting for you. If not, and you need a reference, you've got it."

"Thank you," it is my turn to be embarrassed. "I'm planning on staying in Sleepy Hollow to run my father's bookstore, but I appreciate it."

"Well, good luck," Mr. Grankowski claps my shoulder, "with wherever life takes you."

I watch him walk away, trying to puzzle out how he could be so forgiving after learning that I was sleeping with his wife.

"Come on, Chance," Neil pulls me out of my thoughts and beckons me to follow him out of the courtroom. "The media is outside waiting for a statement. I love that part; it makes me look like Matlock for figuring out the case and getting my client off."

I snort and loosen my tie as I follow him out of the courtroom, "I'll let you do the talking if that's alright with you?"

"I prefer it that way, actually," Neil replies seriously. "You just stand there and look good for the cameras."

I shake my head in amusement, surprised that I can feel humor at all after the past few weeks.

After the press conference, Neil ushers me to his car and says, "Whew, that went better than expected. I might have to open a practice out here in the boonies. The press gobbled up every word I said. Now, please tell me there's a decent pub out here in Hicksville. I'm starving."

Four Months Later

Four months have passed without a sign of Cora. Her studio sits abandoned on Broadway, and I walk past it every single day on my way to Hollow Books. I haven't received a call, a text, or even another letter since Halloween.

It's been four months since my whole world changed; I returned home and met an untouchable girl who set my life ablaze. Somewhere along the way, I forgave Cora; it isn't her fault that she is what she is; I know that now. I didn't realize how much I would miss her; it was like a part of me was missing, and the other half that remained waited for its matching half to return. I wake up in the middle of the night craving her, and every time I walk past the studio, the hollow ache in my chest pangs a little bit harder.

The rest of the town seems to have forgotten Cora if they even really noticed her to begin with.

Two days after Cora disappeared, Beau found an undiscovered manuscript belonging to his ancestor, Washington Irving, in the basement at Sunnyside. It was authenticated to be Irving's first draft of *The Legend of Sleepy Hollow*, and if rumors are correct, it's all about the girl that Washington Irving grew up with and loved who was betrayed by her lover and came back for revenge. I haven't read it. I'm not even sure I can when it hits bookshelves. Beau and I are probably the only ones alive who know that it is Cora's story. At least until after the article that David at the Gazette hired me to sit down and interview Beau and his family for hits the newsstand.

For a town obsessed with the late, great Washington Irving, everyone is buzzing about the manuscript's upcoming publication. They've all neglected to notice that one of the storefronts on the main street sits dark and untouched, still decorated for Halloween.

I woke up this morning deciding enough was enough. Just because nobody in this town knows or is willing to tell me where I can find Cora doesn't mean that I can't track her down. I've been an investigative journalist for years, traveling all over the world for stories.

After throwing back half a pot of coffee, I lace up my winter boots and pull on my North Face jacket. I drive into town, parking in front of her studio while I contemplate my options.

Other than my article, Beau refuses to talk to me about Cora. Cora's assistant, Andi, left town to pursue a career in modeling in the city, so he's out. Stacey has been a great friend since Cora went away, but she only knows what Cora told her in a voicemail message before disappearing – that she's away tending to a sick family member and that she's not sure when she'll be back. Cora farmed out the work for Stacey's to a competitor in White Plains, although Stacey swears that the minute she hears that Cora is back in town, she's firing her new photographer. Even if that means pushing her spring wedding until next fall.

Our mutual editor at the Gazette, David, hasn't heard a word from Cora since she turned in her last assignment on Halloween.

Besides that, I don't think Cora knew anyone in town that well. Sighing, I glance at the entrance to Cora's studio while drumming my fingers on the steering wheel as if the rhythm will dislodge an idea of how to track her down.

Cora did mention a woman, someone with a raspy voice, who found her in the in-between and brought her back to the living. If I could track down this person, if she's still alive, maybe she can help me get Cora back.

Starting the car again, I drive with no set destination in mind, and before I know it, I'm pulling into the parking lot by the Old Dutch Church. Cora was really uneasy the night we went through the cemetery for the ghost walk, so this seems like an excellent place to start.

Jenna, my former classmate, is on my mind as I get out of the car and start through the snow-covered cemetery. After the charges against me were thrown out and Chief Devries was removed from his position, a special investigator from Albany was brought in to clean up the mess in town. The investigator listened to Cora's deposition, and it wasn't hard to figure out the twelve-year-old case she was referring to, so the old case file was dug up, and it turns out that Devries had a bunch of DNA samples from the crime scene that were never processed.

The samples were sent off to a third-party lab, and it was determined that none of them belonged to Jenna's boyfriend. He was released from prison just in time for Christmas, reunited with his family after twelve long years.

"Are you looking for something, boy?" A tired, old, raspy voice startles me out of my thoughts, and when I look up, I realize I'm standing in the middle of the Headless Horseman's Bridge. A wrinkly older woman, standing at an imposing four-foot-three-inch height, blocks my exit from the covered bridge. Her gnarled hands are curled into the bunchy fabric of her long brown dress. A yellow scarf covers her limp gray hair, but she's missing a jacket, and her feet are bare on the damp wooden slats of the bridge under her feet. No living person could be standing before me dressed the way she is and not be cold. It looks like I've found Cora's mysterious savior.

"I'm looking for Cora," I tell her, "and I know that you know where she is. She told me who you are."

"I highly doubt that, boy; the girl doesn't even know who I truly am. Why are you searching for her now? What took you so long?" the woman asks sharply. "It's been four months here in the land of the living."

"I made a mistake," I admit, "It took me a while to understand and stop blaming Cora for what she is, but I'm here now, and that's what matters, so where is she?"

"You're as pigheaded as she is," the woman ignores my question.

"Probably," I concede as I approach her like you would a wild animal, slowly and cautiously. Holding my hands up to show that I'm harmless, I say, "Please, I need to get to her; she shouldn't be facing Brom by herself."

"It's much too late for that." the woman shakes her head. Her milky blue eyes are vague, and they remind me of older people with cataracts.

"Is Cora...?" The words become lodged in my throat as I trail off.

"She's in the in-between. She was strong, though. Brom is gone for good this time," the woman informs me, showing pride in her protégé coloring her words and making her seem less rough.

"You have to take me to her or at least tell me how I can get to her," I insist. "I need to bring her back to the living. She needs to know that I love her."

My confession shocks me, but apparently, it doesn't shock the strange little woman. She merely shrugs and says, "You can't go to where she is. It's not allowed. I've offered to bring her back, but she's refused me so far. You're fools, both of you. Too stupid to see what the fates have planned for you. You being a son of Ichabod Crane's line and all - and Cora being who she is. She would have fared better if she'd left Brom well enough alone, but I guess there's no use crying over spilled milk."

The little weathered crone's babbling isn't making any sense.

"Dammit, this is not up for debate. I need to see her," I demand as I grab the woman firmly by the shoulders to draw her back to the matter at hand.

The woman shakes my hands off her shoulders and tilts her head, "No living being may enter the in-between and come back to the land of the living. Not without coming back changed like Cordelia."

"I don't care, I can't let her go," I cringe at my own words. Cora is right; sometimes, I sound like the sappy male leads in romance novels. It's still better than sounding like Jack Torrance from Cora's favorite book.

"But you did let her go, boy, it's been four months." The woman's eyes scrutinize me, from the toes of my boots to the tattoo-covered tips of my fingers to the way my hair falls into my eyes. She obviously finds me lacking because she says, "Men sure have changed since I was a girl. Nevertheless, despite my opinion and considering the situation, I'll talk with Cora again and try to convince her to come back with me. There are things she does not know. She must return to the living. More than her existence is at stake."

"What does that mean?" I ask. The strange little woman smiles strangely before fading from sight.

"I wanted to go with you!" I yell into the empty cemetery surrounding me. When the woman doesn't reappear, I mutter, "Fine, I'll wait here for as long as it takes."

Sitting down inside the covered bridge as the wind whistles through the cracks in the wood, chilling me to the bone, I prepare to wait as long as it takes.

CHAPTER TWENTY-ONE

CORA

"Cordelia," Bathsheba's raspy voice seems to sing my name as she tries to coax me out of the dark in-between. It's been no more than five minutes since her last tactic failed after I first dragged Brom through the veil with me and sent him to the fiery pits where he belongs. A dozen large, eager gray hands grasped for him, and he howled as he fell into their clutches. Strangely, they left me untouched.

"You're not thinking this through," Bathsheba continues. Though to me, it's only been a matter of minutes since I left the land of the living and entered the dark nothingness of the in-between, this place warps time. I don't know how long I've really been gone from Sleepy Hollow.

"I did what you told me to," I remind her. "I sacrificed myself to end Brom."

"That's not at all what I told you to do," Bathsheba huffs.

"Oh?" I question her. I hate talking to her in the in-between. I can't see her or anything at all, which scares me more than anything despite my cool indifference. Maybe there is no fiery pit waiting for me. Perhaps this darkness is my eternity.

"I told you to allow yourself to love, and then you would see what the right thing to do was," Bathsheba rasps. "Falling in love and fighting to protect those that you care for is one of the hardest sacrifices to make. I meant for you to sacrifice your immortality and allow yourself to really live, not condemn yourself to eternal darkness, you foolish girl."

"What are you talking about?" I can't hide the frustration in my voice.

"That boy loves you, Ichabod Crane's great-great-great-great-grandson. You know the one I'm talking about, the tattooed boy. Aren't you tired of using men to get revenge on Brom? All those years of storing up souls and energy paid off, obviously, since you dispelled Brom faster than any other Dispeller or Gatekeeper I've ever worked with before, but don't you ever wish to stop fighting your feelings and allow yourself some normalcy?"

"Chance is a descendant of Ichabod Crane?" I ask incredulously.

"Don't sound so surprised," Bathsheba says dismissively. "You don't honestly think it was the scenery that drew the first Chance to Sleepy Hollow, do you? It was written on the cards from the very beginning. Your soul was meant for Ichabod's mate from the start, but you both missed the signs. Then, the minute that Trina spurned Ichabod for Brom and Brom killed you, it tied all of your fates together forever. It's why you're so drawn to the men in Ichabod's line, both your Chance and his father before him. Your writer friend was more intuitive than he knew. The descendants of those three families will always feel a relentless tug, ushering them home to the Hollow."

"Does Chance know?" I ask, more to myself than to Bathsheba.

"That I do not know," Bathsheba replies anyway. "My concern is solely for you. You've taken so many lives, but now you have the chance to bring life into the world. Don't squander that chance. Give up your immortality and return to the living, Cordelia. Live your life with that boy. You've already created a family with him. You just aren't aware of it."

"That's not possible," I deny. "I'm not alive, I can't—it's just not possible." I flounder for words.

"You have a life growing inside you, Cordelia," Bathsheba interrupts my denials. "You have to return to the living, for your sake and that which you are carrying. It's time to give back."

"Fine, I'll go back," I relent as doubt begins to creep in, "but I still don't believe what you're telling me. I'm not wholly alive. I couldn't have conceived with Chance. It isn't possible. And what were the others that you mentioned, a Dispeller?"

I hear Bathsheba's impatient sigh, "In truth, I lied to you. You're not a Gatekeeper. You never were. What you've become is less of a choice and more of a birthright. When a Crooked One is born human, before the death that changes them to monsters, an equally powerful creature called a Dispeller is born. Dispellers are the light to Crooked One's dark souls. You and I have had the added benefit of being dead when our time came to seize your destiny. It makes you stronger and harder to kill. All these years, while you have lived off the deaths of men, your true calling is to return your Crooked One counterpart, Brom, in this case, to where he belongs, like I mentioned to you when I told you that you were a Gatekeeper, but there's one main difference. Once a Gatekeeper completes their task, it's the end. Their souls move on to the ether, and their mortal bodies return to the earth. A Dispeller is blessed by the Gods, able to return to the living once they've defeated their Crooked One and driven them back to the underworld. Now that you have succeeded, you will return to the land of the living as a human. You will be mortal and live as one, die as one."

"Why didn't you tell me all of this before?" I demand. "You've been keeping it from me for more than two hundred years!"

"It's better that you didn't know; besides, I wasn't positive that you were a Dispeller until the end," Bathsheba's voice becomes louder as I feel myself being pulled toward an unknown force like I'm being sucked into a vacuum.

Suddenly, I can feel my body again, sharp slivers of pain cutting through me as the dark in-between explodes around me, warm golden ribbons of confetti shredding around me as my heart lurches against my ribcage painfully.

"Clear," I hear someone yelling before the pain becomes so overwhelming I lose consciousness altogether.

———

"You know, after your letter, I could have just left you where I found you," Beau's voice rouses me from unconsciousness.

I crack open my eyes, and my eyelids flutter rapidly to adjust to the bright lights of a hospital room. Looking down, I find myself lying in a hospital bed wearing a vomit-green colored hospital gown—a mess of tubes run up and down my arms. I've never actually been in a hospital. My immortality ensured that I never got sick and that any injuries healed up on their own without medical attention. I'm disappointed to find that it's not as attractive inside as it looks on television.

"How did I get here?" My voice comes out as raspy as Bathsheba's.

"I found you lying in the snow near my great ancestor's grave. You were in bad shape, so I brought you to the local hospital. Your heart flatlined, and they had to shock you back to life and stabilize you before they could airlift you here to the city," Beau quickly recounts how he stumbled upon me. He looks tired and rumpled, like he's been by my side for quite some time.

"How long have I been in the hospital?" I ask as I try to sit up. I instantly regret it as my body reacts painfully in response.

"A couple of days; they had to sedate you because of your

injuries," Beau scratches the stubble on his chin. "I'll go get the doctor and let her know that you're awake."

He gets up to leave but pauses in the doorway, "You could have just told me you were in love with Chance. I would have understood."

"I didn't want to believe it myself," I feel a hot wave of embarrassment crash over me.

"We'll talk about it later," Beau sighs, "there are more important things to think about right now."

Beau ducks out of the room, returning a few minutes later with a doctor who barely reaches Beau's chest and looks as if she's only twelve years old.

"Hello, Ms. Whitt. I'm Dr. Kincaid." The doctor's smile looks too bright and false as she pulls up my chart on her tablet. You were fortunate that your brother found you when he did. You were pretty banged up when you were airlifted in from Tarrytown."

"My brother?" I ask, eyeing Beau suspiciously.

"Yes," Dr. Kincaid looks at Beau briefly before turning back to me, "Mr. Irving told me that he found you out in the snow after you'd gone out snowshoeing and didn't return. In addition to the initial stopping of your heart, you have sustained a dislocated shoulder and a bruised collarbone, as well as a major gash to the head. We had to give you a transfusion because you did lose a significant amount of blood, but thankfully, you and your baby will be alright. There's no further damage to your heart that we can detect."

"Baby?" Beau echoes, a strange, strangled look on his face.

"Yes," Dr. Kincaid confirms, looking at her notes, "I'd say you're about four months along, making you due around mid-to-late July. Does that sound about right?"

"Yes," I close my eyes tightly. I'm pregnant. Bathsheba was telling the truth. How the hell did this happen? I don't even know if Chance will want to see me now; how is he going to react when I tell him that our screw-up at the bed and breakfast created a baby?

Beau sits down quickly, looking like he's going to be ill.

"Do you remember how you got injured, Ms. Whitt?" Dr. Kincaid asks, oblivious to Beau's and my inner turmoil.

Lying has always come easily, weaving together seamlessly into credible stories. "I was snowshoeing through the cemetery, and my chest began to feel tight, and I must have lost my footing. I remember reaching out to catch myself on a headstone, but I must have slipped and hit my head as I went over the top of the headstone. I've always been a little clumsy."

Dr. Kincaid nods, "You're fortunate that the head injury wasn't worse and that you didn't suffer a heart attack. In the best-case scenario, we should be able to discharge you in the morning. How does that sound?"

"Sounds great," I smile weakly.

"I'll let you rest," Dr. Kincaid pats my hand. "If you need anything, just push the call button, and one of the nurses will come in and check on you."

"Thank you, doctor," I say as she steps out of the room and closes the door.

"Snowshoeing?" I exclaim once I make sure the doctor is out of earshot.

"What?" Beau asks faintly. "It's a popular winter activity, very true to the area."

"You do know that I was born, raised, and died in Sleepy Hollow during a decidedly non-snowshoeing time." I shake my head. "I've never even seen a snowshoe in person. Those are the things that look like giant tennis rackets that you put on your feet, right?"

"They are," Beau confirms. "You've never snowshoed? That's a shame. All children should learn to snowshoe."

"I'll take that into consideration," I lay back against the pillows. "Why did you tell them that you were my brother?"

"They wouldn't let me up here unless I was family," Beau grumbles. "Didn't think you'd like it if you woke up and I'd told them I was your husband or something."

"Beau, I never meant to hurt you," I wince in pain. "You're my friend, and I can't imagine my life without you."

"But you don't love me," Beau finishes for me.

I look down at the blanket on the bed, feeling guilty.

"So," Beau says slowly as he changes the subject, and I know what's coming: " You're pregnant?"

"I guess so," I reply quietly as I place a hand over my abdomen.

"Is it…?" Beau trails off.

"The baby is Chance's," I sigh. "I must have gotten pregnant the weekend we went away to the bed and breakfast."

"How is that possible?" Beau asks. "How is any of this possible?"

"I killed Brom's spirit, just like I set out to," I explain quietly. "I had to sacrifice my immortality to send him back to where he came from. The only reason I came back was because Bathsheba told me about the child I was carrying. I hadn't thought it was possible, but I guess some things are just meant to happen. When I came back from the in-between, I came back mortal. I can get sick and die just like everyone else now."

"Bathsheba?" Beau grimaces at the mention of her name. "Is that old witch still around?"

I snort, "I forgot Irvie passed down the story about her, too. Yes, she's still around."

Beau shivers in response. "So what are you going to do now?"

"I don't know," I whisper.

———

CHANCE

I'd waited all day after Bathsheba faded away, hoping that she would reappear with Cora. It was only when it became so dark I couldn't see an inch in front of me without the help of the flashlight on my phone, and the temperature dropped so low I didn't even need to be able to see my fingers to know that the tips were turning blue that I started for home. I held a vigil for three days after that, but Cora did not appear. After four days, I was unable to leave the store unattended any longer, so I went back to work, but I've been by the cemetery and the bridge every morning and evening before and after work to look for Cora.

The bell I installed over the door at Hollow Books chimes to let me know a customer has just walked in.

"I'll be right with you," I call out from the back office where I'm cutting open a box of books I received from an indie Sci-Fi author from Connecticut. Over the past few months without Cora, I realized how really empty my life was. My friends are back in the city or further away than that, and I haven't even thought about dating, not when I'm still holding out hope that Cora will return someday. Instead of connecting with people in town, I threw myself into building this store into something that Pop would have been proud of. It took several months, but I was proud when the store finished out the year firmly in the black.

I've done well marketing Hollow Books online, and the addition of books by independent authors brought in a lot more business, especially with the book signings and author readings that packed the store with new customers every weekend in both November and December.

Stepping out of the office with the cardboard box full of books in my hands, I don't notice the customer weaving through the aisle until a low, smoky voice that belongs to someone I thought was lost to me forever asks, "Do you know if you carry any first editions of Stephen King?"

"Cora?" I ask, my tone filled with disbelief. It's really her. Cora stands before me, looking tired but very real. Her wavy blonde hair hangs limply around her face and shoulders, falling onto a cream-colored pea coat. A pair of faded bellbottoms appears from under the hem of her jacket, but they look strangely baggy on Cora. Her eyes are ringed with dark circles, and a thin bandage covers something on her forehead. Though she seems worse than I've ever seen her, she stands in front of me with her hands nervously placed into the deep pockets of her coat.

The box in my hands drops to the floor with a thud, and I step over it. Pulling Cora's face into my hands, I back her into the bookcase behind her and claim her lips. She moans in the back of her throat as I part her lips with my tongue, seeking purchase in her hot mouth. After her initial surprise, Cora's arms wind around my back, holding onto me tightly. One of my hands moves to the back of her head, pulling her closer. My body feels as electrified as a live wire as I lose my head kissing her.

When we break apart, Cora's face is slightly flushed, and she looks up at me through heavy-lidded eyes, looking somewhat dazed. " That wasn't the greeting I was expecting," she says.

"You came back," I say at the same time. "I was an idiot. I should never have pushed you away. Everything was going wrong, and instead of staying with you, I judged you unfairly when what I should have been telling you is that I love you, and I don't care what things you've done in your past."

"You love me?" Cora asks, wringing her hands together in front of her.

I nod and kiss her again, "I do. If I had only gotten your letter sooner, I would never have let you face Brom alone. It took me so long to see how stupid I was for being angry with you, but once I saw through that red haze and found out where you'd gone, I was afraid I'd lost you for good."

"There's something I have to tell you," Cora says as I grab her hand and start tugging her toward the back office. Suddenly, all I can think about is having her under me writhing with desire.

"It can wait," I tell her as I pull her into the office and kiss her urgently. At first, it seems as if she's going to protest, but then she sinks into my touch, clinging to me as I kiss her cheek and the sensitive part of her neck below her ear lobe.

"Chance," she whimpers as I turn her around and bend her over my desk. Pulling her jeans and panties down and letting them pool around her ankles, I pop the button on my jeans and let my cock spring free, the organ already painfully erect, wanting to sink into my woman. I reach into the top drawer of the desk and grab a condom, covering myself quickly before plunging into Cora's eager body.

Cora moans and arches her back as I grip her hips and take her, driving my cock into her at a steady rhythm.

"Fuck, I missed this," I groan as my thrusts increase. Reaching around, I find the sensitive nerve at Cora's core and brush my thumb against it gently.

"Chance," my name is somewhere between a curse and a prayer as Cora pushes back against me, "I need you harder. It feels so good."

I drive myself into her harder as I kiss a trail up her spine, and it isn't long before I feel her break apart beneath me, her orgasm taking her loud enough to be heard in the central part of the store. As it has each time before, watching Cora come undone triggers my undoing as I grit my teeth as her inner walls milk my cock, driving me over the edge.

I relax on top of her for a moment, pinning her to the desk before moving away and allowing her to stand up straight on shaky legs.

We straightened ourselves up in silence, and I realized I had told Cora that I loved her, but she had not said it back.

"I'm sorry," I murmur as I pull her into my arms. "I didn't mean to attack you like that; I just missed you like crazy."

Cora laughs, "You're forgiven, but Chance, there's something I really have to tell you."

"What is it?" I ask, feeling suddenly uneasy.

Cora looks down and runs her hands through her hair, which is mussed by our coupling. When she meets my gaze, I see the nervousness and panic in her eyes as she whispers, "I'm pregnant, Chance."

"What?" I ask as my entire body goes still. I'm sure that I've heard her wrong; she can't have said what I thought she just said.

"I said I'm pregnant," Cora repeats herself, looking afraid of my reaction. "Bathsheba told me when I was in the in-between, and a doctor confirmed it when I woke up in the hospital. I'm about four months along. It must have been the night that we spent at the bed and breakfast."

"How is that possible?" I ask, marveling at her words. "I didn't think, with you being what you are…"

"I didn't either," Cora shakes her head, "but I guess if something is meant to be, it will find a way. I sacrificed my immortality to drag Brom back to where he belonged, and now that I'm back, I'm fully mortal. I'm just like everyone else."

"I don't think you'll ever be 'just like everyone else,'" I tease as I brush her hair away from her face.

"Are you angry?" Cora asks nervously.

"I'm a little shocked," I admit, and Cora's face crumples. Grabbing her chin, I force her to look me in the eye, "Hey, don't look away. I said I was shocked, yes, but I'm not angry. I love you, Cora, and pregnant or not, immortal or mortal, I want to spend the rest of my life with you."

"I love you, too," Cora murmurs as her eyes fill with tears. Sniffling as she wipes her eyes, she says, "Damn pregnancy hormones."

I laugh, "They just make you even more beautiful." Kissing her gently, I ask, "So, is that a yes?"

"What?" Cora asks.

"Will you allow me to spend the rest of my life with you?" I ask. "Will you marry me?"

"Yes," Cora breathes as she begins to cry harder. I pull her tight against me, and I can feel her tiny baby bump pressing against my stomach now. I kiss her forehead affectionately, in awe that I can finally call this strange, infuriating, beautiful woman mine and even more in awe of the life we've created growing inside of her.

AFTERMATH

And so the Headless Horsewoman fell in love and hung up her reins—well, not literally. I found Blood tied to a tree in the backyard of Chance's father's house, which we've now transformed into our own. Chance was a little intimidated at first, but he quickly warmed up to Blood and built a stable for him in the backyard.

When Irvie's "lost manuscript" was published and became an instant bestseller, and Beau's interview was published in the Gazette, everyone knew the true story of Sleepy Hollow, even if they didn't realize I was the living inspiration. Four years later, when Halloween rolls around, Chance and I have a little girl to take trick-or-treating around the Hollow.

"Look, Mommy, I'm a ghost!" Our daughter Amelia races down the front stairs and leaps into my arms as Chance steps out of the house carrying our newborn son in his arms.

"I see that, baby," I coo as Amelia wiggles under the sheet she cut eye and mouth holes out of to make into her costume. "You look positively spooky."

"Do you think I'd scare the Headless Horsewoman?" Amelia

asks innocently as she slides to the ground and tucks her hand into mine.

"Maybe so, baby," I exchange a bemused look with Chance, "maybe so."

Chance laughs and leans in to kiss me, searing me and claiming me once more with his lips.

Bathsheba was right. In the end, the decision to let myself fall in love and live was worth it. I wouldn't trade Chance or our children for a million lifetimes.

ACKNOWLEDGMENTS

When I first started writing *Headless*, I was not in the best headspace. I was feeling angry, bitter, and betrayed, much like Cora, but I took the rage that was inside me and wrote through it. As writers, we all say our latest book is our favorite to date, but writing this book was a whole new level for me, and I'm proud of how it turned out.

This past year has not been easy for me, and I want to take a minute to thank the people who helped me through it in big ways and small: Melanie Singleton, Judy Brandt, Derek Aiello, and Tracy Ruch. Thank you all for being such wonderful friends and for making me laugh when all I wanted to do was cry. I also want to thank Josh and Shal—my own personal Brom and Trina. Without the two of you, this book wouldn't exist.

To the amazing writers I've met through #Bookstagram: Jesikah Sundin @jesikahsundin), Tyffany Hackett (@tyffany.h), and Grace (@blogherosix) to name a few, you inspire me every day and I love talking about all things books and writing with you.

Finally, to my grandmother, Bonnie, and cousin Billy, I love you. Thank you for always having my back.

ABOUT THE AUTHOR

TAYLOR FENNER is the author of eleven Young Adult and New Adult novels and novellas. Her Young Adult Fantasy Retelling, CURSEBREAKER, was shortlisted for the 2017 Ozma Award for Fantasy Fiction, and her standalone fantasy novel, MONSTERS & MIST, is a Literary Titan Silver Book Award Winner and was also shortlisted for the 2021 Ozma Award for Fantasy Fiction.

Taylor is a thirty-something-year-old book junkie who devours books in most genres, although she has a soft spot for thrillers and horror novels.

Taylor lives in Wisconsin with her escape artist cat, Houdini, and a British shorthair cat, Makita, who might have eaten her last owner. Besides writing, by night, Taylor works the night shift as a dispatcher in a possibly haunted police station. When not working on her next novel, you'll find Taylor traveling or planning her next adventure, watching horror movies - she says classic horror is the best - reading or watching shows about creepy history, indulging in sugary coffee drinks, singing badly along to songs on Spotify in the car, and obsessively planning for Halloween starting in July (it's never too early). You can follow Taylor on Instagram, Facebook, or TikTok.